WENDY VELLA

A PROMISE of HOME

A Lake Howling Novel

Also by Wendy Vella

Historical Romances

Regency Rakes

Duchess By Chance

Rescued By A Viscount

The Langley Sisters Series

Lady In Disguise

Lady In Demand

Lady In Distress

The Reluctant Countess

Christmas Wishes

DEDICATION

This one is for the girls, Shar, Cher & Trudi.
Every now and again, the stars align and you strike gold in
your life, and these three are my gold.
Friends, mentors and confidants, my life is richer for
having you in it. Thank you from the bottom of my heart for
your support xx

CHAPTER ONE

"Welcome to Lake Howling, Oregon." Branna made the appropriate baying noise as she drove past the sign, in acknowledgement of the three years she'd spent here during high school. Howlers, the locals called themselves, but she'd never joined their ranks, having been born in Ireland, and way outside the boundaries of the small town. Heading through the corridor of giant redwoods, she came out the other side and saw the lake to her right, glimmering in the late morning sunlight. The town was stretched along the first body of water. The Roar, a general store that from memory stocked pretty much everything from candles to bait, was positioned first, then the Howler, where you got a bed, meal and a drink, plus some dancing, if you could work out the moves that the locals had nailed.

Branna had noticed that not much had changed when she'd attended her friend Georgie's funeral. The main street was still welcoming, the shop fronts quaint and tidy, flower boxes bright with blooms, and all the windows sparkled. The American flag still flew on top of the library, which was a small white building at the end of the street and was, from memory, the oldest in Howling, beside that sat the church. It was tourist season; the cabins would be packed with people wanting to hike in the woods, get onto the water, or pull something from it.

The office of Cooper Law, which was where she was headed, sat in the middle of town. Branna swung her van into a parking space, grabbed her purse, and climbed out. The heat settled around her as she stretched her hands above her head. After driving for days with only brief breaks to eat and sleep, all she wanted was to reach her destination.

"Welcome, Branna."

Lowering her arms, Branna searched the face of the woman now standing before her, but didn't recognize it, not that she'd come to know many people in her three years here. She was about 5'5", Branna's height, wore crisp white capris with an ironed crease down the fronts of both legs and a collared short sleeved shirt, and she had her grey hair neatly tucked into a plain white cap.

"Thank you."

"I'm Elizabeth Heath, dear. Georgie and I were very close. I'll be calling on you once you've settled in, to make the handover and welcome you to the club."

"Club?" Branna had no idea what the woman was talking about. "Handover?"

"Book Club. Georgie nominated you." The woman reached out to pat her hand. "But don't think about it now; you settle in, and I'll bring all the paperwork along in a few days."

"Paperwork?"

"Must be off, dear, or I'll be late for the hike. The woman then hurried down the street away from her. Branna wondered what the hell all that was about. Shaking her head, she pushed it aside to deal with later.

The Hoot Café had a large front window, through which Branna could see several people seated at tables eating and drinking. To the left of the building, she saw another door, and on that was a plaque telling her that this was the entrance to Cooper Law. Pushing it open, Branna felt the relief of stepping out of the heat into the cool interior as she made her way up the narrow flight of steps, through another door, and then into the reception area.

"Good afternoon, how may help you?"

The name plate on the desk said Penny Bilks, and she was a perky brunette with a wide smile and white teeth.

"Hi, my name is Branna O'Donnell, and I would like to see Mr. Cooper, if it's convenient?"

Penny looked at her closely, blue eyes skimming over Branna in that way one woman did to another, and she smiled.

"You probably don't remember me, but I was Penny Wilkinson in high school."

Branna looked closely and drew a blank. "Ah...well I was only here for a short time."

"Three years, I remember," the brunette said, jumping to her feet with what Branna thought was an excessive amount of energy. "Your daddy was my teacher for a year while you were here."

So, her thoughts of slipping into Howling weren't going quite as planned, Branna thought, eyeing the brunette and wondering what would come out of her fuchsia painted lips next.

"Okay, sure," Branna said, because she had no idea what else to say. She wasn't good with people; in fact, she kept pretty much to herself, which had been quite some feat living in Washington, but still, for the most part, she'd nailed it.

"Good to see you again, Branna," Penny Bilks held out her hand, which was tipped with long, fuchsia-tipped nails.

"You too, Penny." Branna shook her hand, then released it as quickly as she could.

Breathing more easily when Penny had disappeared through a door behind her, Branna then ran her hand through her hair and wondered what she looked like. Compared to the pristine Ms. Bilks, she probably came in a poor tenth. Looking down at her worn cut-offs and old grey T-shirt, she thought she should care, but really didn't. At least her sneakers were clean with no holes.

"Mr. Cooper will see you now."

Branna shook the hand of the big man who walked towards her as she entered his office. His smile was genuine, and he wore his suit with ease, even for his size.

"Pleased to see you have arrived, Miss O'Donnell; a lot of us admired your daddy, and thought he did a lot for the school in his short time here, and, of course, now that he's famous, we love him even more. His laugh was loud and rumbled up from his stomach.

"Thank you." Branna wasn't getting into a conversation about her estranged father with anyone, so she said nothing further.

"As Georgie's friend and lawyer, I knew of your relationship with her, and let me say, I know what you meant to her, just as I'm sure she was special to you."

Don't cry, Branna gritted her teeth and nodded.

"I need you to sign a few things, and then you can be on your way to Georgie's cottage. I hope you plan to stay?" His eyes were gentle and kind, and Branna saw he was genuine in his enquiry.

"I-I hope to stay awhile, but my plans are unsure at this stage."

"Georgie had some money invested that will come to you also; the details are in here, plus her Mustang, Geraldine, of course."

Branna had been looking at the papers on his desk, but at hearing the word Mustang, her head shot up. "She told me she sold the Mustang!"

Mr. Cooper laughed again.

"That 1966 Mustang belonged to her beloved husband, Dan, Ms. O'Donnell. No way in hell, if you'll excuse me for cussing, would she ever part with it. She kept it locked in that big shed behind her house."

Branna knew where it had been kept; she'd polished it, driven it, and learned to change a tire on Geraldine, just as she'd learned a whole heap of other life lessons at the hands of Georgie May Brown.

They talked a bit more, he about the will, she asking questions that she thought she should, when, in fact, fatigue was making her head a bit dizzy. Make that fatigue and a bit of shock over the fact that Georgie had left her the house, money, and Geraldine.

"Well, that about wraps it up, Ms. O'Donnell. You need anything, you just drop by." Mr. Cooper stood and accompanied her back out to the reception area.

"You hand those keys over now, Penny, and Ms. O'Donnell can be on her way," he added, stopping beside the other woman's desk. "I'll be seeing you around." He then shook Branna's hand again and went back into his office.

"I'll walk you down, Branna. I need to get Mr. Cooper a mystery muffin for his afternoon snack." Penny handed over a bunch of keys, then made for the door with Branna on her heels.

Branna let Penny chat as they walked back down the stairs and out onto the street, as her mind went over everything she'd just learned.

"Hey, watch out!"

Branna turned at the cry from Penny and saw a bike heading towards her. The boy tried to swerve, but it was too late, it hit her, knocking her off her feet. Her left hand hit the concrete first, and then her head. She must have blacked out, because when she opened her eyes, Penny Bilks was staring down at her.

"Stop, stay down, Branna; we need to get Doctor McBride here to look at you." Penny tried to stop her from rising.

Hell no, ignoring the vicious pain in her wrist and head, Branna regained her feet.

"It's okay, I'm all right."

"You're bleeding." Penny steadied her as she wobbled. "You need to see a doctor now."

The boy whose bicycle had hit her didn't seem hurt. He was picking it up and moving towards her.

"Michael Tucker, how many times have you been told not to ride your bike on the sidewalk!" Penny snapped at him.

"I'm sorry, Ms. Bilks. Is she okay?"

"I'm fine, really," Branna added, as he looked doubtful. Branna slowly pulled out of Penny's grip. "No need to fuss, Penny." Backing away from them, Branna reached her van, and then with a final wave, she climbed in. Forcing a smile onto her face, she managed to back out and direct the car out of town before she let out a long painful moan.

"Mother of God, that hurts," Branna hissed briefly, looking at her wrist. It had started to swell, and her head was throbbing so much her vision felt blurred.

Heading through town, Branna passed the bus stop she'd spent three years of her life waiting at every morning, and then the park that was used for any occasion that warranted it, then headed along the lake. She passed cabins and houses. The bulk of Howlers lived in a cluster to the right of the main street, spread backwards and up into the hills. Ten minutes from town, the houses had thinned until she reached a left turn that led her down a narrow road, then with another right, she headed parallel to the lake, and minutes later she was driving slowly up the old gravel drive that led to Georgie's house. *Not Georgie's, yours,* Branna thought.

The house was down a long driveway with overgrown trees on both sides, and huge towering redwoods at its rear. Reaching the end, Branna rubbed at the knot of emotion in her chest as she saw the small weatherboard cottage the color of gingerbread, trimmed in white. Parking the van, Branna took a moment to just look at the place that, for so many years, had housed the one person she loved to distraction.

"*Come here, Branna love, come and heal all the hurts inside you. Find peace, and happiness will follow. My soul will rest easy knowing my home is now yours, Branna, and know that I will be there to share it with you.*" Georgie had left these words in a letter to Branna, a letter that also told her she had inherited the house.

Georgie May Brown had been one of the two people that kept her sane when she'd lived here. At Georgie's hand, she had learned so much more than her love of writing. Here, she had learned life skills.

Grabbing her purse, while trying not to use her sore arm, she let herself out of the van, then made her way onto the front porch. The two chairs she and Georgie had sat in for hours were still there. Fumbling around for the keys in her bag, she found them and opened the door. Her hand shook as she placed it flat on the wooden surface and pushed it wide, then walked into a room full of memories.

Everything was how she remembered it, right down to the lace doilies scattered around the arms and backs of the furniture. She walked slowly from room to room, trying to ignore the thumping in her head, and when it got too much, she found Georgie's medicine supplies and swallowed a couple of pills.

It felt strange to be here without her friend. Strange that there were no cooking smells or the sound of classical music.

"I miss you so much," Branna whispered.

Branna made it to the sofa she had slept on a few times, and fell onto it. Kicking off her sandals, she pulled the blanket off the arm and managed one-handed to throw it over herself. She would unpack later; for now, she needed sleep.

***

Jacob McBride walked into The Hoot with only one thing on his mind. Chicken pie with a cheesy crust. Jake liked food, but he was downright dedicated to this pie, and that was why he only allowed himself to come here twice a week, three tops.

"Hey there, Jake, what's happening?"

"Penny," Jake gave the shapely brunette a nod. "How's it hanging?"

"I'm a woman, Jake, things don't hang, and we get real pissed off if they do."

He and Penny had been friends since high school, and he'd been teasing her for at least that long. She didn't give him too much angst, and that was reason enough to continue their friendship, considering he wasn't big on talking, or for that matter, building any more friendships these days.

"Got it. Don't mention things hanging to women," he added, standing at the counter as Buster bagged up his order without him even drawing a breath. That was one of the pluses in a whole heap of negatives that was good about living in your home town again; everyone knew what you liked.

"I have news," Penny drew out the S for dramatic effect.

"Hurry it up there, Buster, a man's starving here," Jake said, with one eye on his pie and the other on Penny, hoping she'd just leave so he could eat in peace, or he could leave before she started in on her news.

"When aren't you starving?" the man behind the counter asked. He had cropped dark hair, a thick neck, and linebacker's shoulders, but Buster Griffin was saved, in Jake's opinion, from being downright intimidating, by soft green eyes and long girly lashes that during high school had got him into plenty of fights. There was also the apron he wore continually as proprietor of The Hoot.

"You remember how I told you Georgie Brown left her place to Branna O'Donnell?" Penny said.

Jake was pretty sure she hadn't, but nodded anyway as he took his first bite. He thought about Branna Rose O'Donnell as the pastry melted in his mouth…her soft pale skin, thick black hair, and pretty green eyes. He remembered she'd intrigued him. Rosebud, he'd nicknamed her just to get a reaction, which he had; she'd fired up every time he'd used it.

"Bet that pissed Brian Reynolds off. He's been at Georgie for years to sell it to him," Buster said, before Penny could speak.

"He's a real estate man, Buster, and knows a good deal when he sees one," Jake added.

"Well, anyway," Penny waved a hand about to get their attention. "She just arrived back in Howling today to pick up the keys. She gets the Mustang too." The last was said with a sneer, which made Jake roll his eyes.

"I offered Georgie good money for it two years ago, Penny, and she turned me down. Let it go already; I have."

"Anyway," she waved her hand about again. "She looked tired and scruffy, but still has those endless legs and that pretty face. I was always jealous of her for looking beautiful in those hideous clothes she always wore, without a scrap of makeup, while the rest of us spent hours getting ready for school. Wasn't real chatty either."

"Can imagine that didn't endear her to you none, Penny," Buster muttered from behind the counter, which made Jake salute him with his pie."

"You saying I'm a gossip, Buster?"

"I'm sure you were going somewhere with this O'Donnell story, Pen. How about getting there before we retire?" Jake interrupted before they got into it like they often did.

"I don't remember much about Branna O'Donnell, but I do remember she was not real loose with her tongue, that's for sure," Buster added. "Being that way myself, you tend to notice it in other people."

"I remember her, and she was belligerent in high school, can't imagine that much has changed over the ensuing years," Jake said, and then took a larger bite for his second. He tried to make it last, but usually failed.

"Get you with the big words," Buster said.

Belligerent or ensuing?" Jake questioned.

"When she left the office," Penny said, ignoring their conversation, "She looked a bit preoccupied after talking with Mr. Cooper, and learning what Georgie's legacy entailed."

"Strange how she got everything, don't you think?" Buster said.

"Not so strange when you realize that she and Georgie talked every week on the phone, and she was always sending her gifts. Georgie went up to visit Branna too, once a year since she left Howling."

"How do you know this stuff?" Buster said, looking at Penny.

"Branna did all that?" Jake whistled. He'd been gone for most of those years, and only returned briefly on holidays. "I guess that explains the legacy then."

"Anyway, that's not the whole story," Penny added.

"Do we need the whole story?" Jake eyed the chocolate muffins that were the size of his fist and filled with a soft gooey caramel center. This he knew, as he'd sampled them…many times.

"Branna O'Donnell walked straight in front of Michael Tucker, who was riding his bike on the sidewalk again. He knocked her off her feet; the sound of her head hitting the concrete, Lord, it made me shudder," Penny said.

Penny wasn't above exaggeration to make a story good, but Jake could see she was sincere in this.

"I think she hurt her arm too, but here's the thing, Jake. She just climbed to her feet with my help, and after I steadied her, she told Michael she was fine, and then got into her van and drove away."

"And the problem here is?" Jake said, looking at Buster, who was now polishing the glass on his cabinets while listening to Penny's story.

"There was blood on the sidewalk, Jake, quite a bit of blood. And she was unsteady on her feet, and her eyes looked kind of funny when she glanced my way."

"Why didn't you make her go to visit Mum?" Jake swallowed the last mouthful, closing his eyes as he savored it.

"I don't know anyone who quite worships my chicken pie like you do, Jake."

"God's truth, if you asked, I'd probably marry you, man."

"Ha, yeah, maybe we could make it work." Buster, like Penny, was an old friend of Jake's.

"She wouldn't go, Jake, turned white at the thought, and then just up and left me and Michael Tucker standing right there on the bloodied sidewalk.

"That much blood?" Jake drawled.

Penny rolled her eyes. "The point is, I think someone should check on her. What happens if she's got one of those concussions and no one looks in on her and she's up there dead for weeks?"

"Yes, because Georgie lives about two day's hike from here, and then there's the trek over the mountains," Buster drawled. "But it'll be the wolves that get her."

"The snow's gonna play hell with the rescue party," Jake added.

"Will you two be serious?" Penny snapped.

"What's the problem here, Pen? You and Branna suddenly buddies or something? If she's hurting, she'll find her way to Mum at some stage."

The breath whistled through Penny's teeth as she tried to haul in air.

"It's not about whether I like or dislike her, it's about this being Howling, and how we look after people who live in our town, Jake. What if she's up there alone in Georgie's house needing medical help?"

"Weren't her and Annabelle friends in high school? Maybe she'd call in and see her?" Buster suggested.

"That was ten years ago!" Penny shrieked.

"You think they didn't keep in touch?" Jake asked.

"They didn't even talk to each other at Georgie's funeral, Jake, which pretty much tells me they didn't."

Jake thought about the funeral, ran through the people he remembered, but drew a blank on Branna O'Donnell. "She was there?"

Penny nodded. "Dark glasses, black hat, pale face, and black dress."

Jake and Buster fell silent as they tried to remember.

"Oh for pities sake, you two have got to be the most unobservant men in America!" Penny said.

"That's a bit harsh, don't you think? I mean, I happen to know that Billy Lee wasn't observing much when he missed that mighty fine pass I threw to set him up for the winning touchdown that lost us the game on Saturday. What you reckon, Buster?"

"Billy Lee couldn't observe a Semi bearing down on his scrawny ass from a foot away," Buster added.

Jake nodded as Penny ground her teeth together.

"So, if you could, that'd be great, thanks, Jake, seeing as you pass the end of her drive on your way home."

"Could what?" Jake questioned.

"Go see if she's okay, you being a doctor and all, and her closest neighbor; you'll be able to check if she needs help."

He looked from her to Buster and back again. "Why would I want to do that?

"Because you know how to."

"I'm a mechanic now, Penny. I don't practice medicine anymore."

"Pffft, that's just you playing around," she waved her hand about and headed for the door. "So, maybe take her to see your mom if you think she needs an X-ray." Penny pronounced it x er ray, which used to annoy the hell out of Jake when he still gave a shit.

"I'm not going." The door swung shut on his reply, but Jake knew she'd heard him. "Why did I come back here?"

"It sure as hell wasn't for some privacy."

Jake snorted at Buster's words. "Why is it so hard for this town to understand I don't want to be a doctor anymore?"

"Because you're one of their favorite sons, and they had big expectations for you, and refuse to believe you're not living up to them."

"What do I have to do? Take out an ad, run naked down the main street yelling that I'm a fucking lunatic now, and not fit to look after people?"

"Bad night, bud?"

Jake was disgusted to see that the hands he ran down his face were shaking. "The worst." He still saw the blood all over them.

"Well, snap the fuck out of it, because I'm bringing the Jeep over later, and you need to stop it making that noise."

Sucking in a deep steadying breath, Jake forced himself to calm down. "Buster, the Jeep is one big noise."

"Whatever, just make her run sweet again."

"I gave up miracles many years ago."

"I didn't," Buster said softly, giving Jake a steady look.

"Whatever," Jake headed for the door, needing to get outside in the fresh air so he could haul in a deep lungful. "Bring the Jeep over later, and I'll put it back together with some duct tape." Lifting a hand, Jake left the shop and climbed back into his pickup. He waved to a few people, and wondered why no one in Howling had seen the changes in him. Why didn't they acknowledge that he wasn't as friendly as he'd once been? Why did they not ask him why he'd turned his back on medicine? Instead, they brought their cars to him if they needed fixing, and when Barry, Howling's mechanic, snow plow, towing service, and search and rescue expert had too much business.

Heading out of town along the lake, the houses started to thin and he felt the tension inside him ease as he left the people behind. He'd be home soon, and he could work on the cars, and hopefully not see anyone else until he wanted to. Seeing Georgie's purple letterbox approaching, Jake decided he'd drive right by. It wasn't up to him to check on a woman he didn't know or care about. Hell, she was probably fine.

Any impact to the head can disrupt the normal function of the brain. People with concussion need to be seen by a doctor, and symptoms can include severe headaches, nausea or repeated vomiting and, in some cases, one of the pupils can appear larger than the other, and in severe cases, the patient can experience slurred speech.

"Stop it, for fuck's sake; you're not a doctor anymore!" Smacking the wheel with his hand, he passed the driveway and then jammed his foot on the brakes. He'd often said things like that to his patients, and now, when he wasn't practicing medicine anymore, this kind of dialogue would pop into his head when he overhead someone talk about an injury or medical condition. It drove him crazy.

Throwing the pickup into reverse, he spat out a few curses, then turned into the overgrown driveway. He'd see if Branna

O'Donnell was okay, then leave. He could be nice if he had to; it just wasn't something he was too good at anymore.

He'd spent a bit of time at Georgie's, as had most of the kids in town. She'd been a woman with a large heart and a huge capacity for giving. She had tutored kids who struggled to read, and helped others learn to spell. Pulling to a halt behind a white van, he climbed out. The place was overgrown now. Georgie had been in the hospital for a few months before she passed away, and while the town had tried to keep it tidy, it had slowly started to get out of hand. Looking at the shed behind the house, he wondered if it still housed the Mustang. He loved that car.

Knocking on the door, Jake spent a few minutes surveying the weatherboards. They looked in good condition, just in need of a coat of paint. When no one answered, he knocked again, this time louder, but still no reply. Then he made the wooden door shake on its hinges as he pounded it with his fist. If she didn't open soon, he'd see if he could find a window to get in through. Seconds later, he was rewarded with the sound of it opening.

"Why are you pounding on my door?"

He'd always liked the gruff little burr of her voice. Maybe it was because he'd not had much contact with anyone else from Ireland. Whatever the reason, her accent had always made him smile.

"Hey, Branna, remember me?"

Her focus wasn't great, but the green eyes eventually settled on him. "Jacob McBride."

"Penny told me you hit your head, and she thought you may need to visit the doctor?"

"No…thanks," she tacked on the last word reluctantly, then started to close the door.

Bracing a hand on the wood, he leaned in a little. "Your head looks like it's hurting you, Rosebud."

"It's fine, now go away," her words didn't pack too much of a punch because she was whispering; obviously, the effort of speaking was not helping her condition.

"You still got that attitude working for you, O'Donnell." Jamming a foot in the door to stop her shutting it further, he gently pushed it open, sending her back a step.

"Please, leave my house." This time, her words had a bit more force, even though they were said through her teeth.

"Yeah, give me a minute and I'll do just that, Rosebud." He watched as she staggered backwards and then lowered herself into a chair, the effort making her wince.

"Branna or Miss O'Donnell, my name is not Rosebud."

"Your fault. You introduced yourself that first day in class as Branna Rose, and it stuck."

"We're not in school anymore, McBride."

"Tell me about the pain in your head, Branna," Jake said, ignoring her words, as he pulled out his mobile and switched on the flashlight app before moving to squat before her. Once there, he pried open the eyelids she'd recently closed and shined the light into them. Her pupils didn't react as they should as he flashed the light across them. In fact, the pupils weren't constricting at all. "Vision blurred?"

"What are you doing?" She tried to bat his hands away, but he didn't move. Instead, he eased her forward to inspect the cut on the back of her head. "Take your hands off me."

"I don't go for skinny, belligerent women," Jake lied, regaining his feet to walk around the back of the chair to get a closer look. Penny had said her legs were fine, and he couldn't disagree; they were long and shapely coming out of those ragged cut-offs, and she filled that shirt out nicely too. "You have way too much hair," he muttered, parting the thick mass of black curls until he saw it. Not huge, maybe an inch, but it was matted with blood and may need a stitch.

"Ouch! Stop, that hurts." She tried to push his hands aside again.

"Surely you're not still pissed with me for reshaping your eraser into a phallic symbol?" he was moving over her body now, checking for other injuries. Reaching her left wrist, her breath hissed.

"Why are you doing this to me, McBride?"

"Because Penny asked me to, and while I'm not big on interacting with anyone much these days, here in Howling, when a friend asks you to do something, you usually end up doing it, no matter how reluctant you are," Jake added. "Does your wrist hurt to move it?" he questioned. It was definitely damaged, but he didn't know how badly. *The most common wrist bone to break or fracture is the carpal bone. Symptoms sometimes include pain and swelling around the wrist. Okay, fuck, will you let up?*

"Yes, now leave."

"But you're such good company." He moved around the house until he found one of Georgie's scarves hanging from the coat stand. He quickly fashioned a sling for her, then slipped her arm through it. When he finished, she made a gagging sound.

"You going to be sick, Rosebud?"

She pushed at his chest and tried to rise, but he simply lifted her into his arms and took her to the bathroom. Raising the toilet seat, he lowered her to the floor, then stood back as she threw up.

"Is there no end to this humiliation?" she whispered when it was over. Sitting back on her heels, she tried to glare up at him, but failed miserably. She was shaking and pale, and he didn't want to feel sorry for her, but he did.

Rinsing a washcloth, he then wiped her face.

"Now, I want you to listen to me, Rosebud, because you were an intelligent girl in high school, and unless you did drugs or some other substance abuse, I can't imagine your brain capacity has dimmed too much." Jake squatted before her so their eyes were on the same level.

"I was an English professor," she whispered.

"There you go," Jake added, wiping her face again. "So, you should get that you need to see a doctor, because you have a concussion, and while I don't think your arm is broken, it sure as hell is not right."

"You a doctor or something?"

"Or something," he lifted her into his arms, which wasn't too hard, as she didn't weigh much.

"P-put me down." Her words were weak and he ignored them. "Where are you taking me?"

"I think we just covered that." He gave her a quick look as he walked back out through the door he had just entered.

Her eyes were the color of fresh cut grass, so bright they'd always given him a jolt, and he remembered that her jet black hair had always been plaited in a long fat braid down her back.

No ribbons or clips, just a plan black band had secured it at the bottom. She'd had no soft edges in school, just a belligerent girl with a serious attitude, and that air of sadness that had clung to her. Of course, everything changed with she had a microphone in her hand. The girl had sung like an angel.

It had always amazed Jake that she chose to join the school band, yet avoided communicating with other students whenever possible. He'd watched her once, been dragged in by Newman, because he had the hots for some girl doing backup vocals and playing the tambourine. He'd been shocked when Branna had stepped up to the microphone. Seeing Annabelle playing keyboards told him who was responsible for her appearance, but nothing had prepared him for her voice; all the hair on the back of his neck had risen when she sang her first note.

"No, I won't go to the doctor." She was trying to get out of his arms now, but he was bigger, so he just tightened his hold. "I don't like them."

"Don't be foolish, Branna."

She squinted up at him as they walked out into the sunshine. "How did you know about my fall?"

"Penny told me."

"She had no right; now put me down." She was squirming against him.

"You're starting to annoy me now, so quit it."

"I don't know the doctor here, and I don't want some quack touching me."

"I'll be sure to tell my mother that." Jake pulled open the passenger door.

"Your mum's still the doctor here?"

"Sure is," Jake said, as he put her on the seat and did up her seat belt. Closing the door, he sprinted around the truck to get into the driver's seat, because he couldn't rule out the fact that she might try to get out. Starting the car, he backed out just as she got the door open.

"What are you going to do, jump?"

She slammed it shut, then moaned.

"I bet that hurt your wrist?"

"Go to hell."

"What's your problem with doctors, O'Donnell?"

"I don't like medical people."

Jake shot her a look as he backed out of the driveway. She was huddled against the door, shivering and pale. Sighing, he pulled the blanket out from beneath the seat and laid it over her.

"My mother's a good doctor, Rosebud, and I can personally guarantee she has no rusty needles or thumb screws in her rooms…and she's got a great bedside manner."

"I don't remember her place. Does it have that bad smell?"

Pulling out of her street, he headed back into town before answering that strange question.

"No, it smells clean and has nice beige walls and magazines dated before 2010."

"I don't want to go."

"But you need to," he added.

Jake reached Howling and lifted his hand to acknowledge Ben Tiller, who stood at the curb waiting to cross. He watched the man's eyes flick from Jake to the top of Branna's head and back. Frowning, Jake drove on. By tomorrow, there would be questions, and he was fairly sure by the end of it he'd be sick of fielding them…such was life in a small town. He'd have to lay low for a few days until something else fired up their thirst for gossip.

"I'm an adult; you can't make me go if I don't want to."

"Well, now, Rosebud that sure as hell sounded like an adult talking." Swinging into the driveway next to The Howler, he drove for a few minutes down the long winding concrete strip, then turned into the parking lot in front of Yelp Medical Facility. Climbing out, Jake went around the hood to open the passenger door. It was locked. Pulling the keys, he had just pocketed back out with a loud sigh, he unlocked it, and opened the door. "Real mature, O'Donnell."

"I hate you." He could barely hear the whispered words as he bent to slip his hands beneath her thighs and pick her up. She was shaking so hard he could feel it through her entire body. This was about more than concussion; this was a reaction to fear, plain and simple, and he had firsthand knowledge of fear and what it could do to you if you let it take root.

"Ungrateful is what you are, Rosebud, and me being a good Samaritan and all."

"I can walk," were the next words out of her mouth, which made him snort. She was shaking and her breathing was now a rasp. "I have to tell you something." Her head lay on his chest as he walked towards the doors.

"I'm listening."

"I'm scared of doctors, hospitals, clinics, needles, and anything to do with all of the above."

"No kidding."

"F-fuck you, McBride."

"That took me straight back to twelfth grade."

"Pl-please, don't make me go in there," she whispered.

He looked down at her and the terror in her eyes made something jolt inside him.

"They're good people in here, Rosebud; they'll be gentle…I promise."

Her good hand suddenly grabbed a fistful of his shirt. "Don't think I can do this."

"Trust me."

She tilted her head back to look up at him as he opened the doors. "Why?"

"Because I give you my word that no one inside these walls will harm you in any way." He'd said the words solemnly, almost as if they were an oath.

"I'll try." After that, she rested her head on his chest again, but didn't relax any. In fact, the knuckles on the fist she had in his shirt were white.

"This is my favorite shirt, O'Donnell; you rip it, you buy a new one."

"It smells."

"Sweat, baby, pure and natural essence of McBride."

Using the hand under her to turn the handle, Jake nudged it with his foot and walked inside. He put Branna in one of the waiting room chairs, the one furthest from the doors, in case she got the urge to make a run for it, and then made his way up to the reception desk.

"Mum busy, Cici?"

"Her next appointment just cancelled. She and Annabelle are going over supplies."

Jake looked behind him at Branna, who was slumped in her chair, face the color of paper, hands shaking, looking like a puppy locked outside in the rain.

"I'll take Branna through if you want to get some forms ready."

"Sure thing."

"I can walk," Branna said, taking the hand he held out to her. He pulled her upright, then slipped an arm around her side as she swayed a little. His mother's office wasn't far, and he saw her blonde head bent over the desk with Annabelle's darker one as they entered.

"Heard things were quiet, so I've drummed you up some business."

Both women looked up as he spoke. His mother smiled, Annabelle frowned, and Branna whispered the words, "I'm going to die."

CHAPTER TWO

Branna's head was thumping and her arm ached as they walked into the doctor's office, but all she could feel was terror. Horror that the words in her head had come out of her mouth made her want to turn into the big body at her side and beg him to take her out of here, beg him to hold her tight, so the fear didn't make her do or say more foolish things.

"Well, now, my day has suddenly brightened, Annabelle, because here comes one of the most handsome men in all of Howling."

The lady walking towards Branna looked familiar; the blonde hair was streaked with grey, and she was tall with big shoulders. She hadn't changed much since Branna's father had forced her to visit the doctors years ago when she'd fallen ill. She had the smile and face of an angel, but to Branna, she could easily pass for the devil. She remembered thinking that Doctor McBride, like all doctors, had that pleasant façade, but underneath she'd be like the others, and soon cause her pain.

"No bias involved either," she heard someone drawl. Looking to the desk, she saw another woman, who, on closer inspection, she remembered very well. Annabelle Smith.

"None." Doctor McBride gave her son a smacking kiss on the cheek before looking at Branna. She flinched as the woman lifted a hand towards her, pathetic person that she was. She then turned her face and buried it into the large warm chest at her side.

"Get me out of here, Jake, please," Branna begged.

"This is Branna O'Donnell, Mum," the beast said, wrapping an arm around her waist as she tried to leave. "She had an accident. Seems she got knocked over and hit her head hard and hurt her wrist." Branna knew there would be all kinds of silent signals going on over her head, but she didn't care; her eyes were shut and she was pressed into a solid chest, even if it was Jake McBride's. Closing her eyes, she tried to put herself somewhere else, like she'd done after the accident. A place where there was no more pain.

"Branna, honey, I've had personal experience with that chest, and I know it's a fine place to rest, but you really need to let me look you over now," Doctor McBride said.

Oh, God.

Her hands gripped Jake's shirt again as she looked up; she couldn't help it. At least if she was anchored to him, in some weird way, she thought maybe she would stay safe.

"Your head hurting you, Branna?"

"It's killing her," Jake answered for her.

"Hey, Branna, remember me?"

Opening her eyes, she looked into the face of the other woman in the room who had once been her only friend in Howling.

"Annabelle, you know I-I have to go, that I can't stay here."

Annabelle Smith was tall with golden brown hair that tended to curl in the rain and brown eyes that melted when she saw animals. Well, they once had anyway, and she was also one of the few people who knew why Branna was terrified of doctors.

"Doctor McBride is the best, Branna. How about you come sit in the chair and let her take a quick look at you? Then she'll give you something for your sore head."

"I-I don't th-think I can, Annabelle."

"Sure you can, and while I'm still pissed with you for leaving me without a word, after ten years I've just about forgiven you, so why don't you let me, Jake, and Doctor McBride here help you."

The side of Jake's shirt stayed clutched in Branna's hand, the other Annabelle held, and they all made their way across to the chair, while Doctor McBride chatted to her son about his favorite meatballs that she was making him for dinner that night. Branna latched onto the silly conversation like a lifeline, focusing on each word to distract herself from what was to come.

"Finish it with a brownie and chocolate sauce, and I'll be persuaded to look at Dad's Bronco before I leave."

"Deal."

Branna sat with Annabelle on one side holding her hand and Jake on the other.

"I'm just going to have a look at you now, Branna. If at any time you want me to stop, you just say. If something hurts, you just let me know, and if you feel sick, then you just turn to your right and throw up on Jake's shoes," Doctor McBride said.

"My mother, the caring face of Howling. If only your patients really knew you like I do."

Branna had a brief vision of her mother and quickly pushed it aside.

Doctor McBride talked as she checked Branna over, her words directed to either Belle or her son, and Branna sat tense and silent while she did so. When she touched her head, Branna bit her lip.

"We need to give that a cleanup, Annabelle, and maybe a stitch or two?"

"No needles…please," Branna heard the plea in her words. She was pathetic. How could a person of twenty eight still be traumatized by events that happened fifteen years ago? She hated herself for the weakness that still plagued her.

"It's all right, Branna, I'm not going to hurt you," Doctor McBride said gently.

"You sure are a scaredy cat, Branna O'Donnell. If I'd known in school you were this easy to crack, I would have tried harder."

"I'm not a scaredy cat, Jake McBride," Branna said through gritted teeth. "And grown men don't speak like that, you wimp."

He continued to poke at her with verbal jabs, which she tried to field, as his mother worked on her head. It helped.

"Don't you remember, Annabelle? Rosebud here had that thing for Nick Fletcher. She kept looking at him all gooey eyed until he asked to change classes just to get away from her."

"I did not," Branna gritted out. "That was the other girl with the really big…ah—"

"Yes, they were certainly a fine pair," Jake sighed. "Kaylee Summers, we were all in love with her, except Nick, who, as it turned out, was in love with Mandy Griffin."

"D-didn't she h-have a funny thing going on with her eyes?" Branna swallowed, as she felt something dig into her head. It didn't hurt, but still, just the thought of a needle anywhere near her was terrifying.

"You take a nice deep breath now, Rosebud. That's it, now another," Jake said, pulling his shirt free of her grip and then clasping her hand, her fingers sliding between his.

"Kaylee had a ton of vision therapy, which corrected it, and she's grown up and out some since then. Mr. and Mrs. Fletcher now run the art gallery here in town. He's lost his hair and puffed out a bit himself."

Surprised by Annabelle's words, Branna momentarily forgot her pain. "You're not serious? Nick, the hottest thing in pants, Fletcher?"

"The very same," Belle said.

"I thought I was the hottest thing in pants back then."

"No," Branna said, shooting Jake a quick look. "You only thought you were; he actually was."

Belle whooped with laughter and Doctor McBride chuckled.

"All done with your head, Branna. Annabelle will take you to get an X-ray on that arm now, to check it doesn't have more damage than we can see."

"Jake didn't think it was broken, Doctor McBride," she felt compelled to say, in case it persuaded the doctor to change her mind about the X-ray.

"He's probably right, but as I'm still the doctor around here and he insists on wasting his talents by putting those skillful hands of his into a gallon of motor oil each day, then we go with my instructions."

Branna's head hurt too much to wade through the tension behind Doctor McBride's words, especially as the fingers holding hers tensed briefly before relaxing again. Looking up, she saw that Jake was looking at his mother, his black eyes steady and unreadable.

"Once she's done there, Annabelle, get her settled in a bed."

"Bed? Why do I need a bed? Do you even have beds here?" She glared at Jake. "You told me this wasn't a hospital."

"Hospitals traditionally are big and smell sterile. As you know, this building is the size of a small house. Therefore, it is classed as a medical facility, Rosebud." Jake helped her to her feet. "And you need a bed because someone will have to monitor you for the night."

"You took a bad head knock, Branna," Doctor McBride added. "Annabelle will run through the instructions I expect you to follow soon, and when you leave, you'll need to take it easy for a few days too. We'll get you some pills for the pain, then Annabelle will keep you company through the night."

"No!" Branna moved away from Jake and the doctor. "Th-thank you for caring for me Doctor, but I'm not staying here overnight."

"Yes," Jake stepped forward and took her arm before she'd made it to the door. "You're doing exactly what the doctor tells you to, Branna."

She looked at his handsome face, saw the determination and strength, and felt her heart sink.

"I don't want to."

"But you will." He pushed aside the hair that had fallen over her cheek, and his hand felt warm against her skin. "Care to tell me why you don't want to stay?"

"Because I—"

"It's all right, Branna," Annabelle stepped forward. "Really, I'll be here with you and we'll catch up on the past ten years. You'll grovel some, and then I'll forgive you, and we can start being bitchy about the townsfolk; it'll be like old times."

Jake released her as Annabelle took her arm, and soon she was being directed down the hallway towards X-ray with her old friend at her side and her stomach filled with anxiety.

She kept her eyes closed throughout the procedure, which didn't hurt, but still caused the memories she had buried deep inside her to surface. She saw the lights, heard the words, felt the pain of those months she'd spent in the hospital all over again.

Someone has to tell her soon that her mother's dead.

Branna had heard these whispered words while she lay in her hospital bed, her head floating from medication, her body broken.

"All done Bran, now we'll get you settled in a bed." Annabelle took her arm again, and drained of energy, she let herself be led into a small room that had four beds; all had big soft pillows and bright yellow and blue striped covers. Admittedly, it looked nothing like the one that she'd stayed in for so many weeks, and unlike then, she wasn't broken inside and out.

"See, it doesn't look anything like a hospital ward. No machines buzzing and clicking, no trays being wheeled about," Annabelle said, as she nudged Branna down onto one of the beds. "You know that wrist is going to take a while to heal, Branna, right?"

"How long?" Branna questioned.

"Well that's up to you and whether you take Doctor McBride's advice or not."

"I have to wear that?" Branna eyed the brace and sling Annabelle placed beside her on the bed.

"You're not going to give me trouble the entire time you're here, are you?"

"Probably," Branna sighed. Now that she wasn't being poked and prodded, she felt a bit more relaxed. Taking the pills Belle held out to her, she swallowed them down then took a mouthful of water. She was still scared, but she was also exhausted, and the latter was pulling her eyes shut.

"Now, I'm going to be waking you through the night, Branna, so don't slug me when I do."

She gave Belle a weary smile; the day was suddenly catching up with her. "I'll try not to."

"How's the worst patient to enter the hallowed halls of Yelp Medical Facility doing, Annabelle?"

Branna was too tired to open her eyes as Jake arrived at her bedside.

"How's the pain, Rosebud?"

"It's okay, starting to ease."

"I need you to promise me not to make a run for it tonight."

She sighed and then opened her eyes, and there he was. Mr. Way too Hot, McBride. Hair tousled, shoulders broad, and a slightly lopsided smile that was making her insides feel strange, which Branna put down to the pills. He'd always had that effect

on her, even in high school, when she'd pretty /
everyone.

"Go away and torture someone else, McBride."

"A simple thank you will do."

Perhaps it was the fear, or the pain, or the fact that finally the realization that she had uprooted her life to come here was hitting her, but suddenly Branna felt the hot sting of tears behind her eyes. Closing them, she struggled to hold them back, but they slipped beneath her lashes and down her cheeks.

"It's all right, Rosebud." He talked softly about concussion and delayed shock, then using a tissue, he mopped up the flood of humiliating tears until finally Branna ran out of them.

"I- I'm actually a strong person," she whispered.

He was still standing above her, and Branna felt that horrible tug of need she used to feel when she sat behind him in class. She hoped like hell it was just because she was having a bad day.

"Thank you, Jake."

He smiled. "That's it? Thank you, Jake? After the torment I've endured at your hands I get a 'thank you, Jake?' You've wept on me, bled on me, abused me, and let us not forget that I've carried your considerable weight a considerable distance."

Branna heard Belle snort somewhere in the background.

"I think the least I deserve is for you to sell me the Mustang."

Belle's snort became a shout of laughter.

"You want the Mustang?" Branna asked Jake.

"I'll give you a fair price."

Branna was lying down, which was a distinct disadvantage against this man; she needed to be upright so she could get a good glare going on.

"You're asking me now, when I have a concussion and can barely form a rational thought? That's low, McBride."

His smile wasn't as bright as it had once been; it was just a small tug of his lips now, and she wondered what changes had taken place in this man's life since she'd been gone.

"Rosebud, that old thing's just taking up room in your shed. Let me get it out of your way. I'd be doing you a favor."

"Geraldine is a 1966 Ford Mustang 4speed manual 289 V8, McBride, not an old thing, as you put it, and it's mine," Branna said, squinting up at him. His face didn't register shock that she, a woman, knew things about a car; he just looked at her with those black eyes.

"There was always something sneaky about you, even in school. I reckon it's just had time to develop since you left Howling."

"I could always outsmart you, McBride; glad to see some things stay the same." Closing her eyes as she ran out of energy, Branna managed a small smile. "But, I do thank you, Jake, for everything you did for me today, even though I may have been a bit difficult."

"A bit," he snorted. "You owe me, Rosebud, and payment will be a drive in that car."

Branna was pretty sure her smile wouldn't slip until she fell asleep.

The night was long, and by the time Annabelle woke her for the last time as the dawn was breaking, Branna thought briefly about letting the curse that was forming on her lips loose, but Nurse Smith looked tired too, so she swallowed it instead.

"Okay, Branna, that about does it; the torture is over for both of us. Now, go back to sleep, and when you wake I'll get you home." Annabelle yawned after these words.

"You go get some sleep too, Belle."

"Will do, and I'll be right over there," she said, pointing to the bed beside Branna's.

"It's good to see you again, Belle," Branna finally found the courage to say the words she'd being thinking about through the long night. They hadn't talked, because mostly Branna had slept, but it was still comforting to have her old friend here.

"You too, Branna, we'll catch up soon."

She wanted to, but it had been so long since she'd had a real friend like Annabelle Smith, in fact, probably since she was last in Howling, that she wasn't really sure if she could still do it. She lay quietly as Annabelle settled into sleep and was soon breathing deeply, only then did Branna rise and swing her legs over the edge of the bed.

She felt like a wreck; her head hurt; she needed a shower, and her arm was in a really uncomfortable brace. Looking about for her clothes, she found them on a chair. Slowly and with one hand, she managed to remove her hospital gown and pull on her clothes. Finding some paper and a pen, she wrote Annabelle a note saying she'd gone home. Slipping on the sling that Jake had told her she had to wear along with the brace, she headed for the door.

The doors opened from the inside and then locked behind her as Branna made her way outside into the cool morning air. Shivering in her shorts and tank, she looked up and down the street. As usual, she'd reacted without thinking things through, and now it seemed she was going to have to walk home. Unlike Washington, Howling didn't have ten taxis ready to pick her up the minute she stepped off the curb.

Making her way down the long driveway, she let the cool, crisp and quiet morning air settle around her. Howling had always tugged at something inside Branna. Once it had made her long for what she couldn't have. Long to belong to somewhere and to someone. When she'd first arrived to go to high school, she'd been numb with grief from the death of her mother and hoped this small town would help both her and her father heal; she'd soon realized that hope was foolish.

Reaching the end of the drive, Branna headed down the main street. There was no litter or drunken people coming home from the night before; here, all was quiet. Howling was a town where you could settle and be safe. Your children would be happy and allowed to run down the streets and go to the shops without fear of something happening to them.

As the years had passed for Branna, the town of Howling had become stronger in her head, not weaker. She'd often remember things from here, places and people, and it had been those memories, along with Georgie's wishes, that had made her leave Washington, pack up her life, and come here. If it didn't work, she could always leave, but Branna had wanted to at least try and see if she could one day call Howling home.

She heard the car from some distance, and then a worn old green jeep pulled up beside her and the window was rolled down.

"Morning, Branna."

The man looked familiar. His close-cropped dark hair was different now; in school it was long, reaching his shoulders. His smile wasn't wide, but then she remembered that too as always being that way. In fact, Buster Griffin had always looked solemn, when, in actual fact, he had a dry humor that had often made Branna laugh in school. He was still built like a bull, big and solid, but strangely, he had been one of those people who she'd always felt comfortable around.

"Hey, Buster, you're up early."

"I own the Hoot Cafe, Branna."

He was also not a man of many words, she remembered, which suited her just fine.

"You break yourself out?"

"I did." She wasn't about to ask him how he knew she was back. This was a small town; everyone knew everything about everyone…her arrival would have been telegraphed around town minutes after she'd driven through the redwoods.

"Get in then, and I'll take you home."

He made it sound like it was something he'd done regularly, that they had seen each other just the other day, not ten years ago. The door swung wide, and Branna didn't hesitate. Climbing in, she was relieved that she didn't have to walk home, as her head was starting to hurt and her wrist was aching. She had some nice strong pain pills that she would take once she'd made up her bed.

"Jake's gonna serve you up when he finds out you've done a runner," Buster said, as he made a U-turn.

"I didn't do a runner; I discharged myself."

Branna shifted in the seat as Buster snorted. He was right, Jake wouldn't be pleased, especially as he'd asked her to stay in the clinic, but then maybe he wouldn't care, and why should he anyway? It wasn't like they were even friends. She only remembered snatches of yesterday. Her memory was pretty fuzzy, but she remembered him carrying her, and holding her hand. Pushing aside the guilt, Branna looked around her for the source of the wonderful aroma that was filling the small car.

"Buster, where's that amazing smell coming from?"

He reached one beefy arm behind him and pulled a huge basket into the front, placing it between them.

"They're a new muffin I'm trialing in the café. Have one."

Her stomach rumbled at the thought, so Branna picked up one of the sweet smelling treats and took a bite. Her mouth was filled with cinnamon and chocolate.

"Buster, will you marry me?"

"Jake already asked me, so, sorry Branna, it wouldn't be right."

She laughed and then took another bite, and another, until soon she had eaten the entire muffin.

The rest of the short trip was accomplished in comfortable silence, as neither of them were talkers, both content to enjoy the peace and quiet of the morning.

When they arrived at Georgie's driveway, she said, "stop at the bottom, Buster, I can walk up." Of course, he ignored her, as she'd known he would. The people of Howling understood manners; Branna's father had once told her that.

"Well, thanks again, Buster, for the ride and the most delicious muffin I've ever eaten. I'll be coming into your bakery later to get a few more."

He handed her another muffin silently, then turned the car around and left. Branna stood there in what was now her small corner of the world and breathed. This was going to be her home; she'd make it so. The place she could live and write in peace. The little house wrapped around her as she walked inside, and she felt Georgie again.

Thank you, my dear, dear friend, Branna thought, as she walked slowly through the house again. Thank you for giving me a place to belong.

Jake always woke early; it was a habit he'd formed after five years in the army that he'd never kicked. His nightmares hadn't woken him, and to his relief, seemed to be getting further apart, so he felt rested and ready to take on the day. His run had taken him away from town and round the lake. Then, after a shower and breakfast, he made his way to the huge barn at the rear of his property. In there were cars that needed his time. Split radiator hoses and misfiring engines, all things he loved to fix, now that he was no longer fixing broken bodies.

The words flashed a vision through his head of a soldier and the arm he'd amputated. It wasn't the worst of the flashbacks he experienced, but still, it always shocked him to suddenly be back there. He could smell the blood, feel the heat, and hear the anguished cries. The flashbacks snuck up on him when he wasn't prepared, and he hated the way they made him want to drop to his knees, curl into the fetal position, and cry like a baby.

"Hey, boy, what are you fixing today?"

Coming out from beneath the hood of a car an hour later, Jake watched the long easy strides of Patrick McBride as he wandered in. He'd look like that one day. Like Jake, his father was tall, but his hair had started to pepper with grey over the last few years, and there were other signs of age, but all of them sat well on the man. At fifty-two, he was still handsome and there was no man Jake respected more. It made him sad that he'd never be the man his father now was; he didn't have it in him anymore.

"Hey, Dad, you're up early."

"Your mother makes me walk with her some mornings if I don't pretend to be asleep when she wakes."

"That sucks."

"Sure does, but the upside is that I get a cooked breakfast before she heads to the clinic."

"Always a plus."

Ducking back under the hood, he knew his father would be on the other side soon.

"How's Katie?"

His father appeared and started poking about as he usually did, which Jake didn't mind, as he was good with cars like him.

"It's her break in a couple of weeks, so she'll be home to annoy us for a while."

Katie was Jake's younger sister, and she was in L.A. at the police academy. They were close, and he missed her, as she did him when he'd gone away, but he also knew that like him, Katie would find her way back here when the time came to settle.

"Your mum was telling me that Branna O'Donnell was in the clinic. Sounds like a nasty knock to the head."

"Yeah, stubborn woman. I had to force her to see Mum after I'd checked her over. It was pretty obvious she was concussed."

"You remember her dad, son?"

Jake thought about that as he put a clamp on the fuel line. He could picture a man with Branna's hair and pale skin, but not much else.

"He never taught me at school, but Buster had him, and said he was a hard ass who didn't put up with any crap," Jake said. "I remember him telling that Simon Duffell off for knocking Lilly Belcher off her feet and not stopping to help her back up. He had me shaking and he didn't even raise his voice."

"He writes those crime novels under the name of D.J. O'Donnell."

"Really? I love those books," Jake said.

"Me too, have every one."

"Hand me that screwdriver, Dad."

"Your mother and I always believed there was something off with those two," Patrick said, handing over the tool.

"Off how?" Jake stood to look at his father. He didn't gossip or involve himself too much in the community of Howling, but people still talked to him and tried to draw him back in. But he was genuinely interested in hearing about Branna. She'd intrigued him in school, and after what they'd been through together yesterday, he had to say he was still intrigued.

"They weren't close with each other, Jake, no hugging or kisses on the head, "Patrick said. "They were about as comfortable as strangers. I always felt sorry for that little girl; she looked lonely the few times I saw her."

Jake thought back to when and if he'd seen Branna with her dad, but his memory couldn't pick up anything, which was probably because, at the time, he was interested in Macy Reynolds' breasts.

"She wasn't one of the easiest classmates I ever had," Jake said, getting under the hood again.

"Remember you moaning about her a time or two."

"She didn't smile much and was usually frowning or looking pissed off. She had a wardrobe filled with clothes that were from the seventies, and was about as approachable as a mountain lion," Jake said.

"Did you ever wonder why, son?"

"I was sixteen, my main motivator was getting Macy to bend over so I could see down her blouse. Shallow as it makes me sound, Dad, I have to say that Branna O'Donnell's moods didn't worry me too much."

"At least she had Georgie."

"Yup, that woman was pretty much Mum to every child who needed one in Howling," Jake added.

His father agreed as Jake's phone rang. Wiping the hands his mother said were his most precious gift to the world, and why the hell wasn't he using them for the greater good, on a rag, he pulled his phone out of the pocket of his overalls.

"Morning, Buster, you thought any more about my proposal?" A string of abuse followed his words, and then the smile fell from Jake's lips as Buster came round to the reason for his call.

"What!" Jake couldn't believe what he was hearing. "You told her how stupid she is, right?" he added. "Thanks, I'll catch you later, Buster."

"Problems?" Patrick McBride said.

"Buster found Branna O'Donnell walking down the main street as he was heading to work this morning, which I'd guess was close to 5 a.m."

"Your mother is going to be furious."

"Yeah, well, it doesn't endear her to me none either, but she's all grown up now, she can go to hell her own way. I'm not lifting a finger to help her again."

"I'm sure she had her reasons, son. Your mother said she was terrified just being in the clinic."

Jake had seen the fear in those green eyes as she'd clung to him. She'd been terrified, but that wasn't his problem either; he had enough of his own. Looking at the screen as his phone rang again, he didn't want to answer it, but knew he had to or she'd just keep calling.

"Morning, Mother."

"Yeah, Buster just rang me," Jake said, as he dropped his head back and looked up to the roof of his barn as Doc McBride talked. "Can't you go over?" Jake listened as she said how busy she was and how worried she also was about Branna O'Donnell. Jake felt the weight of her expectations settle around him. He was happy to disappoint most people in his life, but his parents were a whole other ballpark. They'd cared for him and pretty much been the best parents a person could ask for, so he owed them. Add to that the fact that he was breaking his mother's heart by walking away from what he'd trained to do, and the guilt factor weighed more than a 1966 Mustang.

"I'm working here, Mum." He gave it one more shot, then listened a while longer as she talked at him. "I can't believe you pulled out the tears," he muttered into the receiver. "Yeah, yeah, all right already, I'll do it." Shutting off the call before she could launch into another reason why he should go check on Branna O'Donnell, he shoved it onto the bench. Pulling off his overalls, Jake then made for the sink.

"Problems?" Patrick McBride stood behind him.

"Because Branna broke herself out of the clinic, your wife thinks I need to check on her because she's too busy to do it herself."

"And you don't want to?"

"I'm not a doctor anymore, Dad, but no one seems to get that fact."

"It's harder for your mother to understand than it is for me, son. She wanted you to take over from her one day, and still can't believe you won't."

Jake dried his hands, then turned to face his father. "I can't, Dad; I can't do it anymore."

He saw the sadness, the pain of a parent knowing his child was suffering, but his father didn't push; he wasn't made that way. Both he and the doc hadn't asked what had happened to change their son into the broken man he'd become, and Jake hadn't volunteered the information. He wasn't ready to go there, and wasn't sure he ever would be.

"I understand that, but you can do this for your mother. It'll take you twenty minutes tops, then she'll be happy. And you go easy on the O'Donnell girl, Jake, not everyone grew up with parents who cared."

"What does that have to do with Branna leaving the clinic? It was foolish, Dad, and dangerous. She has a head injury, and the studies I read on that kind of thing were not something I would ever dismiss lightly."

"It means some people don't live within the guidelines we do, and pushing aside the medical aspect of this, if Branna is as scared as your mother said she was about being in the clinic, then that probably outweighs common sense."

"It was still a dumb thing to do," Jake said.

"Maybe, but I'm sure she had her reasons, so go easy," Patrick Mr. Bride added. "And before I forget, your mother asked me to invite you for dinner; we're having steak."

"Sounds good," Jake waved a hand over his head before walking outside and jumping into his pickup. He kept telling himself to calm down, let the anger go, but as he pulled into the driveway a few minutes later, his insides were set to a slow boil. He didn't need this shit in his life. Didn't want to think like a doctor, or, for that matter, care. He'd come home to try and sort out his head and heal, if that was possible, but he wasn't holding out too much hope. In fact, he was fairly certain he was going to end up the hermit of Howling, holed away in his shed with two dozen cats and people arriving with food now and again. Right about now, that sounded like a good deal.

As he reached the end of her driveway, he saw her, and his hands clenched on the steering wheel. "You have to be shitting me," he said through his teeth. She was carrying a large suitcase over the ground towards the front door.

CHAPTER THREE

Branna was dragging a suitcase from her van into the house when she saw Jake McBride's pickup come into view. She'd hoped that the McBride's would just leave her alone when they heard the news that she'd left the clinic without being discharged. She hoped they'd get so pissed off they'd wash their hands of her. Seems that wasn't the case, if the storm cloud slamming the door of his pickup had any say in it. Dropping the case, she stood straight as he approached.

"What the hell are you doing, you crazy Irish woman?"

Yesterday, her head had been too fuzzy to really check him over, but today she wasn't so lucky. In school he'd been big, but his body hadn't filled out yet, but now it definitely had. He was one of those rare men that were big and graceful; she admired his long, even strides as he stalked towards her. Curls the color of chocolate caramel stood off his head, eyes black as midnight, large fists clenched. His movements were easy, even though he was angry. He wore a worn grey T-shirt with a tear in the shoulder over a broad chest and old shorts that stopped above his knees…and he was indecently handsome.

"About what?"

He stopped before her and drew in a deep breath through his nose, which Branna guessed was because his teeth were clenched.

"You're not in Washington now, Branna, you're not just a number; people here actually care what happens to you, and breaking out of the clinic in the middle of the night is not endearing you any to me or the rest of the community," his words were deep and angry.

She didn't want to feel guilty about what she'd done, but damn, he was making her.

"Annabelle woke and panicked, my mother thinks you're probably lying injured in a gutter somewhere, and if I'd have seen you walk out of that clinic, I'd have blistered your ears so bad they'd still be ringing."

She'd never seen Jake McBride snarl. In school, he was the good guy, the boy everyone wanted to be near. He'd had a way about him that drew people to his side, and he'd pretty much been nice to everyone, except her, because she hadn't wanted anyone to be nice to her, and she definitely hadn't reciprocated in the kindness stakes the few times he tried. In fact, not that much had changed, she realized, except that age had taught her how to be polite while keeping everyone a good arm's length away.

She felt a stab of remorse, thinking about Annabelle and Doctor McBride; she hadn't meant to upset them, she'd just hated being in that clinic and wasn't used to taking other people's feelings into consideration, so she'd just done what she needed to do and left.

"That's a threat, McBride and I'm reporting you."

"Good, and I'll tell Cubby Hawker that you have a head injury and are a few brain cells shy of the regulation dozen."

He really was mad; a muscle was ticking in his jaw and he looked mean, but Branna refused to let herself be impressed with just how awesome he looked. She was not going to fall into that trap again; school had been bad enough. She'd spent too many hours lusting after this man, who was then a boy, and trying to hide it.

"Cubby Hawker is the local sheriff?"

"And a mighty fine one."

"Wow?" She tried to picture the little tubby red-haired boy she'd known as an authority figure and came up short.

"You do realize that you have a head injury, right?"

"I'm fine, McBride. Go home and tell your mother that." Branna picked up her suitcase, then let out a yelp as two hands lifted her off her feet, and suddenly she was heading towards the house with her feet dangling off the ground.

"Put me down!"

He did, in a chair, and then knelt before her so their eyes were level, and Branna's throat went suddenly dry at the anger that pinned her back in the seat.

"I read a study on head injuries when I was in med school, and that was after I saw a student hit his head from a fall. The same day, he hit it again, this time playing ball with his friends. Two days later, he was dead, and I wanted to know why. Turns out, he had brain bleed.

"Jake, there's no need for this; truly, I'm fine."

"Recite the high school pledge for me."

Branna smiled, she knew that off by heart, as they'd had to say it every day before class. Opening her mouth, she tried to speak, but nothing came out, because she couldn't pull the words from her head.

"How about, naming three of your teachers in our final year?" he asked.

Branna literally drew a blank, and he knew it, as she mumbled that she couldn't remember because it was so long ago, which, of course, was a lie, as she remembered everything. It was her curse. Her brain refused to reject things. It stored and catalogued, and she could recall any fact, no matter how much she wanted to forget it.

"The thing about head injuries, Branna, is they come back and bite you in the ass if you don't take the proper precautions. Now, while it's my opinion that, because you're an adult, it's your right to make dumb decisions and go to hell your own way, it's not my mother's. Unfortunately, she does care about the choices you make, and she's one of the few people I give a damn about, so I'm not having her beating herself up because some thick headed Irish idiot won't do as she's told."

"B-but I feel all right." She was shocked that she couldn't remember those things, and trying to find them inside her head was making it hurt.

"Well, obviously, you're not." Standing, he went out the door, and she wondered if he was leaving, now that he'd made his point, but he was simply collecting the suitcase she'd left outside, as he reappeared seconds later.

"You don't have to—" He ignored her and stomped up the stairs to drop her case in the bedroom. Over the next thirty minutes, she watched him unload every item in her van. She tried to stop him, but he just carried right on, and Branna was too tired to fight him. Truth be told, she was shocked over her failing memory. That, above all things, had stopped her from leaving the chair.

"Where does this go?" He held a large leafy plant that was as tall as him, which made him have to speak to her through the fat shiny leaves.

"In here, please."

He placed it in the corner, and Branna admired his tight muscled butt as he bent to put it down. He really was a fine looking man, if a really angry one. She'd been without one so long that it was hardly surprising she was enjoying the view. After all, she was breathing, and pretty much any girl with a pulse would appreciate the man before her.

"That's it, now you don't move from this house; you don't lift anything or watch too much TV." His dark brows had drawn together as he glared down at her. He wasn't even breathing heavy from all that lifting; no sweat slicked his brow. "No driving either, I don't want the citizens of Howling hurt."

"No driving?" Branna queried.

"No, if you need anything, call someone."

She wasn't about to point out that she didn't have anyone to call here in Howling, except maybe Annabelle, and she wasn't really sure where they stood, which was pretty pathetic, considering she'd lived here for three years.

"Where's your phone?" One large hand extended towards her, and Branna was fairly certain he'd pat her down it she didn't pull it out of her back pocket and hand it to him, so she did.

Handing it back to her minutes later, he then turned on his heel and left. No goodbye, no raised hand, no see you around, he just left, started that big green pickup, and rolled out of her driveway.

Looking through her phone, she saw he'd put the clinic number in it, but not his. What had happened to the Jake McBride she'd known all those years ago? The man who now carried his name seemed angry. Visions of yesterday filtered into her head, the way he had carried her, the hand that had run down her back, and the feel of her fingers in his. Those were the actions of the boy she'd once known, so he was obviously still in there. But something had made him change so that now his smile wasn't as bright.

Resting her head, Branna let her eyes sweep the room. Georgie and her husband Dan, plus Annabelle, had been the only ones in the three years she spent in Howling who'd seen through the surly young girl she'd been, and it had been with them that she'd finally found peace. It had broken her heart when Dan had died while she was here. After the death of her mother, to lose him had nearly destroyed Branna, as it had Georgie, but they had clung to each other, and through that found the strength to go on.

The little house was still full of their things. Georgie's clothes had gone, but everything else was still here. The chairs she and Dan had sat in were still in the same place with the little lace head covers. Georgie had made those and tried to teach Branna to stitch some herself, but after much scolding and hilarity, she'd failed. Instead, she'd brought out the knitting needles, and

Branna, surprisingly, had been good at that, and still knitted today.

Climbing out of the chair, she made her way to the sofa, where she pulled the cream knitted blanket she'd made Georgie off of the arm, then curled up and let her mind drift and let the memories settle around her.

The sound of a car woke Branna. Sitting upright, she rubbed her eyes. Her head felt better, steadier. Searching her memory for the high school pledge, she still drew a blank, however, which was unsettling.

"If you make me coffee, I may just forgive you by Christmas, and as that's still a good few months away, you have some work to do."

Branna found herself smiling as Annabelle Smith appeared in her doorway. Unlike yesterday, she was dressed casually today, as a concession to the heat; she wore a floaty pale pink tank top and white shorts that showed off the endless length of her long legs, teamed with white sandals and her toes painted to match her top; she could have stepped out of any fashion magazine. Over her shoulder was slung a buttery colored bag.

"You still got that color thing happening, I see, Smith," Branna climbed off the sofa.

"Always will have, and don't change the subject." She walked into the house carrying a brown bag from which delicious smells were coming.

"Coffee, now!"

"I've got a head injury," Branna complained, as she walked to the kitchen. "Be gentle."

"You play another trick like that, and it'll be more than a head injury you end up with."

Branna struggled one-handed to put the coffee on, then took a deep breath before facing her old friend.

"I'm sorry, Belle, really sorry; it was never my intention to hurt anyone. I just needed to get out of there; you know how I am in those kinds of places, and the reasons why."

"You're not fifteen anymore."

"I know it," Branna sighed. "But I'm no better for the years that have passed; in fact, I'm probably worse."

"Worse how?"

Belle started getting cups and rinsing them out, as they hadn't been used in some time. She then started foraging through the supplies Branna had brought with her.

Branna leaned on a cabinet and watched while she tried to think about what to say. She wasn't big on confidence sharing; she wasn't big on friends either, for that matter. In fact, this woman was probably the only true friend she'd had since her mother's death, but Belle knew pretty much everything there was to know about her. Over the three years they had been friends, Branna had unloaded her fears, her angers, and everything else that was personal to her onto her shoulders, and Belle had simply listened and not judged, then offered the one thing Branna had needed, friendship.

"Come on Bran, spill, you know I'll get it all out of you anyway."

She laughed, and it felt good. Branna could feel the comfort of what they'd once had again, the teasing and companionship that had always been there for them.

"Going to Washington was what I wanted when I left here. WSU offered me anonymity, a place to be a face but nothing more. I worked hard and passed with flying colors, but I never formed any connections like I did here with you and Georgie and Dan, and over time it was just easier to be that way. I guess when I walked out of the clinic yesterday, I did so without thinking about you or Doctor McBride, because that was what I've always done. I'm not good about thinking of anyone else but me," Branna said honestly.

Belle added the milk. "It bothered me that you were going to WSU two years younger than everyone else, and with all those issues you always had."

"Two years was a lot at that age," Branna conceded. She'd skipped grades because of her intelligence, which had done more to hinder her than help.

"And there was me thinking that you'd be partying in Washington, making friends, and doing the wild thing," Belle said.

Branna took the cup she was handed and followed Belle back to the living room. She took Dan's chair, so Branna took Georgie's, which was now hers. Belle put the bag of delicious smells on the small table between them.

"Did you get these from Buster? Because he picked me up this morning and gave me a muffin that tasted like ambrosia."

"No other place like it. That man can bake."

Branna bit into the muffin and made a small appreciative noise. "So, why has Howling's most adored son turned into the ice-man, Belle?"

"Ha, ask me about the national deficit; it'd be easier than trying to understand Jake McBride."

"Yes, I noticed how surly he's become."

"You two should get on fine now; he avoids people too." Belle swallowed a mouthful of coffee and sighed. "Jake trained as a doctor, then went into the US Medical Corps, and I know he was in Iraq, because I work with his mother and she was scared the entire time he was there. Then, one day, a year ago, he came home and started fixing everyone's cars, and he's still doing it, much to Doctor McBride's confusion."

"Okay, so that explains the flashlight thing he did with my eyes, and the lecture I got this morning about head injuries, but not why a trained doctor is now a mechanic."

Belle thought about that for a few seconds as she took another bite, and Branna realized that she was happy to be sitting here with her old, maybe still, friend. She was not on edge with Belle; sharing confidences and gossiping wasn't making her itch like it normally did with anyone else.

"I don't actually know the details, because Jake keeps his problems pretty close to his chest, and while we're friends, Buster and that Texan Tomcat are the only ones he talks to. His mom won't talk about it either, just gets all choked up if you try to. So, I just let it go, but I have to say, it eats the hell out of me not knowing what makes that man tick," Belle said.

Branna laughed. Belle loved to know everyone's business, always had, even in school.

"He's certainly filled out some."

"He's a hot, sexy hunk of man is what he is, and that belligerent attitude only makes him hotter," Belle sighed.

"Don't hold back."

"Don't tell me you haven't noticed, Branna O'Donnell. That man should come with a warning, he's so cute."

He was, but Branna wasn't about to acknowledge the fact.

"Have you and he?" Branna waved her hand about.

Belle sighed. "No. We thought about it, but both decided it would just be wrong as we're more like brother and sister."

"His sister was my age, if I remember right. She wasn't like him, though, kind of serious and into sports, right?" Branna said.

"Katie, she's in L.A. at the police academy."

"The siblings have got that whole services thing going on."

"Surprising, really," Belle said. "Neither parent followed that path."

After Jake, they talked about Belle and what she'd been doing since school, but like her, Annabelle Smith wasn't an open book when it came to her family. Branna knew she had two brothers and they'd lived with her uncle after her mother died. Her uncle was a gambler and hopeless guardian, and Belle had pretty much raised her brothers herself.

"I'm a writer now," Branna said.

Belle gave her a long look before saying. "Just like your daddy."

"I don't write under my name," Branna added, not wanting to draw any parallels between herself and her father, although there were a few of them to make, if you looked closely.

"Well?"

"Well, what?" Branna knew very well what Belle wanted.

"What name do you write under?"

"Rosanna Howlling, two LL's," Branna added.

Belle whistled loud and long. "Even I've heard of you, and I'm more of a magazine girl. The people of Howling already worship your daddy because he's famous, and as shallow as we are, there's no other reason. But you," Belle laughed. "You're going to get the keys to the town when they realize who you are."

"Don't tell them," Branna pleaded.

"Oh, now even you can't imagine that information is not going to get out and spread like wildfire."

Her shoulders slumped. Hell, yes, Branna knew they'd find out; there was nothing sacred in Howling.

"Surely, it's good if they know? Don't you want to sell more books?"

"Maybe...yes, hell, Belle, I just want to live here peacefully and integrate back into the community."

"And you will, just as a celebrity," Belle said, her eyes twinkling.

Branna muttered something unflattering, which made her friend laugh. She couldn't remember a day she'd enjoyed more as she sat there with her old friend. They drank coffee and talked, and it felt like the times they'd shut themselves in her bedroom and stayed there for hours.

"So, got a microphone in your hands any time in the last few years?" Belle questioned, which made Branna shudder.

"No, and I only played in the school band because you cheated in that bet, Annabelle Smith."

"I did not cheat, O'Donnell, and you know it. I was just the better card player of the two of us."

"You hustled me, Smith, plain and simple. 'Come on Bran, if you beat me at cards then you don't have to join the band with me; surely that big brain of yours can do that.'" Branna remembered the bet like it was yesterday; Annabelle had duped her, big time.

"Hey," Belle lifted her hands in the air. "I didn't have to disclose that my uncle played poker for a living; we didn't set out rules or anything."

"Ha, ha," Branna poked out her tongue. "So, to answer your question, no, I have never again sung a note, unless it's in the shower...alone," she added. "That band thing traumatized me."

"Shame," Belle got to her feet. "You sure could sing."

Branna rose too.

"So, we've got this friend thing going again, Bran, you got that?" Belle said leaning on the door frame. "No more bailing on me without a word, no more secrets; you remember the rules, right?"

"I got it."

Belle hugged her hard. "I missed you."

"Missed you too, and I'm sorry I didn't keep in touch."

"That's okay, I was fairly busy having sex and going to wild parties in Portland at nursing school to give you too much thought," Belle added. "Now, remember, you don't take that sling off until the doc tells you to, and nothing that strains your brain for a few days."

"I got that message from Jake," Branna said, thinking of his scowl.

"Oh, and before I go, I thought you should know they're forming a high school reunion committee, so run if you see anyone coming towards you with a clipboard."

"High school was an hour and half from here on a slow yellow bus. Why is anyone from Howling organizing it?"

"Two words, Macy Reynolds."

"She's still here? Wow, I was sure she would have gone on to win a Miss something contest and marry a movie star."

"Howlers don't stray far, Bran, as is evidenced by your return." Belle flicked up a hand and then she was gone, leaving Branna smiling.

The smile was still on her face when she climbed the stairs to go to bed. Three years she'd lived here in Howling, and at the time she'd thought them some of the worst and best of her life. She'd been angry after the death of her mother, and hurting because her father had turned away from her in his grief, but here she'd found friends. Branna had believed she'd never be a real Howler, because she'd been born in Ireland, but maybe she was wrong. Belle had said Howlers don't stray far from home, and she'd been talking about her, Branna O'Donnell.

Climbing into bed, she turned off the lamp and closed her eyes. She wasn't sure how long she'd stay, or even if she would, but for now, this was the right place for her to be…right here under Georgie's roof.

"I'm here, Georgie," she whispered. "Let your soul rest easy, my friend."

CHAPTER FOUR

"I like this one better than last week's mystery muffin, Buster, what's in it?"

"The key word there, Branna, is mystery."

She was sitting in the corner of The Hoot, Buster's cafe, at one of the tables he had set up to look out the big window to the mountains and redwoods beyond. It was early, and the day crisp, but in here it was warm, especially with one of Buster's coffees and a muffin in front of her. She'd been back two weeks now, and life was starting to settle into a routine.

"But you can't keep it as a mystery muffin if it's going to be a regular in your cabinets," Branna protested.

"It won't."

"What? Why?" She looked down at the piece she had left. It had to be a regular or she'd never get to taste it again.

Buster's sigh could have felled a forest. "Branna, we've had this discussion four times, and you've only been back in town two weeks. The mystery muffins are a treat for those game enough to try them; they're not a regular thing."

"Give me the recipe then, so I can make it again."

The loud scoffing sound coming from behind the cabinets made her frown.

"I can bake."

"Annabelle told me you burn things," Buster said.

She rolled her eyes, even though Buster couldn't see her. "One thing, when we were in high school. I burnt the popcorn, and she had to take the blame as we were in her house and her uncle wasn't too happy with the smell."

"That's not how I heard it." Buster appeared behind the counter. Those beautiful eyes narrowed. The man had the longest lashes she'd ever seen; women would pay good money for those.

"I can cook, I tell you, and one day I'm proving it," Branna gave him a glare.

Branna had always felt comfortable around Buster, and that hadn't changed. She came in here to sit in silence and read. If he chose to talk, they did; if not, he grunted hello and good bye, and that was where it ended.

"You better have those pies cooked, Griffin!"

She hadn't seen him since the day he stormed out of her house, and now there he was, standing just inside the door with the sun surrounding him. The table she sat at wasn't tucked completely out the way of the door, so she had a partial view of Jake McBride, big and beautiful, eyes narrowed and looking downright unsociable as he entered.

"You're early; I just pulled them from the oven." Buster disappeared back into the kitchen as he spoke.

"Had some stuff to do in town and my stomach is gnawing on itself, so feed me." He saw her then, and she was certain he would have walked back out if the pie wasn't important to him. He gave her a nod, but didn't add any words.

Another scruffy T-shirt stretched across his shoulders, this one bearing some army slogan, and he'd pulled on cargo shorts that had seen better days, on his feet he wore trainers, also worn. The silence between them stretched uncomfortably, but as neither of them were inclined to speak, they both let it settle into a heavy thickness.

"Jake, this is Branna."

Jake snorted as Buster appeared with a tray of sandwiches. "You want coffee? I'm making Branna another one."

"Ah, sure," he shot her a look. "How's the head?" The words were thrown at her in dismissive way, as if to say, I don't give a shit, but anyway…

"Good, thank you." Branna then reeled off the high school pledge, and named three of her teachers, remembering how he'd asked her those questions the other day, and she'd been unable to answer them.

"Nice," he looked at the chair across the table from hers, then pulled it out and folded his large body into it. "What about the wrist?"

"Your mum said I had to wear the brace for a while yet, because of the damage I've done to some things inside."

"Tendons and ligaments," he said.

Buster dropped a plate loaded with food in front of Jake and a mug of steaming black coffee before each of them.

"He won't tell me what's in the mystery muffin," Branna said, filling the silence, because now that Jake was close and looking at her with those intent black eyes, she felt uncomfortable. In fact, she wanted to squirm in her seat.

She'd been like this in school when he was near; her face used to flush and she'd feel off balance. Branna hadn't wanted to be infatuated by Jake McBride. In fact, she'd done everything she could not to be, but nothing had helped. So, she'd tried to avoid him or have a really bad attitude whenever he approached her, but nothing had worked.

There was no doubting that he'd been hot in school, but there'd been other equally handsome boys too, but it was Jake that had got to her, Jake that she'd secretly lusted after with the ferocious heart of a teenager.

"Mystery is the key word there, Branna."

"Buster said that."

"Well then, he's probably right."

She watched as he ate half the pie in one bite. His teeth were large and white and Branna had the disturbing vision of them nibbling on her ear.

"I'm sorry!" She hadn't meant to say it so loudly, but she knew she needed to apologize, and now was as good a time as any.

His dark brows rose at her words. "About what?"

"For the way I treated your mother and Belle, the way I treated you when I should have been thanking you for looking after me, and instead was being awkward and ungrateful."

His smile wasn't the light your face kind that it used to be, but she saw a glimpse of the boy she once knew.

"I do awkward and ungrateful. My best friend's the master at it, and as it turns out, I've perfected it myself over the last few years," Jake said.

"Valid point," these words came from the depths of the kitchen, confirming Buster's status as Jake's best friend.

"Still, please accept my apology anyway."

He did that other disturbing thing he'd done in school then, looking at her as if he could read every thought spinning around in her head.

"Accepted. It's not like I wasn't prepared anyway."

"Prepared?" Branna questioned.

"You weren't up for Miss Congeniality in school, Rosebud, so I figured unless you'd had a personality transplant, not much had changed."

"I was fifteen!" Branna literally spluttered out the word. "You show me any kids of that age who are congenial! And, furthermore, I didn't have the compulsion that you had back then to have everyone fall at my feet. You went through your days flashing that smile at any unsuspecting female, or male for that matter, and being bloody accommodating to everyone but me; it was enough to bring up a person's lunch!"

Buster's laughter sounded like a rusty hinge.

"And there was me thinking you hadn't noticed me in school; fair warms my heart to see how wrong I was," Jake drawled. "And, for the record," he leaned closer to Branna. "I tried to be accommodating, you just didn't reciprocate."

He was deliberately taunting her, and yes she should laugh and brush it off, but the cold look in his eyes told her that to him there was no humor involved. His mood was dark and he wasn't about to sugar coat anything, especially not to her. In fact, if she got up and left, Branna was fairly certain, it would just about make his day.

"Hard to believe the man before me is the same boy I once knew," Branna said, hitting back at him. She didn't understand what had happened to Jake McBride, but something had, and it had shaved off all his light edges and replaced them with dark ones. "You sure grew up different from what I imagined."

"Well, I guess shit happens to all of us, Rosebud, even the golden boys."

He was angry, even though his voice sounded like he was messing with her, and it wasn't recent anger either, this was deep-seated. Branna understood what she was seeing in him, because she'd battled it for years herself.

"I never said I thought of you as a golden boy."

"It was implied."

"Like hell," Branna snapped.

"Well, at least you stayed the same. Belligerent, rude, and you still got that flower child look going." Shards of black ice ran over her from top to bottom, as he took in her loose flowing top, faded cutoffs, and leather sandals.

Branna had taken years to put the emotions from her past in a place that could no longer hurt her, but looking at this man, she felt them return; she felt the helpless anger and confusion of her time at Howling resurface. Swallowing a large mouthful of coffee, she took a few seconds to get herself back under control. There was no way she would allow Jake McBride to provoke that kind of reaction in her again…ever.

"Listen, McBride, I think we've established we weren't buddies in school, and I'm fairly confident that's not going to change any time soon, even with your new hot, bad boy, I don't give a fuck attitude." Branna kept her voice level. "So, here's the thing, thanks for looking after my head and putting on the polite act that day, but in the interest of us both finding some peace in this town, how about we agree to stay the hell away from each other?"

"And there was me thinking we were hitting it off just fine."

His lazy smile made her hands twitch to slap him. Pushing back her chair instead, she walked out of the bakery without another word.

Jake watched the door close behind Branna, then slowly took another bite of his pie. The action was a reflex, and the pie that he loved so much now tasted like dust. His eyes followed her along the path in long angry strides until she disappeared from his sight.

When had he become an asshole?

"That went well." Buster sat in the seat Branna had just left.

"Not one of my finest moments," Jake said. "She used to annoy me in school, and it looks like not much has changed, especially as I've lost my ability to sugar coat things."

"The thing is, Jake, I like her. She's sure not a talker, and when she comes in here we've not passed more than a few words, but she's a comfortable person, and I don't want to see her hurt, especially as it's my belief that girl has suffered a whole world of hurt already."

"Jesus, did you just string an entire sentence together unprovoked?"

Buster's look told Jake he knew that he was deflecting the conversation away from himself.

"You're going through shit, Jake, but you have the support of your friends and family to help you through the hell you're battling; that little girl has no one and never did have." Buster's eyes were somber as he looked at Jake. "Her daddy, according to my Aunt Vi, was a cold unfeeling asshole, and if memory serves, Branna O'Donnell only had Annabelle and Georgie as friends, while you pretty much claimed everyone else in Howling."

Jack ran a hand over his face as shame washed over him. Not many people could pull emotion out of Jake these days, but Buster was one of them. He didn't push or smother him, and usually when he spoke Buster made a lot of sense, like now.

"I'm just not real good company anymore; maybe I should stay home?" Jake looked into the sympathetic eyes of his friend.

"Maybe, but then I can't imagine you're all that happy with your own company either."

"Also true," Jake agreed. "She come in here much? Branna?"

Buster ran with the change in conversation. "Most days, until she can start running again, then she said it will be less often."

"She runs?"

"Yeah, seems she's one of those sicko healthy types like you."

"Says the man who pumps weights and sits on that rowing machine for hours."

"True, but I don't run," Buster added with a smug look.

"Wonder what she does for a living?"

Buster settled back in his chair. "Annabelle said she was a teacher and is now a writer of some kind."

"No kidding, just like her daddy. What else you got?" Jake knew the grapevine would be working overtime with a new person in town, especially with Branna having lived here before.

"Annabelle wouldn't say; she reckons Branna is a private person and didn't want everyone knowing her stuff."

Jake snorted. "Someone will get it out of her, or dig up the information; that's how this town works."

"Yeah, not much for gossip myself."

Jake pointed his cup at Buster. "You're the biggest gossip of the lot, but just hide it behind that piss off face of yours," he teased.

"I don't have a piss off face; I just don't understand the need to be yammering on constantly like some."

"I hope you're not accusing me of yammering." Jake climbed to his feet to take the dishes and put them in the sink. "Because I've never yammered a day in my life."

"Whatever."

"See you at seven." Lifting a hand, Jake made for the door.

"She's planting stuff and digging holes. I told her to call me if she needs help," Buster said, as he headed back into the kitchen.

"And you're telling me this why?" Jake turned to look at his friend.

"Just on the chance you wanted to apologize for being a bastard."

"I am a bastard, Griffin, when are you and the rest of this town going to realize that?"

Buster said something that Jake missed as he walked out of The Hoot.

"Hey there, Jake."

"Macy," Jake dug around in his pocket for his keys in the hopes that the woman who'd just walked up to him would take the hint and let him leave.

"The committee thinks you'd be a good man to take the microphone on the night of the reunion," Macy Reynolds-Delray stated.

"Not really good at public speaking, Macy. If you need any cars tuned, however, I'm your man. Plus, I'm not feeling too social these days," Jake located the keys and started towards his pickup; Macy followed, tottering on her heels.

Macy Reynolds, now Reynolds-Delray, was the girl who had it all in school. The girl that every boy lusted after; she was certainly the person he'd had plenty of uncomfortable nights dreaming about. Homecoming queen…every girl in school wanted to be her friend. Of course, that club had been exclusive. She was still beautiful, but now it was a forced beauty and the eyes beneath those long fake lashes were cold. Carefully pampered, her hair was colored almost white, her breasts looked bigger, which could mean she'd had some work done, but he wasn't sure. She looked about as real as one of the dolls his sister had loved as child.

"It's one night, Jake, at the school you attended." Even her voice had lost that enthusiastic, if highly annoying, pitch…this one was cold and emotionless.

"Sorry, Macy, I'm busy."

"I hear Branna O'Donnell is back too, and she's a teacher and writer," she added, stopping on the curb beside his pickup. I'm going to ask her to do some handouts and advertising for the committee."

Why was he surprised that Macy knew this about Branna? Small towns could ferret out even the most closely guarded secret.

"You do that, Macy. I'm meeting mum for lunch, so I'll see you around." He didn't look back, just climbed in and fired it up and headed out of town. He had a barn, plenty of loud music, and cars that sounded a whole lot better than running into more of the good folk of Howling. Driving past the end of Branna's driveway, he pushed his foot down on the accelerator; he wasn't going anywhere near her again. Something about her flashed warning signals inside his head, and then there was the fact that he couldn't look at her and not want to strip her naked.

***

Branna was still cursing herself when she pulled Georgie's hat on and walked outside.

She'd overreacted to Jake today and that annoyed her, because it meant that all those years she'd worked hard at forgetting, or at least locking all those feelings away, hadn't worked. Well, they had, but now they weren't anymore, because of him, Jake McBride. Why did she care what he thought of her? Why had she ever cared? She'd reacted like an emotional fool, and then stormed out of the bakery like a child throwing a tantrum. That was not the woman she had become, the one who'd spent years perfecting the imperturbable façade.

The problem was, she couldn't get him out of her head. What had changed him into the man she'd seen today?

Stomping around the back of the house, Branna found the garden and began tugging out weeds with her good hand. Georgie would be pissed if she saw her treasured garden being strangled to death by the bloody things, and even one-handed it was good to be doing something, anything to drive the memory of those cold, angry dark eyes out of her head.

Jake McBride was hurting, Branna had seen it, but why?

She'd been working a while when she felt someone watching her; looking over her shoulder, she saw a young boy. Skinny, lots of brown curls, and wide brown eyes.

"Can I help you?"

"Penny said I needed to come and say sorry for knocking you over with my bike."

Branna got to her feet and arched backwards; she was stiff from bending for so long.

"Well, say it then."

"What?"

"Sorry I knocked you over and hurt your arm and made you bang your head," Branna said.

"Yeah, that," the boy mumbled.

"It's not an apology if you don't actually apologize."

His brown eyes studied her for a few seconds.

"Georgie said you were the difficult type when you wanted to be."

"Yeah, well from where I'm standing, you don't appear very accommodating either," Branna added.

He got off his bike and rested it carefully on the ground, which told Branna he treasured that thing, as most kids just dropped theirs when they climbed off.

"What's your name?"

"Michael Tucker. What're you doing?" he added, coming forward to look down at the small patch she'd weeded.

"Baking double chocolate muffins." He snuffled a little laugh that made Branna smile.

"I could help, seeing as I hurt you and all."

"Now, that's an apology." Branna pointed to the shovel she'd found leaning on the house. "You get that and start digging a hole over there so I can plant something in it."

He did as she asked, and soon they were both working.

"What are you putting in?" Michael asked.

"I'm thinking a small row of trees around the back to shelter the garden first; it was something Georgie always wrote to me that she wanted done, but just never got 'round to it."

"She sure loved her garden."

"Why aren't you in school?" Branna looked at him as she asked the question, and was glad she did, because he looked guilty as hell.

"We don't got to go in today."

"I don't have to go to school today," Branna corrected him. "So, the school just decided to give you all a break?"

"Yeah."

"I don't think so," Branna added. "You're playing hooky?"

"I hate school; it's boring." He dug the spade into the dirt with force.

"You're breaking my heart, Mikey. You want to try working for a living? Then you'll have something to moan about."

"You're not working."

"Why is it boring at school?" Branna asked, ignoring his statement, as she did need to get back to work, but hadn't found the enthusiasm to do so yet.

"They don't teach us anything new, so I just sit there all day bored."

"How old are you?" He was tall and thin, all knobby elbows and knees.

"Ten and a half."

"You smart or something?"

"Maybe." He muttered the word, and Branna wondered if he was like her. "You read, Mikey?" If he was like her and Georgie had found out, chances were she'd got him reading all the books she loved, like she'd made Branna do.

"Molly Browning says reading's for people who ain't got any friends."

"Ain't is not a word; therefore, don't use it."

He stopped digging and looked at her again, with those big brown eyes that could melt a person in seconds.

"Georgie used to talk like that."

Branna swallowed the lump in her throat at the mention of her dear friend. "Yes, well, she was right."

They carried on in silence for a few more minutes.

"So, I'm guessing this Molly Browning's real perky? Pretty face, popular with the boys, plenty of giggling friends hanging around?"

"Kind of, she's not that pretty, though. She has real pointy ears that she tries to hide under her hair. She can be pretty mean when she wants to be, but Georgie said there will be something nice inside her somewhere."

Branna had also received that particular speech from her friend.

"So, what does your mum think about you playing hooky?" Branna sat down on the dirt, because she was tired all of a sudden and her arm was beginning to ache, even though she'd been using the other one.

"She's in L.A. for work."

"Someone has to be looking after you. What will they say?" Branna questioned him.

"Gran won't find out, she doesn't leave the house much, and Connor doesn't care about that kind of thing."

"Connor being?" Branna slowly dragged the information out of Mikey, until she found out his gran cared for him, while his mum traveled about with her job, and Connor was his uncle and sounded like a size ten asshole, but she kept that to herself. The man didn't seem to work, just lounged about, living off his sister and grandmother. There was another uncle who was a lawyer and lived in Boston, and an aunt who lived in Portland. Reading between the lines, it sounded like Mikey pretty much did as he wanted with no one watching over him. Not an ideal situation, but Branna was pretty sure he wouldn't get into too much trouble here in Howling.

"You looked in there yet?'

Dragged from her thoughts, Branna looked to where the boy was pointing and felt her heart sink as she saw it was towards the large shed behind them.

"Not yet."

"You want me to go in with you?"

He knew, Branna could see it in those intelligent brown eyes; the boy knew she didn't want to go into that shed and see the car that had meant so much to her dear friend. Seeing that would bring it all back again. It had all started with that car.

"I don't know if I'm ready, Mikey," Branna said, surprised she'd told him the truth.

"She said you were strong."

Branna closed her eyes at his words. He may be ten and a half, but he had the insight of a far older person. She rose to her feet and swiped at her butt to remove any lingering dirt. If Jake McBride saw her now, it would just reinforce his belief in her '70's look, especially with Georgie's large straw hat on her head.

"You go inside for me and get the keys that are beside the front door on the rack then, Mikey." Decision made, Branna started towards the building that had been standing silently waiting for her to open it since she'd arrived. She heard the thud of his feet approaching seconds later.

"I've forgiven you for knocking me down, Mikey, so you don't have to beat yourself up about it anymore." Branna patted his head as they walked towards the shed.

"You should have been watching where you were going anyway."

"You're not actually trying to blame me?" Branna watched his agile little fingers slip the key into the padlock and heard the click as it opened. She felt the pressure in her chest increase, as he pushed the doors wide.

"Come on," Mikey urged her forward.

"All right, gee, you're a nag." Branna took the hand he held out, and gripped it hard as they walked inside. She felt the tension inside him too, the anticipation of the memories they both knew would be waiting for them.

"Georgie and I used to drive into town and get ice cream up until six months ago, and she used to let me change the gears sometimes," Mikey said, leading her to where Geraldine stood beneath the pale green cover.

"She found me sitting on the side of the road crying," Branna said, remembering that day as if it were yesterday. Her life had changed because of it. "I remember hearing Geraldine's motor purr as she opened the door and asked me if I needed a ride anywhere."

"Why do you think she was so special when so many aren't?" Mikey's words were low and gruff, and she could hear the emotion in them. Branna didn't fight the tears as she normally did, instead letting them fall.

"She saved me too, Mikey. I don't know what would have happened if Georgie hadn't found me."

"I was breaking into her house, had the back window open with one leg over the sill when she caught me." His voice was choked as he battled the tears.

"I miss her," Branna whispered. "She made sense of everything for me."

"Me too, it's like the sun's gone down now, Branna, like there's no light left anymore without her here."

Branna didn't willingly touch people. She'd always found that touching people made you feel things or made them believe you felt things, and she didn't want that, didn't want people to think she cared. She hadn't wanted that since her mother died and her father turned his back on her. But right now, she knew what Georgie wanted from her, could almost feel the pressure of a hand on her shoulder urging her to give Mikey comfort. Tugging on his hand, she pulled him into her body and held tight.

They cried, both of them, loud and long, needing to grieve for the woman who had saved them and given them love and a reason to live. This was their time to mourn. Branna hadn't allowed herself to do that. The sorrow and pain had lay in her stomach like a hard knot, tied really tight. She had worried that if she let go she'd never stop, but now, with the tears streaming down her face, she only felt relief.

"Shhh now, Mikey, it's all right." She kissed the top of his head like Georgie used to do to her, and patted his back until his cries stopped. She felt calmer, as if the tears had begun to release the sorrow and pain from her body.

"I miss her."

"Me too, Mikey. So much that it actually hurts inside, but being here with you, and talking about our friend is helping, don't you think?"

He nodded, his arms still wrapped hard around her waist. "I-I have to tell you something, Br-Branna."

"What?"

"Georgie told me before she died that out of all the children that had come through her life, me and you were hers, and that we would find each other because we're made the same way, and we need each other."

"S-so, I'm stuck with you…is that how this is going to work, Mikey?"

"Seems like."

She wasn't sure, but thought that the boy sighed and his body lost its stiffness as he leaned on her, and Branna bent down and held him close. *I hear you, Georgie, and yes, he's now part of me, just like he was you.*

"Okay, but I'm not the pushover she was. As far as big sisters go, I'm pretty hard ass."

His chuckle was the sweetest sound. "You speak like me, but you sound different."

"It's an Irish accent, squirt, but I've been in America so many years it's softened. Now, you get into that house and find the key to Geraldine; we need to start this bad boy up, and maybe get my purse, in case we do and we can get ice cream."

"Wow, cool!" He ran in a flash of limbs from her towards the house, and Branna took the time to collect herself. She didn't like excesses of emotion; they played hell with your ability to function.

She began to walk around the shed, looking at the tools that Dan, Georgie's husband, had hung carefully along one wall. It was still immaculate, each thing in its place. Memories bombarded her; she saw Dan laughing as she tried to hammer a nail into the school project he was helping her make, saw Georgie walk in through the doors, the sun at her back, all that red hair alight with light streaking through it. Dan would drop whatever he was doing and sweep her up in his arms, kissing whatever part of her face he could reach.

"I miss you both so much," she whispered. Her fingers touched as she moved, running down the long handle of a tool, or along the edge of the work bench. This had been her haven; this had been the sanctuary that a broken sixteen-year-old had needed.

"I didn't meet Dan, but she told me about him."

"He was special like her," Branna said, coming back to where Mikey now stood beside the Mustang. "Had a really deep laugh that made everyone want to join in."

"Georgie told me about him, and showed me pictures."

They worked together to remove the cover, and then there it was, the beloved Geraldine.

"Why's it called Geraldine?"

"Dan's mum was called Geraldine, and as they had no kids, he named his car after her."

It was pale baby blue, with red leather upholstery, and it was hers. Branna smiled, a genuine one that started in her belly and traveled through her body.

"The battery's on the work bench…you want me to put it in?" the boy said.

"You know how?"

Mikey snorted and she was pleased to hear the sound, because her heart had just about broken hearing the pain of his cries and feeling the sobs that shook his body. She knew Georgie had given her the house because she had loved Branna, but she also realized now that there was more to that gift, and that perhaps this boy had been part of the legacy.

"Georgie taught me stuff."

"She was a pretty handy lady, that's for sure." Branna lifted the hood, and he placed in the battery, then connected the terminals.

"Okay, squirt, let's fire her up."

They both climbed in and Branna turned the key and she roared to life, which made them both laugh like crazy for some strange reason.

"I may not be able to drive this time, Mikey, with my wrist still being sore, but—"

"Is that Jake McBride?"

Following the finger Mikey had pointed out the doors of the shed, she saw the dark green pickup truck appear, Jake pulled it to a stop beside the barn and Branna refused to acknowledge how good the man inside looked as he climbed out. The sun played with his curls and surrounded him as he walked the few paces to the entrance; the expression on his face wasn't as mean as the one he wore this morning, which made her relax a little.

"Jake loves this car; he asked Georgie if he could buy it once," Mikey said.

"Just the once?" Branna switched off the ignition as she looked at Mikey, who was looking at Jake. She sighed when she saw the hero worship in his eyes. It was just like school all over again. He collected admirers like other people did stamps, only now, he didn't seem too keen on keeping his collection going.

CHAPTER FIVE

"You're trespassing, McBride," Branna said, going on the attack.

He bent to look into her open window and she fought the childish urge to wind it up as those dark eyes studied her. Branna could see the lines around them, and the small scar under his chin, and this close he was devastating. A big hunk of male that to most women would be irresistible, but she was not most women, nor was she still a besotted teenager. Therefore, Branna absolutely refused to find him anything but irritating, especially after their last encounter.

"I'm sorry," he said solemnly.

His words took the wind out of her sails, just when she was going to launch another verbal volley. They were only two simple words, yet she knew that for this new version of Jake McBride, they were two of the hardest to say, just as coming on her property to say them hadn't been easy either.

"Okay," Branna said, and saw the flash of relief cross his face, that she was not going to challenge him further.

"Hey there, Mikey, how's it with you?" Jake lowered his head to look at the boy, the intent expression changing. His smile was genuine, as was the soft look in his eye as he looked at the child.

"Real good, Jake, we're going to get ice cream."

"Nice day for an ice cream, it has to be said." He kept smiling, one of those slow ones that made the recipient's, who unfortunately was Branna, insides turn to liquid by the time it reached his eyes. It was especially potent, because she knew they were rare these days. It seemed Jake McBride still had some of the boy inside him, if only for a child.

"The apologies are done with, so you can leave now, McBride." Branna had always found that confrontation was the best way to deal with attraction or any kind of intense emotion, and as she was feeling a little vulnerable after her crying jag with Mikey, she thought defense was what she needed right now.

"You should try a simply hello, Rosebud, it's how we do things in the US of A."

His drawl was deliberate, as were the eyes he ran over her face and down her neck. Heat trickled over her body and landed right between her thighs, but she ignored it. Her body may betray her when he was near, but her head would remain clear and her expression calm.

"Hello, now go away; Mikey and I have places to go."

"You see, now there's where the problem starts for me, Rosebud."

Branna pushed her spine back into the seat as he braced himself on the roof and leaned his head further in the window. God, she could smell him now, that sexy man scent of outdoors, sweat, and the bite of citrus, which she thought may be coming from his hair.

"Wh-what problem?" Branna cleared her throat as his smile grew wider, and she wanted to close his head in the window to wipe it off. Turning away, she stared at the steering wheel instead.

"This is a stick shift, and you have an injured wrist that currently is in a sling, which I'm glad to see you had the sense to wear; so, to my way of thinking, that rules you out of driving."

"Then we'll take my van; its automatic," Branna said.

"Now, that would be a shame, seeing as you're both ready to go, seated right here as you are."

"We can take it out when I get better, McBride." Branna looked at him again and saw the spark of humor in his dark eyes, even though his face was still serious.

"Tell you what. I'll do you both a favor, seeing as Mikey has his heart set on taking Geraldine out. You shift your cute little butt over, Rosebud. Mikey, you climb in the back, and I'll drive you both into town for that ice cream." Jake opened the door as he spoke. "It'll be a sacrifice, as my day is full, but for friends that's what you do, make sacrifices."

Some may be fooled by that innocent face, but Branna was not one of them.

"Gee, Jake, that's real good of you," Mikey said.

"You're not really falling for that line of bull are you?" She looked at the boy, who had done as Jake asked and climbed into the back seat.

"Jake's one of the good guys; Georgie told me he was."

"She was usually such an astute judge of character; still, we all make mistakes one time or other," Branna said these words softly, but Jake heard them, because he snorted.

"Said if I'm in trouble to go to him, even if he looks angry, which she said you do a bit these days, Jake, no offense," Mikey added.

"None taken."

"And that I could count on him."

She looked out the side of her eye and saw Jake's jaw clench then release after Mikey had finished speaking.

"She's right, Mikey, if you need me you only got to holler."

"Well, now that this touching moment has come to a close, you can take your offer and—"

"Come on, Rosebud, stop being difficult and move over so I can get in." This time, he pleaded…looking like a small boy who was about to touch his favorite toy for the first time.

"I wanted to be the one to drive it." Branna hadn't meant the words to sound whiny, but knew they did.

"I know you did." The hand he placed on her head was brief, but still it comforted her, which annoyed the hell out of Branna. She didn't want anything from Jake McBride, least of all comfort. "But now that she's yours, you get to drive her whenever you want to."

"Don't get any ideas," Branna said, moving to the passenger seat. "This is a one-time thing, McBride."

He was in the car so quick she hadn't even settled herself.

"Always makes me laugh when I hear you talk American, but sound Irish," he said.

"If you're going to insult me, I will rescind my offer."

"Okay, so there's the brain box with those big words I remember." Jake was running his hands over the steering wheel and dashboard as if he was stroking the fur of an animal.

"Rescind is not a big word."

"For a jock like me it is."

"Thought you were a doctor, Jake?" Mikey said, leaning over the seat between them. "That's what Georgie told me."

"He's just playing dumb, Mikey, but it's something he does well, as you can see."

"Nothing you can say will hurt me right now, Rosebud."

She swallowed her smile as he turned the key in the ignition and then pressed the accelerator and laughed at the throaty roar of the engine. An old memory slipped into her head of one Christmas, when her mother had bought her father a remote-controlled airplane. He had looked just as Jake did now. Pushing the disturbing thought aside, she watched Jake's hands put the Mustang into gear.

"We ready?" he said, smiling, and this one reached his eyes.

"Yes," both Branna and Mikey said.

He eased them out of the shed and down the driveway, and once he was on the road, he put his foot down and the car surged forward, pushing Branna back in her seat.

"If I die right now, it would be as a happy man."

They both knew that was a lie, because whatever demons were driving Jake McBride these days were stopping him from being happy, and it would take more than a drive in a car to change that.

"Why do you call Branna, Rosebud?"

"It was his idea of fun in high school, Mikey. Something he used to torment me."

Jake took his eyes briefly off the road and rested them on her. "Now, that wasn't the reason at all; it was because you were cute, and when you introduced yourself that first day you said your name was Branna Rose O'Donnell, and I thought Rosebud suited you better."

Branna hadn't expected that. "He tormented me like Molly does to you, Mikey," she said, to cover her confusion.

"Yeah, Molly's real good at embarrassing people," Mikey said.

Bitch, Branna thought, realizing that she already felt something for this serious little boy.

"And, for the record, I didn't torment you; you just took everything I said and twisted it around. Any time I tried to make friends with you, you instantly thought I was being mean, or trying to have fun at your expense," Jake said, shooting her another look.

Branna thought back to those days in school, when every morning she opened her eyes she wondered if she had the strength to get through another day. Everything had just seemed too much effort without her mother. She knew that Jake had tried to be friendly with her a few times, but her attraction to him, and her jealously because he seemed to have everything she wanted, like a family, popularity and plenty of friends, had made her unreceptive.

"You shaped my eraser into a…a," Branna said, waving her hand about, aware of the fact that they had a ten year old listening to their every word.

"One fingered salute?"

"Yes." Actually, what it had been was a penis, but she wasn't mentioning that word in front of the boy.

Jake's laugh was a deep rumble that she felt in the pit of her stomach and refused to acknowledge.

"While we're on the subject of school, I'm wondering why you're not there, Mikey?" Jake asked.

Branna raised an eyebrow at Mikey, who, in turn, slumped lower in his seat. "He's playing hooky."

"Why'd you tell him that?" Mikey demanded.

"Because it is wrong to lie, Michael, and the sooner you understand that, the easier your life will be." Branna felt Jake's eyes on her as she spoke.

"So, it's true, you are a teacher." Jake changed down a gear as they turned a corner, then pushed his foot down on the gas once more, sending them forward in an exhilarating rush.

"Were," she corrected.

"You're a teacher?" the boy moaned. "But, you're kind of cool."

"Surely one of the few teachers you've had in your short school career must have been cool?" Branna said.

There was a short silence while Mikey thought about that before answering.

"No, not that I can think of. But Mr. Hope was okay, I guess, but he's retired now. He used to throw equations at me for fun whenever we passed each other in the halls. Some of them were real hard. He had me IQ tested."

"God save us, another one," Jake whispered.

Shooting a nasty look at him, Branna said. "I had Mr. Hope for a year, and he had me IQ tested too, but that was in high school; surely you're not there already?"

"He helped out here at Howling Elementary for a few years when he left the high school," Jake said, answering her question.

"What did you score?" Branna held her breath as she waited for the answer.

"One hundred twenty-eight."

"Me too." She couldn't breathe as the memories of those early days filled her head. She'd been a freak, her classmates had said, when someone found out her results. Was Mikey suffering like she had?

"Take a breath, Rosebud, he's doing okay," Jake's words were gentle.

She gave a jerky nod and filled her lungs with air.

"You like mathematical equations, Mikey?" Branna asked the boy.

"Sure, who doesn't?"

"Normal people."

"Shut up, McBride, why the hell you think you're normal is beyond me. I remember you in the science lab doing all those weird things with test tubes."

Branna couldn't stop the laugh as he waggled his eyebrows at her.

"So, getting back to you taking a day off, just because," Jake re-entered the conversation. "Your gran know about it?"

"No."

"How about Connor?"

"Connor's a dickhead."

"Lady present, bud, mind the language."

"Sorry," Mikey mumbled after Jake's rebuke.

Branna waved her hand about to indicate she'd accepted his apology, but stayed silent as Jake talked to Mikey. Her head felt fuzzy, and her stomach ached. It was like she was back there during those early days when she'd found out her IQ was above average. It had just added to her difficulties, especially as she'd already been different, and it had given her yet another reason to withdraw into herself.

"So, how often are you taking these unscheduled days off and why?"

Mikey's sigh was loud and long in answer to Jake's question. "A couple every month."

Jake whistled.

"I get the mail before gran or Connor see it, and the phone's been cut off, so they can't ring."

"It's a small town, Mikey, eventually the school will give up sending letters and call 'round to see your gran."

Branna watched Jake's large, steady hands handle the Mustang with ease as he questioned the boy. She didn't want to feel any degree of comfort or companionship around this man; Branna had a feeling that if she did, she'd be in all kinds of trouble.

"It's boring," Mikey said.

She was impaled by Jake's dark gaze once more, and then he looked at the road, which meant Branna could breathe again.

"Sound familiar to you, Rosebud? If my memory serves, you were bored in school too."

She had been, even though Mr. Hope had tried to keep her brain busy. What she hadn't realized was that anyone else had noticed.

"He needs some accelerated classes, and if they're not available, then they need to give him some work above the general class stuff," Branna said.

"Molly and her friends will laugh at me more."

"Not if she doesn't know." Branna had had her fair share of teasing when she'd been given extra work, but she'd make sure that didn't happen to Mikey, even if she had to go the school to sort it out herself. "What's your teacher like, surely she'd be happy to help?"

"Miss. Todd is okay, I guess, but she gets angry with me if I answer all the questions, so I don't answer any now. Plus, the work she gives is so easy I have it done before the others, which makes them get angry and makes her think I cheat."

"You may want to duck down in that seat, sport, we're just about in town, and if people see you, word will get back to your gran," Jake said.

Looking over the seat as Jake pulled into a parking spot, Branna noted Mikey was now slouched so low, only the top of his head was visible. She wouldn't let this sweet little boy suffer because he had a brain; she'd find a way to help him.

"What flavors are we all having?"

"Lemon," came a small voice from the back seat.

"Lemon!" Jake scoffed. "Men don't eat lemon."

"Good thing I'm a boy then."

Branna giggled, the sound slipping from her mouth before she could stop it.

"I'd forgotten about your laugh."

"What's wrong with my laugh, McBride?" Branna questioned.

"Not a damned thing."

She dropped her eyes as heat filled her cheeks. No, no, no, she would not be enamored with this man again; she simply refused to.

"Be back soon." He got out of the car while she was scrambling with her thoughts, and made his way to the store in that slow gait that looked as if he'd just ridden in from a day on the ranch.

"Why is Connor dumb?" Branna asked.

"He just is."

"How old is he?" Branna watched Jake bend to pick something up, the material of his old shorts pulled tight across his butt, which she had to admit was fine.

"Twenty two."

"I can't believe he's dumb if he's your uncle." Jake was reaching into his back pocket for his wallet now. It was the gesture of a trillion people, mainly men, every day, but on him it was sexy. After today, she was steering clear of that man, Branna vowed. Maybe she needed to have an affair that would push him from her head.

"He's not really dumb, but he acts dumb." Branna heard the disgust in the boy's voice.

While she talked with Mikey, she let her eyes drift around the streets of Howling. She and Belle had spent many of their days wandering along them. They'd sat for hours at the edge of the lake and hiked through the trails with the redwoods standing over them. Annabelle Smith had the best friend a girl could ever have.

From the day Branna had walked into the high school, kids had started in on her:

"You talk funny."

"My dad said the only thing Irish people did well was grow potatoes."

"Hey, O'Donnell, top of the morning to ya."

The words didn't hurt her now, and almost seemed funny, but back then Branna had already been raw with grief and anger and too young to deal with the pain.

She'd been locked in the cubicle in the girl's bathroom one day crying, when Belle had found her. "If you're going to let them do this to you every day, O'Donnell, it's going to be a long school year for you." Branna had heard those words through the door and simple curiosity had made her open it, and there had stood Annabelle Smith, her savior.

"Branna O'Donnell, just the woman I wanted to see!"

If she hadn't been daydreaming, Branna would have seen the woman coming towards the car, and recognized her as Macy Reynolds-Delray, because not much about her had changed in the years since Branna had left Howling. She quickly got out before Macy saw Mikey hiding in the back seat and walked to greet the homecoming queen.

"Hello, Macy."

"Welcome back to Howling," the woman said with a fake smile that went nowhere near her eyes. "I was hoping to get your help with the reunion. We need some flyers done up, and maybe something for the press. I wondered if I could leave that with you."

Macy waved a perfectly manicured hand about, as if they'd seen each other yesterday and Branna would simply fall in with her plans, like most people had always done. Her blonde curls were styled beautifully, although on closer inspection, Branna thought that maybe there was a bottle of dye involved now. Dressed in a tight emerald satin sheath that clung to her ample breasts, she wore matching heels so high that they would have given Branna vertigo. She looked ready to go out for an evening, not walk down the main street of Howling at midday, but even in school she'd managed to make her uniform look like a prom dress.

"Sorry, Macy, I won't be attending the reunion," Branna said calmly.

Just like in school, Macy didn't hear what she didn't want to, and simply carried on talking.

"We can get the high school logo to you as soon as you like."

"Macy!" Branna raised her voice to get the woman's attention. "I don't think you understand. I will not be attending your reunion, nor will I be helping with posters and press releases."

In school, Macy would have cried crocodile tears, and sniffed a lot, while making a scene that drew all her friends to her side; not now, however; she just looked at Branna with cold eyes.

"I'm sorry that you feel that way about the school that educated you, Branna."

"Three years, Macy, it was not the only place I received an education, and certainly not the most memorable," Branna said, with a bit more feeling than was warranted.

"Well then, if that's the way you feel, I'm sure it's not my place to change your mind."

Branna felt like she'd just kicked a puppy, hard, with large boots on. The woman didn't flinch, nor did she censure her, but she felt as if she'd just let Macy down badly, and had no idea why that bothered her so much. The old Macy Reynolds would have made a scene, but not this one; she kept her face expressionless.

"Hey, Macy," Jake said, as he stopped at Branna's side.

"Jake." Macy flicked her hand in the air and then walked away.

"You want to take this, Rosebud, before it melts?"

Dragging her eyes from Macy's retreating back, Branna took the cone and licked a drip before it fell.

"You have to admire a woman who can walk like that in stilts."

"Amen," Branna said, watching Macy walk with the ease of someone who'd worn heels for years and hadn't fallen off them once.

CHAPTER SIX

"How did you know I like peanut butter?"

Jake got a lick of his own before he answered Branna's question.

"You liked peanut butter in school."

She was disconcerted by his remembering she liked peanut butter. Jake saw it in the way she dropped her eyes. They climbed back into Geraldine and he fired her up, then he took a few seconds to savor the sound of the engine.

"You and Macy have a nice little reunion before I arrived?"

"Let's just say we came to an understanding we never reached in school, although she didn't make a scene at my refusal, just made me feel like a cad for not accepting."

He snorted as she looked at the retreating back of Macy Reynolds. "Cad?"

"Sorry for using a word the stretches your vocabulary, shall I say heel?"

"Always the wise ass, O'Donnell," Jake muttered, backing Geraldine out of the parking spot.

"You can't eat and drive." Her protest was muffled, as she was licking her ice cream. The sight of her pink tongue wrapped around the cone made Jake shift in his seat. The woman was already sexy enough without watching that mouth do what it was.

"Sure, I can, and if I get stuck you can change the gears. I thought we should probably get the truant in the back out of town before anyone sees him," Jake added.

Her super-sized brain hadn't thought of that, so he headed Geraldine back the way they'd come.

Jake had stewed on how he'd treated Branna. It wasn't her fault he was an asshole these days, nor was she the reason he'd changed, and he'd treated her unfairly. The man he'd become wasn't so far from the one his parents had raised that he couldn't feel shame for his behavior, so he'd decided an apology was necessary, and it had nothing to do with the fact that she occupied far too many of this thoughts.

So, he'd climbed into his pickup and driven to her house. Jake had seen the door open to the shed when he'd arrived. As he'd approached the Mustang, he'd picked up on the fact that both Mikey and Branna had been crying and looked like two lost kids who needed a hug. The heart he'd thought was now cold and slowly dying, had kicked into gear, and he'd wanted to pick them both up and sit with them in his arms until he drove the worry and sadness from their eyes, which if he'd been honest had scared the shit out of him, but a small part of him had relished the warmth that had filled his chest.

She got to him, always had, and now that he was older, it was worse. She'd always put up so many barricades, it was a wonder anyone could get through them. Annabelle, Jake knew, had always been able to, but not him; she'd always kept him at a distance. He was like that now too; he didn't let people in, wanted to be left alone to brood, but seeing that in another person made Jake wonder about the man he'd become. A man filled with anger for something that he'd had no power to change.

She took another swipe at her ice cream and he nearly groaned as heat filled his body. She was turned towards him, her long legs curled on the seat as she talked to Mikey about something. He wanted to stroke them, run his hands over the smooth skin and under the edge of her shorts. Instead, he ate and drove, listening to Branna question the boy. He felt at peace, which was something that had been in short supply lately, and again should scare him spitless.

"Can you spell pococurante, Branna?"

"Pfffft, give me something hard," she said, spelling the word. "Pococurante, meaning indifferent, nonchalant."

"Laodicean," she fired back at Mikey, and as Jake didn't know what the word even meant, he kept eating and thinking. What had happened in her life since they'd last met? Were there lovers, boyfriends? Where was her father?

"Laodicean," Mikey spelled the word slowly. "But I don't know the meaning," he added.

"It means indifferent in religion or politics," Branna said.

Jake was pretty smart himself. You didn't go through as many years as he had studying medicine, then his army training for the medical corps, and not know how to handle a textbook, but these two were out of his realm. He could hear the excitement in the boy's voice as Branna questioned him, switching from math to English. Jake would have liked a few science questions, possibly could have held his own then, but it didn't seem to be on the agenda.

The lake appeared again as he reached the end of Branna's road and swung onto his own. Pulling the Mustang onto the grass under a tree, Jake wondered if she knew that they were neighbors.

"Ha, I got you there, Branna," Mikey crowed.

"So did not," she teased as they all got out of the car. "Three-fifths, plus one-fifth, plus four-fifths, equals one and three-fifths."

Mikey's face screwed up as he thought through what she'd said. "Okay, maybe you're right."

"I know I'm right." The boy got out of the car and swaggered around in front of Branna, making her laugh again. He then ate the last of his cone in one mouthful. "I have to go now; I need to get home before Gran starts to worry." Before either of them could say anything, he'd run away, his thin legs flying as he headed back up the road toward Branna's house.

"Bye," Branna called, but the boy didn't stop.

Jake moved to the edge of the bank and sat on the warm grass. Branna, however, kept her distance, still standing a few feet away.

"I'll be doing the same now, McBride. I have things to do."

"It's your car, Branna, seems odd that'd you walk home when I'll be driving that way myself." Tipping his head back, he watched her frown.

"Well then, drive me," she added.

"Any chance I can finish my ice cream first?"

Her sigh was to tell him she wasn't happy, but she sat seconds later, dropping down beside him, but making sure to leave a decent space between them. They sat in silence, finishing their cones. The water was cool, even in summer, and he watched the wind skimming along the surface. This was his place, his home, even when he'd gone away to med school and then the army, he'd thought about it every day, and wondered why he'd been so eager to leave. It was his bolt hole now, the place he'd come to heal.

"I never really looked when I was here before." Jake turned to watch Branna as she gazed over the water to the mountains beyond. "I never took the time to see what was special about Howling. But it is special, Jake, magical almost."

"You've only been back a few days, Rosebud."

She curled her tongue around the cone and heat licked through Jake again.

"I know, and I could do without some of the Howlers, McBride, and I hate that everyone knows my business, but this place is nice. I love the hills that surround it, I love the trees and the lake, and I like that it's slower than the big cities."

"Washington, right?"

She nodded.

"What's Mikey's story, Jake?"

He finished his ice cream, then bent to wash his hands. He got the signal that personal questions were not allowed, which annoyed him, but he could hardly complain, as they were off limits with him too.

"His mother travels with her job, so his grandmother cares for him. She's in her eighties, so it's hard on her, especially as two of her children live out of Howling, and the one that does live here is pretty hopeless."

"Connor?" Branna questioned.

"Yeah, he's not a bad guy, but tries to play at it. Helps Buster out now and again when he's busy, but he dropped out of school, and hasn't held down a job since then. I haven't had that much to do with them, only what I hear through Buster and mum."

"Mikey needs to be challenged, needs that stimulation, or he'll grow bored, and that's when the trouble starts," Branna said.

"Is that what happened to you?"

"No."

"No, you didn't get in trouble or you didn't get the correct stimulation." She threw him a suspicious glance to see if there was any double meaning in his words.

"Yes to the first and no to the second."

"Buster told me that you and your dad were teachers and now you're both writers," Jake added.

"So, Belle told me you started out a doctor and now you're a mechanic?"

"Come on, Rosebud, throw me a bone here; I'm just trying to be nice."

"I thought you weren't doing nice anymore?"

"I can still pull it out when required."

"I hate that about small towns," she added with a fierce frown.

"You don't like it when people are nice?"

"I hate it when people appear nice, so that they can find out everything about you, right down to your shoe size," she corrected.

"And yet you came back."

She sighed again, and looked over the lake once more as Jake studied her profile. She was fine-boned, small ears, and nose, curved chin, high cheekbones. Her skin was beautiful, soft and smooth, a hint of color in the cheeks.

"I had to," she said the words slowly.

"Why?"

She got back to her feet. "Because Georgie wanted me to. Now, can you drive me back, please?"

It was the please that did it. They were soon back in the car and traveled the short distance in silence. He reversed the Mustang into the shed, as the early afternoon sun warmed Georgie's garden. They both got out and he covered the car, then shut and locked the doors.

"Thank you for letting me drive her; it's been a dream for some time." Jake stood close. "Reluctant as I am to hand them back, here are your keys."

He dropped them into her palm and then closed his hand over it when she started to pull away. Her green eyes widened as she looked up at him.

"I'm sorry if I was rude or hurt you, Branna. Things have changed with me, and it's those things that make me mean."

"I-I overreacted. My head was sore and my wrist hurt—"

"I did want to be your friend in school, Rosebud, no matter what you believed."

She didn't know what to say to that, so she tried to pull away instead.

"Let me go, McBride."

"You scared of me, Rosebud?"

She tried to scoff, but it was a weak effort. Lifting one had, he cupped her cheek, using his thumb to tilt her chin upwards.

"No!"

"Yes." He touched her lips with his. Soft and sweet was Jake's first thought. His head filled with her scent as he deepened the kiss. Wrapping the other arm around her waist, he pulled her into his body. Jake knew it was a mistake, as neither of them wanted or needed this in their lives now, but he couldn't seem to stop himself.

He took her mouth, and Branna could do nothing to stop him, and after the first touch she could do nothing to pull away. In seconds, her head was filled with this man who possessed her lips. Soft, it was a caress, and with each kiss, the contact grew deeper, stronger. Branna heard a moan and knew it was hers, knew that it was she who was pressing her body into his. She was on fire, her skin consumed with hot primal heat and lust; the urge to rip his shirt open and touch his chest had her hands clenching. His tongue stroked hers, slow and steady, each touch designed to heighten her desire, pull her deeper into the vortex of passion she felt. It had to stop while she could still think; she had to pull away. Wrenching free, she stumbled back a step.

"Don't." The hand she held up as he closed the distance stopped him.

"I won't apologize for something we both enjoyed, Branna."

He looked sexy, hair tousled, eyes heated, body hard and ready to give her what hers ached for. One kiss and she was ready. Looking at his big hands, she knew they would take her to heaven if they ever touched her naked flesh. Branna knew that, but ultimately they could also send her straight to hell.

"It won't happen again," she vowed.

He tilted his head slightly, as if to read what was in her eyes, so she lowered them, and waited for him to leave.

"It will."

She didn't answer, just watched as Jake turned and walked towards his pickup. Branna had just filled her lungs with a deep calming breath when he retraced his steps.

"Wh-what are you doing?" Digging her toes into the soles of her sandals, Branna braced herself as he stopped before her. He lifted the hand that wore the brace and fitted it back in the sling gently.

"You don't do anything that strains this until my mother tells you to, Rosebud. Same goes with that thick Irish head of yours. No running until you get cleared to do so. Use some of that superior intelligence and rest until you're well enough to do otherwise."

"Don't look after me, Jake; I don't need you to."

"I can't even look after myself these days, so I think you're safe there, O'Donnell."

"What happened?" She hadn't meant to pry, hated it when people did it to her, but suddenly the pain inside him made her hurt too. His eyes traveled over her face briefly.

"They're my nightmares, Rosebud, and I don't share."

He never spoke again, simply got into his pickup and drove away, and Branna wondered how her life had become more complicated in the past few days, when coming here should have resulted in the opposite happening.

***

"You gonna play a card, Newman, or knit something?"

"Don't get your panties in a twist now, Tex."

Jake sat back on the legs of his chair. Cards night in his parents' basement was a monthly event. There were five of them, three school friends, one of Jake's army buddies, and his father.

"I tried your latest dressing yesterday, Newman, on my ribs, you know the one with your pretty face on it. Have to say, it's your best yet," Ethan Gelderman the 5th said. Big and dark, he was a Texan down to his handmade gator cowboy boots.

"It's the saffron, adds the punch," Newman said, having had plenty of practice answering these comments. He was born Paul Theodore Newman to parents who'd idolized their only child from day one, and to a mother who loved his namesake just as much. He'd put up with his fair share of ridicule, it had to be said, but was easygoing enough to handle it. The ladies liked his blond curls, and the fact he was a successful businessman helped.

Buster snorted, then tugged his visor lower to hide his eyes, which was a sign to all of them that he had a good hand. "You wouldn't know the difference between a cinnamon pod and saffron, Newman."

"They grow that stuff on trees? Ha, who knew?"

"You girls gonna lay a card while I'm still breathing?" Patrick McBride glared at the players then tweaked his faded, lucky cap. Once red, but now pink, it had the words, Number One Dad, embroidered on the front; Jake and his sister had given it to him for his birthday one year. Which one is a little hazy right now, as Jake had lost count of the beers he'd consumed.

Ethan hummed a couple of bars of *Raindrops Keep Falling on My Head*, but the taunt rolled off Newman's large shoulders, as he placed a card on the table that made them all groan.

"Well now, son, you just about ruined my next mouthful of beer."

"Never my intention, as you know, Mr. McBride. Your son, however, now annoying him should be a national pastime," Ethan added.

"So, I've been back in town a day before mum tells me you've been seen driving Geraldine with Branna O'Donnell seated beside you, McBride," Newman stated.

Jake hadn't seen Branna for a week, but the hell of it was, he'd wanted to. It was fair to say he'd shared a few kisses in his lifetime, some of them pretty good too, but that one with Branna had made him lose reason.

"We had sex five times, Newman," he drawled. "Once on Geraldine's hood." Jake thought about Branna's legs and the way they looked coming out of those cut-offs she wore. Long and lean, they'd wrap around his waist perfectly.

"Like she'd touch you, McBride," Newman scoffed. I call BS."

"Aww, shucks," Jake added. "And there I was, thinking I was totally convincing."

"I hear she's quite a looker?" Newman took a mouthful of his beer.

"Who is Branna O'Donnell?" Tex rolled the cigar he never lit from side to side in his mouth.

"She's Irish, came to Howling for three years during her high school years, and is the only girl that I know of who never made a fool of herself over Jakey boy here," Buster filled Tex in.

"I love the Irish accent. Rolls up and down your spine, leaving you feeling hot all over."

Jake had to agree with the Texan about that, but he wasn't sure just any Irish accent would do it for him.

"The total female population didn't fall at his feet; there was Lydia Southby, she hated him too."

"Newman, Lydia Southby was sixty at the age of fifteen; she didn't like anyone."

Jake raised his bottle to Buster in agreement.

"Branna's father writes those crime novels," Patrick said.

"Not D.J. O'Donnell?"

"The very man, Tex. You a fan too?"

Tex whistled around his cigar. "Patrick, I have every one of his books and headed down to a see him and get a couple signed, when his tour brought him through Dallas a few years ago."

"She writes too." Jake wasn't sure why he'd said that. "Haven't been able to find her name on anything when I searched, so must be writing under a pseudonym, I'm guessing."

"Well, well, well, fancy our Jake doing a bit of research on his high school nemesis."

"I like to read, and thought I'd support a local, so shoot me." Jake flipped Buster the bird.

Of course, his mother would choose that moment to walk into the room, to the sound of his friends and father hooting with laughter.

"Son, if that gesture was the one I thought it was, I'd be disappointed."

"Newman made me do it, Mom."

Buster snickered.

"I brought pizza, but you have to share." Doctor McBride dropped the boxes in the middle of the table, right on top of the cards, but no one complained too loudly.

"I love you, Nancy." Jake rolled his eyes as Tex then leapt out of his seat so his mother could have it. She had that effect on people. Beautiful at fifty years, the woman would turn any man's head, young or old, but after thirty years, she had eyes for only one man, and he was pulling her down onto his lap.

"Find your own woman, son, this one's mine."

Dutifully, Jake made a gagging sound as they kissed, as was expected of him.

The pizza was good, probably due to the beer, the company the same, and when he stumbled upstairs into his old bedroom a few hours later, Jake wondered what Branna was doing. Had she left behind friends in Washington who she'd collected over the years? Did they used to meet in bars or movies to talk, like he did with his friends? The ones who never turned away from him, even when he'd returned to Howling a different man from the one they'd known.

He doubted the existence of Branna's friends; in fact he doubted the serious, beautiful woman let anyone close, because she sure as hell hadn't in high school. Closing his eyes, he let the buzz of beer lure him to sleep and decided that tomorrow he would see Branna O'Donnell again, just to make sure she was settling in.

***

After the craziness of her arrival in Howling, the next few weeks were relatively peaceful for Branna. She settled in, putting her things about Georgie's house and turning it into Branna and Georgie's house. She found memories everywhere, from photo albums to stories that Branna had written and Georgie had kept. Tears of sadness and joy crept up on her, so that at the end of each day she fell into bed exhausted to sleep long and dreamless. Since her mother's death, she'd managed to avoid crying as best she could, but here, in this house that she'd once thought of as her haven, it was unavoidable; everywhere she looked she found her friend.

She cooked in the kitchen where she'd learned to bake, using the recipes Georgie had collected over the years. She slept in the room she'd stayed in the few times when her father had allowed her to sleep over. It was both harrowing and healing to Branna to be here, to look back into the past with its painful memories in order to find a way forward into the future.

Mikey and Belle had helped her to move a few things out to the shed, which allowed her to fit her writing desk into the back room that had glass doors that led outside to the garden. Belle had hung her mother's picture in the lounge, so anyone who walked inside saw it immediately. "Because she is part of you, Branna, and deserves her place in your life."

She'd given Mikey some things that she could tell meant a lot to him, and a few to Belle, who'd also been a constant in Georgie's life. In time, she'd pack some of the knickknacks away and remove some of the doilies, but for now, she was happy with the blend.

The day after her final doctor's visit, where Doctor McBride had given her the all clear, she woke and pulled on her running shorts and singlet. Lacing up her shoes, she took herself outside as the sun began to rise. Here in Howling, she didn't need music in her ears; there was silence here, no blaring horns or city noise. She stretched, her muscles were tight after so long with no activity, and then she ran down the drive and turned left, which would take her around the lake.

Now this, Branna, will be heaven, she thought, as the sun slowly began to rise over the lake. It was cool, but she was soon warm. It felt wonderful to be running again, especially after days spent bent over her desk. The brace was still on, but Doctor McBride said she could at least now run and type, but if it hurt, she had to stop. She'd done a fair bit of one-fingered typing the past few days and was looking forward to growing her word count before her agent called to give the talk about deadlines and meeting them.

Inhaling the fresh country air, Branna began to hum an Irish ballad, one her grandmother had sung to her as a child. She saw a track that disappeared into the redwoods that she would investigate one day, then passing a driveway she looked up, wondering if she knew the person who lived there. Her stomach dropped to the soles of her shoes when she saw Jake McBride jogging down in his long steady stride. She didn't think he'd seen her, so there was time to turn around, or maybe she should speed up?

"Morning."

Damn, why did he have to be her closest neighbor? Branna didn't stop, just waved her hand over her head and kept running. She didn't want to share her first run, and especially not with a man who had taken up far too much of her thoughts the past few days.

"Nice day for it."

He'd caught her in a few strides. Shooting him a look, she noticed his eyes were bloodshot. She took in those long muscular legs encased in grey running shorts and wide shoulders in a torn, faded T-shirt with Medical Corps U.S. Army on it.

"Your eyes are bleeding, McBride."

"Card night last night."

As she'd never been to a card night, nor wanted to, Branna said nothing further, and he seemed happy to follow her lead. They ran as the day woke around them. On one side, there were trees and grass, on the other a beautiful clear lake with mountains beyond, and she thought that had Jake not been here, she could just about be perfectly happy right at this moment.

He disturbed her; it was a fact and always had been. If he was near, she was aware of him…even if she didn't want to be.

"How often do you run?"

He may be hung-over, but he wasn't breathless, which told her he was as used to running as she was.

"As often as I can…mostly four times a week, but here it'll probably be more."

"How far do you go?"

"5 to 10 miles a run, sometimes less or more. I don't really plan it; it's just how I feel on the day."

He thought about that as they ran, and she knew he was adjusting his pace, shortening his steps to match hers.

"I can run on my own, Jake, if you want to go on."

"I'm good, but thanks. How's the arm? I see you still have it braced."

"Good, and before you say anything, your mum said I had the all clear."

"You don't have to get defensive every time I open my mouth, Rosebud."

Branna exhaled, loudly.

"I'm not good with people, Jake, It's not how I started out; it just turned out that way." Why had she said that? She'd always had a loose tongue around him. He wasn't someone who talked a lot, and he listened when others spoke, but he also had the ability to unsettle a person with just a look...well, her at least. She'd rattled out more rubbish in his presence just to fill a silence than she had in her life.

"Forewarned," he said, and she had a feeling he was laughing at her, but one look told her his face was serious, and she was pleased to see, starting to sweat. "And for the record, I'm not exactly everyone's favorite person anymore either."

"You may believe that in some warped part of your small brain, McBride, but you still are, even with the bad boy attitude."

"What's with this bad boy attitude label you keep giving me?"

She waved her hand about, dismissing his question, as she continued with the matter of his popularity. "Yesterday, I went into The Hoot to have a mystery muffin, which Buster wouldn't give me the recipe for, even though I begged."

"You have a real thing for those, don't you, Rosebud?"

"Each one has been as good as the last, McBride, and this one had ginger in it, but Buster just folded his arms and ignored me when I offered him a bribe."

"What did you offer?"

"Twenty dollars a recipe," Branna said.

Jake snorted. "Offer to scrub his baking trays; that'll do it."

"No, it won't; he's just plain mean when it comes to those recipes," Branna added.

"Getting back to the point of this conversation, Rosebud, I think you were about to explain about me still being everyone's favorite person?"

"Right," Branna added. "I met Mrs. Purvis, who happens to be Penny's mom."

"I know who Penny's mom is."

"Well, she said you just needed some time, and you'd be back to the boy they all knew and loved and doing your doctoring any day now."

"I bet those words were verbatim?" He sounded pissed off.

"The point is, McBride, you may think differently about yourself, but none of them do."

"Them being the entire town?"

"Even the animals."

"You seem pissed about that, Rosebud. Would you be happier if they all disliked me?"

Was she? Maybe in school it had bothered her that he could do no wrong in anyone's eyes, but that was jealousy because no one liked her, but then she'd never given anyone encouragement either.

"McBride, it was an observation. I have no feelings about you, and don't plan on forming any."

"Ouch."

She didn't say anything, and then clamped her top teeth around her bottom lip to shut herself up.

"You ever drop those barriers enough to let anyone in, O'Donnell? Really in, I mean, the fall in love, you're the sole reason I breathe, in."

"You read romance novels, McBride? Because no man I've ever met has said the words 'you're the sole reason I breathe,' before."

The sound of their feet hitting the road was the only noise for a few seconds, and Branna was congratulating herself on the fact that she'd headed him off when he said, "I guess that answers my question."

She wanted to snap something back at him, tell him to stuff his comments somewhere she'd never have to hear them again, but instead, she ran on in silence. She was older now, twenty-six to be exact, and no longer needed to snarl like a rabid dog when someone annoyed her, even if it was Jake McBride...still the hottest guy in town.

They ran on in silence, both lost in thought; he led and she followed, as she didn't know the way, and when her sides were starting to hurt, she looked up and found herself back where they had started.

"You swim, Rosebud?"

"Why?" Branna watched as he pulled off his running shoes and socks, which revealed long feet. He then stood once more, and somehow, he was now inches from her.

"You always answer a question with another one?"

"Do you?'

He snorted, and even with bloodshot eyes and sweat running off his big body, he was sexy as hell.

"Yes or no?"

"Maybe."

"Well then, get your shoes off and that brace."

Branna slapped his hand as he reached for the straps on her arm. "Touch me and I'll drop you, McBride."

"You and whose army, Rosebud? You're an itty bitty thing compared to me."

His smile was slow and easy, and to her, it was the exact one a wolf would give before it gobbled up its prey.

"I'm not swimming in that," Branna shot the lake a look. "It'll be freezing; I'll probably never thaw out."

"I can help you with that." He took another step towards her, but she spun around and started running away. His laughter only stopped when she heard a loud splash as his body hit the water, but she refused to look back. The thought of that body all wet was not one she wanted to have put into reality.

Chapter Seven

She allowed herself a smile as she ran up the driveway. He couldn't see it, so she was safe. The day would be warm and Branna had plenty to do. Her book was coming along, and she wanted to get the border finished around the garden. Humming, she ran inside and straight up to the shower. Stripping off her sweaty clothes, she stood under the hot spray and let it pound her body.

How was she going to cope with him?

The problem was, he was just so good at getting under her skin. He could irritate her with a few words, and just a look from Jake McBride got her riled up. Squirting a handful of soap into her hands she ran them over her body and her breasts tingled. That was the biggest problem; thinking about him heated her up. He was sexy and smart, and she wanted him, and that annoyed her because she couldn't remember the last time she'd wanted anyone.

Shutting off the water, Branna wrapped herself in a towel and walked into her bedroom. The morning sun lit the room in a soft glow. She'd put her furnishings in here too, her big free standing oval mirror, the thick red rug that had yellow and blue splashes of color. Across the bed, she'd draped a soft purple wool blanket and placed colorful pillows.

After drying her hair, which she vowed to cut because she was tired of it getting in her way, she left it long, the ends reaching below her shoulder blades now. Pulling some white lace underwear on, Branna then went to the wardrobe and looked in. She wore shorts most days, but today, after her first run, she felt like putting on a dress.

It was a simple pale green shift that stopped a few inches above her knees. On her feet she wore sandals, and looking down at her toes, she thought about painting them and then thought not, as the vision of Jake looking at them filled her head. She would not dress so he noticed her, ever. Strapping on the loathsome brace, she headed downstairs.

Grabbing an apple, Branna picked up her keys and headed out to the van. She needed a few things from town, and then she'd see what Buster's special muffin was today.

The grocery store was towards the end of town and tucked back behind the row of shops. Making her way inside, she grabbed a cart and started down the aisles.

"The apricots are good this time of year."

An elderly woman was inspecting the oranges, which were right beside the apricots.

"Thanks."

"Make a good cobbler with those if you get some berries as well," the woman added.

Branna was used to walking around a crowded supermarket in Washington without saying a word; she'd frequented the same one for five years and never conversed with anyone unless absolutely necessary. This was another thing that she needed to adjust to here in Howling. It seemed that her, "I don't really like to talk much" sign wasn't flashing neon.

"I was thinking of a chicken apricot dish," she said, surprising herself.

The woman sucked on her teeth, the lines on her face deepening as she thought about what Branna had said. "May work, but I'm not partial to mixing my sweets and savories too much; still, you be sure to let me know how it turns out."

"I will, and you have a good day," Branna added.

Moving along, she began to navigate the canned food section. It was about adjusting. She could do that, and would have to, if she planned to stay in Howling. She didn't want to be known as that woman, you know the one that lives in Georgie's old place. Has thirty-seven cats, doesn't leave her house.

"Hey, Branna, how's the head doing now?"

Penny Bilks gave her a wide smile from across the aisle.

"Much better, thanks, Penny." Branna didn't hold grudges, and in all honesty, Penny's intervention had helped her, she could see that now, even if it did put Jake McBride on her doorstep.

"Good morning, Branna."

Branna turned to look at who else had spoken, and thought about making a run for it. Macy Reynolds was approaching with a man. Dressed in snug-fitting red Capris, a tight stretchy white top that hugged every curve, and a red pair of slip on heels, her perfectly made up face held a cold expression.

"Macy," Branna nodded her head.

"This is my husband, Brian Delray," Macy said. "Brian, this is Branna O'Donnell."

Macy said the words reluctantly, almost to Branna's ears as if she didn't want Branna to meet her husband.

"Miss O'Donnell," Brian Delray held out his hand, which Branna shook.

He had a nice open face, neat dark hair, and soft brown eyes. His clothes, unlike his wife's, were understated, a pair of gray trousers with a sharp edge ironed in the fronts and a pristine white shirt with pale grey pin stripes, and a matching tie. His shoes were polished black leather. Branna could only imagine the life this man led at the hands of the barracuda at his side.

"I hope you're settling in well, Branna. Georgie's place needs a bit of work from what I remember; if it gets too much, you let me know," Macy's husband said.

"I'm sure she can cope, Brian, especially as the house was a gift," Macy's words sounded almost shrill, and Branna felt another tug of sympathy for the man.

"So, how long have you two been married?" Branna asked, when they fell into a heavy silence.

"Six years now, and we're very happy," Brian Delray said with another gentle smile.

"I-I, ah…" Branna felt the heat of embarrassment fill her cheeks. Did he know what she'd been thinking? She didn't know what to say; the thought of this gentle soul being in the clutches of someone like Macy Reynolds was just plain wrong.

"Branna? Branna O'Donnell? How long has it been since we saw each other?"

This day was just getting weirder by the minute. Now, a big dark-haired man, who looked like he'd stepped off of a billboard, was sauntering towards her, his smile wide and genuine. She had no idea who he was, but he seemed to know her. Looking closer, she wondered if he'd gone to school with her. She couldn't remember anyone who had eyes that particular blue, and his accent had a Texan twang to it.

He didn't stop as he reached her, just wrapped his big arms around her, placing a smacking kiss on one cheek. Then, tucking her into his side, he stuck out one large hand to Brian Delray, who was watching the proceedings with a slightly stunned expression on his handsome face, while his wife's mouth had puckered in disapproval.

"Ethan Gelderman the 5th." His words were as smooth as heated honey and rolled off his tongue.

"Brian Delray, and this is my wife, Macy. You're not a local, Mr. Gelderman?"

"No, but I love your little town, Mr. Delray, and it holds even more appeal now that I know the first woman I ever loved lives in it."

She had to fight the urge to laugh. She knew he was making it up then, but why? Furthermore, why was she going along with him when normally she would run a mile if anyone touched her like he was? Funny, how she didn't feel threatened by him.

"Let's go, honey, I'm hungry; hustle that sweet little butt of yours along and we'll head over to Buster's for a coffee," Ethan Gelderman the 5th then said.

Smiling at Brian and Macy Reynolds-Delray, Branna raised a hand before letting him lead her away.

"You done?" he questioned.

"I am, and I have to say, you don't look like Sean Connor, who was my first love. He had red hair and green eyes. Although, they can do wonders with surgery these days, and name changing happens all the time, I believe."

"I got the feeling from Buster and Jake you'd be handful," the Texan said.

"A handful? Are you serious? You were the one who walked up spouting all that rubbish about first loves, Mr. Gelderman, and I'm not entirely sure why?"

"Ethan," he corrected her, "and that little gathering just looked plain awkward, so I took pity on you."

"Do you know Macy Reynolds or should I say Reynolds-Delray, that poor man's wife? The woman standing there dressed like a model?" Branna looked around the supermarket. If she was in the city, she'd have been nudged and shoved a dozen times by now, but here she was able to walk and browse, or had been until a large, way too handsome man had intercepted her.

"Can't say as I've met her before today," he drawled.

"Think fake everything, right down to her personality, and you'll understand," Branna said.

"Now, that I understand, darling. I'm from Texas, after all."

"And you love those kinds of women?" Branna added, looking at his perfect bone structure. The man was a walking advertisement for what woman wanted in their men. Tall, built, devastating smile, and could talk a pair of panties down without breaking a sweat.

"You talk funny," he said, hustling her up to the checkout by putting a hand on her back.

"I'm Irish."

"Jake said you'd lived in the U.S. for years, but occasionally you spout out something from your homeland."

"Sounds like you and Jake had a nice little chat about me."

"He may have misled me about just how damned hot you are, but I'll take that up with him when I see him."

Branna rolled her eyes, because men like Ethan Gelderman the 5th had learned to flirt in the birth canal.

"Morning." The young girl at checkout gave the man behind her an interested look before returning her attention to Branna. She had short white hair, spiked, with bright green tips. She had piercings through her lip and brow.

"Morning," Branna said, as she started to load her stuff on the counter. The Texan tried to help, but she slapped his hand, which kept him out of her cart.

"I learned to drive in your car," the girl added, as she started to scan the groceries and put them in a bag.

"Did you?"

"Name's Jilly, and Georgie taught plenty of the local children to drive in Geraldine; she was kind of the local driving instructor."

"She was a special person, that's for sure," Branna said, still loading her things onto the counter.

"She baked cookies for us too."

Branna thought again of the anonymity she had in Washington; she'd still rather be here, though, because when the interest in her died down, she could live in peace and be left alone to write her stories.

"I liked the vanilla ones the best," Jilly said.

"Absolutely, they were the best, although the double chocolate was a close second."

Jilly made a humming sound of appreciation.

Walking out with her bags and a large Texan a few minutes later, Branna realized that most people just wanted to talk about Georgie. They didn't want anything from her, like she'd first thought they would, only to keep the memory of the woman they all loved alive.

"So, Sir Galahad, I think your good deed has been done for the day; I release you," Branna said, after they'd loaded her van. Out here in the sun, his eyes were amazing, like a clear blue lake and surrounded by long black lashes. His hair shone and he had the look of a fit healthy man who was quite happy with the human he had become, a bit like his friend McBride had once been.

"You owe me a coffee for saving you from humiliation."

"I don't know you."

"Ethan Gelderman, the 5th," he stuck out a hand, and Branna shook it.

"Do I have to drive you there too?"

"The lines are too low here in town to land my chopper on the main street."

"Where do you land it?"

"At McBride's house."

She wasn't sure if he was serious or not, but suspected he could be, as she had heard the thud of a helicopter a few days ago. Heading for the driver's door, she said. "All right, get in, as long as you can handle a woman driving."

"Honey, I can handle anything you want to do to me."

"Do women honestly fall for that kind of thing?" Branna backed her van out of the parking lot, and then headed towards The Hoot. "I mean, seriously?"

"What can I say? It's a gift."

Branna remembered Belle saying something about a Texan who was Jake's friend.

"You're the Texan Tomcat!"

He rolled his eyes. "Annabelle Smith just hates that I haven't hit on her yet, so she made up that name."

Even sitting in the front seat of her van, which could easily pass as a family vehicle, he looked sexy. Funny how she didn't find him as attractive as Jake, though, which was just plain annoying.

"Why haven't you hit on her? She's hot. I'd hit on her if I was into women," Branna demanded.

"My eyes just crossed at that vision."

Branna refused to laugh as she pulled up outside The Hoot, but it was hard. The guy was certainly a lethal combination; however, she felt nothing, which was a shame, because he'd be the perfect man to have an affair with.

"Hey, loser, I want food now!" Ethan demanded as they walked in.

"Go fuck yourself."

Branna laughed at the snarled words from somewhere beyond the counter.

"Morning, Buster," she said.

"Sorry, Branna, I thought it was the Texan card swindler the 5th who'd walked in."

"Did you know Buster was a sore loser, Branna? Real sore, takes it right to heart."

The muttering continued out back, until they were forced to go see what he was doing, as he didn't seem to want to serve them. Buster was hunched over his laptop, tucked in at a table around the back of the café. Sun was pouring in the window, and he was the only one in the room.

"Business a bit slow today?"

"Just had a rush," Buster didn't look at her as he answered.

"Any chance of some service? I want to try the mystery muffin," Branna said. "And I'm willing to clean your baking trays for the recipe."

"Not happening, and help yourself to whatever you want." Buster frowned at the screen.

"What are you doing?" Branna moved to look over his shoulder.

"Trying to get my website up and running. I want to sell stuff online, do some catering, but it's harder than it looks, and costs too much to get it done by someone who actually knows what they're doing."

"Jesus, boy, you just about got out a full sentence out there," Ethan called from his position in front of the food cabinets.

Branna started to ask Buster questions, and soon they were throwing ideas back and forth; she could see what he wanted, but that he wasn't getting close to getting there.

"You want me to fix that bit for you?" Pointing at the page he was having trouble with, Branna saw a few things that needed a different angle, and her fingers itched to change them for Buster.

"Would you?" He was out of the chair so quick it wobbled.

"Sure, I'll take a look."

***

Jake was thinking about Branna as he walked towards The Hoot. She thought she was tough, liked to think she didn't want people in her life, but she'd only been back a while and she had collected Mikey and reconnected with Annabelle. Seeing her van parked outside as he drew near had him swallowing his smile before pushing open the door to inhale the smell of coffee and baking, both coincidentally, which he loved.

"She's in the back."

"Who?" Jake questioned the tall Texan lounging at the counter.

Ethan rolled his eyes and Jake wondered when he'd become so obvious. "I found Branna in the grocery store chatting with some guy who should be named Mr. Perfect and his hot wife."

"Brian and Macy Reynolds-Delray," Buster and Jake said together.

"I stepped in when the conversation got awkward. Apparently, Irish was astonished when she realized who Mr. Perfect was married to. FYI, she's now in love with me," Ethan added.

"It's certainly one of life's mysteries as to why Brian married Macy, that's for sure," Buster said, as he wandered out with a tray of pies that smelled way too good for Jake to resist, so he stole one.

"They're steak."

"I'm changing it up." Jake took a bite and sighed.

"Your woman's doing his website up," Tex said. "It was a pathetic sight when we walked in; Buster was weeping onto his keyboard, so Branna took pity on him."

"She's not my woman." Jake knew Branna couldn't hear them, as the music in the café was loud enough to mute their conversation, but he wasn't taking any chances on her hearing and firing up at him.

"Sure she is," Ethan said.

"Thought you said she was in love you with you?"

"She is, but I'm standing aside for my friend, clearing the way, or you'd never get the girl. Wouldn't be fair on you otherwise, as the odds are not in your favor."

The Texan's blues eyes twinkled, and he knew Jake wanted to bite back, but instead he went for something far tastier that would soon reverse the tables.

"Saw some birds sitting on your tail rotor when I went for a run, and one shat on your windscreen. Nothing I could do about it; by the time I got out there, they'd done the damage."

"What!"

Jake swallowed his laughter as Ethan pushed off the counter, no longer the easygoing Texan. If anything riled him and robbed his ability for rational thought, it was anyone touching his helicopter.

"There's a bucket in the barn, if you want to wash it off, and I'm pretty sure there was no damage done, but…"

The blue eyes narrowed and then he relaxed back onto counter. "Fuck you, McBride."

Jake's laugh was low and nasty.

"For what it's worth, she seems to have your personality traits. Nasty mouth, foul moods, and generally bad tempered," Ethan said, his eyes suddenly serious.

"Leave it, Ethan."

"I've left it for way too long, Jake. In fact, since I was the one who pulled you out of that makeshift hospital with blood all over you and nothing but emptiness in your eyes, I think I have a vested interest in you, my friend. I also believe it's time for you to deal with what haunts you, Jake, and I think she could help you."

"I don't make a habit of agreeing with number five, but in this, I do," Buster said, who also knew about Jake's time in Iraq.

"Jake looked to make sure Branna hadn't suddenly appeared before he spoke. "I don't need this now, Ethan, I'm dealing with it the only way I know how. The flashbacks are getting further apart, but the dreams are still vivid. I would never inflict that on a woman."

Ignoring the pitying look on his friend's face, he walked further into the café. Jake stopped when he saw Branna, because the sight she made was worthy of that, and it gave him time to let the tightness in his chest ease. Seeing her pulled him out of that pit of darkness he sank into when he thought about his time in Iraq.

She was totally unaware of him, hadn't realized he'd even walked in, which let him observe her undetected. The sun brushed the thick black curls that reached her shoulder blades. He'd never seen it loose, and it made his fingers itch to touch it. The dress was another revelation, and while the cut-offs had his vote, this soft pale green thing was something special. She'd curled her legs under her, and the hem was halfway up her thighs, and Jake wanted to get his hands on her; he wanted to run them over all that exposed skin. Two white top teeth trapped her bottom lip, as her eyes studied the screen of Buster's laptop.

"Hey, Rosebud."

Her head shot up, green eyes wide, and then she muttered something and looked at the screen again. But Jake wasn't fooled; he'd seen the flash of interest. He wasn't the only one in this, whatever it was. Walking around behind her, he looked over her shoulder. A picture of Buster stared back at him.

"Damn, that man's ugly."

"He's not; in fact, he's cute."

Her hands flew over the keys as she tweaked this and adjusted that.

"How about a drop-down there, with different options?"

Her hands stilled and she looked at the screen for a few seconds. "McBride, if you're good at this, why the hell didn't you help him before?"

"I offered, we just never got 'round to it, but I guess there's no need now, as you're doing it."

She worked silently to implement what he'd suggested, and when it was done, he suggested a couple more things. His hands touched her shoulders as he leaned over her and she tensed beneath them.

"Relax, I don't bite during daylight hours."

"I'm done; you can move back now." She'd tilted her head back to look up at him.

"Clever girl, it looks pretty good." He wasn't looking at the screen as he spoke; his eyes were focused on her. The soft curve of her lips and the sweet beauty in her face that eased the pain inside him.

"Don't."

"Do," he cupped her chin and closed the distance. It was sweet and brief and ignited him in seconds. She responded, her lips moving beneath his, and when he lifted his head, they were both breathless.

"You're beautiful, Branna Rose O'Donnell." Running a finger down her cheek, he traced the soft blush that stole into her cheeks.

"Haul ass, Buster, she's finished!" Jake grabbed the nearest chair as he spoke, and sat it close to Branna, just to unsettle her some more, before dropping into it as his friend appeared.

"She's made you look pretty, which should get her a lifetime supply of mystery muffins, I reckon."

"I'm pretty." Head now beside Branna's, Buster was soon getting a tutorial on how his new website worked.

"Son, I've seen Texan Longhorns that could outshine you," Ethan said, coming to look at the website too.

Buster snorted. "You're a Texan; everyone knows how you feel about your cattle."

They threw insults around between the three of them, while Branna alternated between giggling, which was a sweet little sound that made Jake's gut tighten, and outrage on Buster's behalf when both he and Ethan attacked him.

"Don't listen to these feckin eejits, Buster, you and I both know who the prince among the three of you is."

"Honey, that hurts right here," Ethan thumped his chest.

She wasn't interested in Ethan; Jake could see that by the way she interacted. He'd seen women stop in the streets, their mouths falling open as the Texan walked by, but not Branna, she treated him like she did Buster.

"And now that I've had my daily dose of fun and laughter, I must return home and do some real work." She climbed to her feet and the hem of her dress settled a few inches above her knees.

Hell of it was, he'd just calmed down, but seeing that hem just begging to be raised, was firing Jake up all over again.

"What do you do, Branna?"

"I write." She picked up her purse. "Books," she clarified.

"So, it runs in the family? I have to say, honey, I'm a real fan of your dad's stuff. Have the entire collection," Ethan said.

"That's nice."

"Do you think he'll be coming to Howling, because I'd be happy to meet him again if he does?"

"Again?" She frowned at Ethan.

"Went to a book signing in Dallas; he's a real nice man, your daddy."

"My dad and I...we d-don't really talk."

Jake could see Branna didn't want to talk about her father. She looked cornered, exactly like he did when people questioned him about stuff he didn't want to share.

"What kinds of books do you write, Branna?" Ethan asked, exchanging a look with Jake she missed. Both Buster and he had noticed her reaction, but the Texan was the elected questioner; he could get anything out of anyone when he used that tone.

"The reading kind."

"I read, tell me what they are and I'll buy a couple." His smile was wide and flashed a mouthful of perfect teeth, as his blue eyes twinkled.

"I don't write under my name, and you may not like them anyway." Branna's words were flat and expressionless. Her fingers gripped the back of the chair Buster now sat in, clearly uncomfortable.

"You'll pardon me for saying this, Branna honey, but isn't the idea to get people to buy those books of yours, not put them off?"

The two top teeth worried her bottom lip again. She didn't want to tell them, but Ethan was making it impossible not to.

"Rosanna Howlling, is my writing name. Howlling with two LL's" she quickly added. "Now, I have to go, so stop bugging me."

Ethan raised both hands as if to say he wouldn't stop her, and with a muttered goodbye, she was gone. Jake watched those long legs disappear around the corner and felt himself relax.

"That girl sure is a puzzle," Ethan said, moving to Buster's left shoulder. "And now that I know her writing name, I'm even more intrigued because I've read every one of her books, and let me tell you, she's a rival for that daddy of hers."

"I've read a couple too," Buster said, bringing up her website.

She was smiling in the picture, and her hair was loose around her head, and Jake reckoned she'd get her fair share of fan mail. They read her bio in silence, and then studied the list of her books.

Buster whistled. "She's as famous as him, that's for sure. Funny how she writes the same stuff."

Jake whistled as he studied the list of books and accolades she'd received.

"Was it just me or did anyone else notice how she froze up when I mentioned her dad?" Ethan asked.

"Noticed it, and I wasn't even looking at her." Buster was navigating his way around her website.

"There's a mystery there, boy." Ethan slapped Jake on the shoulder, "and I'm commissioning you to unravel it, then tell your friends."

"Tough job for sure, but I'll take it."

Two sets of eyes looked at him.

"Well, well, well, looks like our little boy may have been hooked, Tex."

"Ha, not likely, but she's hot and smart, two things that I find hard to resist," Jake said the words out loud, hoping like hell they were true, because he didn't want to feel anything else for Branna.

"And maybe she might help you, Jake, and maybe you might help her?"

"Ethan, I'm not sure what, if anything, will help me other than time."

"You talked to anyone lately? You told me you'd think about it, that it was time to do that again."

"No, but maybe I will soon, I just need to do this when I'm ready. I know you got that buddy who's a shrink, and I'll let you know when I'm ready, I promise," Jake added.

Buster swung in his seat. "Funny how you're a doctor and adverse to a bit of doctoring."

"I'm not adverse; just don't want my veins sliced open before I'm ready." Jake thought about the doctor who'd been assigned to him in those first weeks. He'd made Jake open up, and he'd wept and raged, and nearly punched the guy, and at the end of it he'd felt more tired than he could ever remember; he didn't think he was ready for that again…or ever would be.

"It's fair to say Branna's done a hell of a job on my website." Buster was back to looking at his laptop. "Mystery muffins will be on me for a bit, I'm thinking."

Jake left The Hoot minutes later and jumped in his pickup, then sat there thinking about what Buster had said.

"Hooked? Ha, no way." Shaking his head, he started the car and headed for the clinic to see his mother.

CHAPTER EIGHT

Ally knew he was here; she could hear the rasp of his breath and the stench of stale sweat, both were etched in her memory from their first terrifying encounter, but unlike that night, this time there was no escape. He was going to finish what he started, and tomorrow the sun would rise without her.

Branna was wrenched from the story as someone knocked on her front door. "Bollix!" she muttered.

"Branna?"

"In here, Mikey." She heard the sound of his feet running; the boy rarely walked anywhere. He appeared in the doorway, shirt ripped at the shoulder, dirt on his knees, hair standing on end.

"Good day at school?"

"It was all right, but Miss. Todd put me in detention because I answered one of her questions with too much detail."

"What?" Branna stood and shepherded him out towards the kitchen. History had told her he would demand food in a few minutes.

"She asked if anyone knew what the word notion meant, and I said I did without raising my hand; she's real strict on that kind of thing."

"I used to be big on that too, to be fair," Branna conceded.

"And then I gave her the explanation, because I knew it."

Branna had been thinking that she might pay Mikey's teacher a visit. Just to let Miss Todd know what she was dealing with, and this reinforced it. She'd make the time to call in at the school over the next few days.

"You want some pancakes? I'm starving."

"Yes!"

They cooked, ate, and she quizzed him about words and numbers, then they did his homework. She'd never had a sibling. In fact, since Belle, Branna had never had to think about anyone but herself. It wasn't something to be proud of; it was just the way things had evolved after the death of her mother. To cope with their grief, both she and her father had shut themselves away from each other and neither had found their way back, until they'd simply drifted apart permanently.

She had a pain that was dull and deep in her chest that reared its head when she thought about Declan O'Donnell. She'd had no contact with him since that day he'd come to see her at university, and they'd said horrible nasty things to each other. Well, at least she had. It was funny how they'd both chosen to become teachers, and now wrote crime novels, funny and disconcerting, considering they were estranged.

Occasionally, memories of the father she'd once had slipped into her head, the man who had spent hours teaching her how to make a page of writing come to life. But Branna usually pushed them back into that dark place as soon as they appeared; she would gain nothing from remembering. She was better off remembering the cold, hard man who had turned his back on the child who had needed him.

By the time Branna had given Mikey the extra work she'd created for him, and he'd cycled off, she was ready to pull on her gardening gloves and head outside. It was closing in on early evening, and cool enough to pull a few weeds. She'd hit her writing target for the day, so now it was time for a bit of down time, and much to her surprise, gardening had become this for her. Georgie had loved to garden, and Branna had helped now and then, to keep her friend happy, but now she enjoyed it, loved the feel of the earth between her fingers, and the smells around her. It also gave her plenty of time to think, unfortunately most of her thoughts were occupied with a dark-haired man, who was far too disturbing.

CHAPTER NINE

He arrived on foot; the sound of his shoes crunching on the gravel of her driveway alerted Branna that someone was approaching. Wearing worn shorts and T-shirt, as usual, Jake kept walking until he was at the edge of the garden.

"Ethan would have come, but he's star struck now and doesn't think he could get a word out without stuttering."

Branna stayed kneeling in the dirt, which as he'd walked closer, was the wrong move because he was now towering over her.

"I'd hoped to avoid something like that," she said. "Him being such a delicate little flower and all."

His laugh was deep and unrestrained, which told her he was in a better place than some of the others she'd seen him in.

"Your arm up to gardening, Rosebud?"

"Yes."

"If you don't give it the proper rehabilitation, you could be wearing that brace for longer."

"I thought you gave up being a doctor, McBride?" She'd touched a nerve, because his left hand fisted briefly, and his good mood started to slip.

"I still know how to be one."

"And yet you choose to work on automobiles." Why was she doing this? Pushing him? Maybe because she could feel him getting too close?

The brief silence was thick enough for her to reach out and take a swipe through it. She attacked another weed, because she didn't want to look at him; he was so gorgeous it was making her eyes hurt.

"Why did you choose Howling as your last name?"

Branna's hands jerked at his question. "Because I did, and it has two L's" she was not going there, not with him. "Why don't you doctor anymore?"

"Because I don't want to, and for a writer that's not very good English."

"I'm taking a hiatus like you with the car fixing thing," Branna fired back.

"Why don't you and your dad get on?"

"Because we don't." She dug her gloved hands deep into the dirt. If anything made her irrational, it was talking about her father.

"Why'd you leave the army?"

"Okay, I'm done with this bullshit."

"What bullshit?" She made herself look at him again.

"This, us, me looking at those long legs of yours and wishing we were both naked with them wrapped around my waist."

"I-I ah, thought you were done with all the questions and no answers," Branna's body had started to tingle all over as he spoke, and the vision of them both naked made it hard to breathe.

"We'll get to those answers, but for now I'm done talking." He took a step towards her.

Branna squeaked as he suddenly gripped her arms and stood her upright. He pulled off her hat and threw it onto the ground, and then removed her gloves.

"What are you doing?'

"Shut up." Anger clenched his jaw and darkened his eyes, but she wasn't scared of him; he'd never hurt her...he was one of the good guys.

"Don't tell me to shut up," Branna protested.

He picked her up after throwing her gloves on top of her hat and carried her inside. Making for the stairs, he took them two at a time, even with her in his arms.

"Put me down, Jake." He didn't, and her foolish heart started thumping with excitement as they reached her bedroom. Walking inside, he lowered her slowly down his body so that her front touched all of his and left a trail of heat streaking through her. Then, he kissed her.

It was savage and messy, and she wanted more.

"Don't deny this is where we've been heading since you came back, Rosebud." He pulled her top over her head then put his lips on her collar bone, tracing the edge with his tongue. She was a pool of need and he'd only put his lips there. What would happen when he kissed the rest of her?

"I-I...this is wrong, Jake," she sighed as he moved to the top of her breasts above the lace cups of her bra.

"Nothing this good could ever be wrong, now put that super-sized brain on power save mode and play with me." He eased the strap down and took her nipple into his mouth, and she moaned long and loud and his laugh was dirty.

"I-I'm sweaty."

"Is that what tastes so good?"

She gave up after that. Pushing her fingers into his hair, she gripped his head as he licked and sucked her breasts, each stroke making her wet and aching.

"You've filled out some since school, little girl." His eyes were wicked as he looked at her. "Especially here." His hands cupped her breasts, running his thumbs over the sensitive peaks, making her moan again.

"I could spend a long time worshipping your breasts, Rosebud, but there are other parts of you that need my attention too."

"Not before you take this off. " Branna grabbed a handful of his shirt and tugged it upwards until she had it off his body. Her hands were on him then, running over the hard planes of skin that covered all those wonderful muscles.

"You've filled out since school, big boy."

His laugh was forced as she was playing with his abdomen, stroking each of the defined muscles, her fingers brushing the waistband of his shorts.

They teased and touched, when his lips were on her, her hands were on him. It was hot, at times rough, and Branna had never experienced sex like this before. The feelings were intense and the need ravenous.

When he'd stripped off the remainder of her clothing, he stood back and looked at her, which was disconcerting, because she couldn't remember any of the men she'd slept with wanting to just look at her.

"Do I get to look at you too?" she asked.

He started at her feet and traveled upwards, and by the time their eyes met, she was panting and he hadn't even touched her.

"You're beautiful, Rosebud, perfect in fact."

Branna snorted, but she didn't cover herself. She wasn't ashamed of her body, but she knew it wasn't anything special.

"Whatever, McBride, now get your clothes off."

His smile was gentle as he continued studying her. "You don't believe me."

She closed the distance between them and reached for the zipper of his shorts. He didn't resist, instead running his hands through her hair and down her body as she worked. When she had the zipper down, she dropped his shorts and cupped the long hard length of him through his boxers, running her hand up and down until the breath hissed in his throat.

"You're killing me."

This time it was Branna who smiled. Removing the shorts, she then stood back to look at him, and oh my, he was fine.

Big shoulders, broad chest, and lots of tanned skin over slopes and plains of muscle. The man was a walking fantasy. She touched him again, running her hands down his thighs, then, dropping to her knees, she took him into her mouth.

"Christ!"

Branna stroked the hot hard flesh with her mouth and felt the pressure building inside of him.

"No more, Branna, I can't take it." Lifting her to her feet, Jake then carried her to the bed. "I've been horny since you arrived in town, and if you keep that up, it'll be over in seconds."

This time it was him who was doing the torturing, his mouth and hands running over her until he parted her legs and the delicious torment really began. His tongue stroked the wet folds, teeth grazing the tight bud. She heard her moans turn to sobs as she begged him to do something about the pressure inside her.

"Condom?" he groaned. "I don't have one."

"I'm on the pill, had a checkup, and am clean. You?"

"You kidding me? I was a fucking doctor? And then he was there, his big body on top of her as he eased inside her.

Branna could feel the tension build higher with each delicious slide in and out. Her hands gripped his shoulders as he braced himself on his arms and looked down at her as his body continued to take hers higher.

"God, you feel good, Branna O'Donnell."

His head was thrown back as he pushed into her again, this time harder. Branna lifted her legs and wrapped them around his waist, making the penetration deeper.

"Sweet Christ, Rosebud, you better come for me soon, I can't hang on much longer."

She felt the delicious tension inside her start to peak, and then he rubbed his thumb over the tight hard bud between her thighs and she shuddered as the sensations hit her. Her cries were loud, and soon his joined hers as they both found their release. He slumped down on top of her, pinning her sweaty body to the bed.

Her head was spinning, her body lax, and Branna knew she had never felt as she just had with another man. It was a scary thought and one she would tuck away for another time when she could rationalize it.

Jake rolled sideways taking her with him until it was she that lay on top of him. His arms wrapped around her and held her there as she struggled to get off.

"Stop fighting me; I'm stronger."

She did because she was tired, her body suddenly heavy, lashes fluttering closed. Laying her head on his chest, she heard the steady rhythm of his heartbeat. She'd get off in a minute, when she could find the strength.

Jake opened his eyes as Branna climbed off him. He heard her walk from the room and make her way to the bathroom, and then he heard the shower. Looking out the windows, he guessed they'd been asleep for some time as it was dark. He wondered what thoughts were going round and round inside her head. Rolling onto his back, Jake stared up at the ceiling. She'd blown his mind; it was as simple as that. He'd never felt like this with another woman in all his twenty-eight years. She was awkward, smart, argumentative, and hotter than hell and he wanted her like he did the oxygen that kept him alive. She'd taken and demanded from him in bed, and just thinking of how it had felt when he'd pushed inside her had him pulling aside the covers and heading for the shower. Opening the door, he was greeted with steam.

"You got that water hot enough, Rosebud?"

"I won't be a minute, then you can use it, or you could go home and—what are you doing?"

She stood with her head back against the wall, eyes closed, water running over that sexy body.

"If I was struck down now, I'd die a happy man. Damn, you're sexy, O'Donnell."

"What are you doing?"

"I like to share, cuts down on water wastage." Stepping in, Jake pulled the door closed behind him, caging them both in the steam and spray. Easing her off the wall, he pressed her wet hot body into his. "I look on it as my patriotic duty to my country and to future generations."

"Jake, I don't think—"

"There you go, thinking again."

Cupping one of her breasts, he took the nipple deep into his mouth, which caused her head to fall back on the wall as she moaned loudly.

"You said something about being sweaty." Jake reached for the soap when he'd lifted his head. "Let me clean you up a bit." She tried to stop him as he soaped up his hands and started to run them all over that sweet little body, but he ignored her, and then her hands fell to her sides as she closed her eyes and groaned long and loud.

"At least I know how to subdue you now."

"I'm not subdued."

Her eyes were barely open, the green depths filled with sensual heat that made her look like a sex kitten. She arched towards him as he stroked her stomach.

"Wrap your legs around me." Picking her up, he drove himself deep inside her as she lowered onto his aching flesh. He took it slower this time, enjoying the hot water cascading over them, the steam shrouding them, but most of all the feel of being inside her.

"Jake," her sigh was whispered in his ear as he felt the tremors start to rock her.

"Let go, baby, I've got you."

She did and he did, and it was as amazing as the first time, and Jake didn't think he'd ever get enough of this woman. Lowering her to her feet, he tilted her chin up and kissed her lips before washing off and getting out of the shower. She needed some time, he knew that. Branna O'Donnell was a woman who didn't get close to people; she hadn't in school, and he'd seen nothing to change that opinion since she'd arrived in Howling. Like him, she'd shut people out of her life, but unlike him, she'd had no one continually hammering at her door to get back in.

He was attracted to Branna, and maybe that was because she was like him, but he also knew women, and how their emotions tended to eventually get involved. Jake would just have to make sure that never happened here, lay out the facts right from the start about this…whatever it was, between them. Maybe they could be friends with benefits, but without the emotional entanglements? That sure as hell suited him.

Pulling on his clothes, he made his way downstairs and put on some coffee. Walking through the house, he looked at the changes she'd made. A painting here, a plant there. She'd thinned out some of Georgie's things, and it looked good. He came to a halt beside a large framed photograph of a woman that could only be Branna's mother. She had the same hair and eyes, but the smile was different. This woman had no secrets or sadness haunting her; she was happy from the inside.

"Th-that's my mother."

She was standing behind a chair, her hands resting on the back. Her hair hung around her head; now that it was wet, he could see that it almost reached her waist. She wore a baggy T-shirt and shorts and looked nervous, her eyes filled with shadows again.

"She's beautiful, like you." He dragged his eyes from her before he closed the distance and held her, which Jake knew would be a mistake right about now. Branna wasn't the holding kind. She was the stand and fight type.

"She was the most beautiful woman I have ever known." The words weren't spoken for effect; they were soft and sincere, and came from Branna's heart.

"How long has she been gone?"

"She died when I was twelve."

Two years before she came to Howling. He remembered how sometimes she'd looked so sad it had hurt his chest, but at sixteen, he'd not been able to do anything about it, because he didn't know how to reach out to a girl who was struggling to cope in his town, a girl two years younger than everyone around her.

"How did she die?" He thought she wasn't going to tell him, but then she started talking.

"W-we were in a car and it crashed. I lived and she died."

"Tough losing your mother at that age, on you and your father."

"It was my fault."

The words were whispered, and when he looked at her she'd turned around and gone. Jake followed, finding her in the kitchen. She was getting down two mugs from the cupboard above her.

"Why was it your fault, Branna?"

Her shoulders were hunched, spine rigid.

"It doesn't matter. I shouldn't have said anything."

"Is this another question we're not going to have an answer for?"

"Don't make it sound like it's just me who doesn't like answering them, McBride."

"Point taken."

She messed about with sugar and cream, taking things out of cupboards and putting them on the bench.

"So, tell me anyway," he added.

"This, what's between us, is about sex, Jake, nothing more. No deep and meaningful, no emotional entanglements. Just sex. If you don't want that, then walk away now."

"Not want it? It's every man's dream." So, why wasn't he smiling? She'd said the words that he'd wanted to hear. *Don't rely on me, Branna, I'm not a safe bet right now.* Those words had been on his tongue, and she'd beat him to it, and that just plain pissed him off and Jake had no idea why.

"I still want to hear about your mother, seeing as you started the conversation by saying it was your fault."

She turned away from him to pour the coffee.

"I was arguing with her, telling her and my father, who was in the back seat, that I wanted a cell phone like everyone else had. Why did I have to be the different kid, the one everyone laughed at just because my parents were too mean to buy me one?"

"That sounds like a normal teenage conversation to me."

Her hands were braced on the surface now, body still turned away from him, as the memories hit her.

"She turned to look at me and the car swerved and we hit a barrier. She took the full impact, but my father and I were on the other side of the car and survived."

"And, therefore, her death is your fault?" Jake kept his voice calm. He'd dealt with enough trauma in the army to know what was going on here.

"Yes!" She spun to face him. "It was my fault because I was a spoiled brat. Had I not made such a scene that day, she would still be alive."

"Because nothing else would have distracted her. She wouldn't have wanted to turn to look at her husband or daughter, the two people she loved? Her eyes would have stayed on that road, never deviating. You know that's bullshit, right? That super-sized brain of yours has worked that out by now, surely?"

"Don't try to analyze this, McBride. It's what it is, plain and simple. My behavior killed my mother and drove my father and me apart. End of story, now drink your coffee or leave; I don't care."

She was lashing out at him because she was angry and hurting, Jake knew this. He'd even done it a few times himself, but it still pissed him off. "Thanks for the fuck, Jake; now piss off, is that how this is going, Rosebud?"

The cup she had just picked up was slammed back down again as she turned to glare at him.

"Real smooth, Jake."

He shrugged, but didn't apologize.

"Okay, you want answers? Well, so do I. Why the fuck are you messing around with cars when you're a, and I quote from your legions of devoted friends, brilliant doctor?"

"Swearing doesn't suit you."

"You just swore, and fuck, fuck, fuck you, McBride."

He felt his temper ignite. The rock steady composure that he had once been legendary for deserted him again.

"Why is it that other people can change their careers, but not me?" His growl was loud in the small kitchen, but she didn't flinch. Even through his anger, he could see that she showed no fear.

"Because you spent years and years learning to do what you loved, while the rest of us flitted about trying to work out what we wanted to be...if we ever grew up. I remember hearing you talk about being a doctor in school, McBride. It wasn't a job; it was a passion."

His chest felt tight and suddenly he was there, back in that dirty room trying to stop those children from dying. The school had been bombed and he and his unit were the first on the scene. Jake had worked for hours and hours, trying to save the ones he could. It was after, when he could let himself think, that he'd known he couldn't do this anymore, couldn't see another child or person killed in this thankless war that would probably never end. And then the flashbacks had started.

"I don't want to talk about this." His voice sounded raw.

"Why?"

She was standing before him, but he couldn't see her, only the blood and the small helpless children begging him to take away their pain.

"Shut up!"

"No, I want to know why you walked away from what you love. Jake?" He felt her hand on his arm, but he didn't want it, nor did he want to unleash the anger inside him on her.

"I have to go."

"So, I had to bare my soul to you, but you won't do the same with me. You asked and I told you, McBride, when I've never told another person what I did to my mother."

"You didn't kill your mother." His chest was so tight it hurt to talk. He could feel it creeping up on him; soon he'd start shaking and sweating.

"You having a flashback or something?"

"What?" He focused on her face; maybe he could will it to stop.

"You're pale and sweaty and your eyes have gone weird."

"Weird how?" He could feel his chest rising and falling as his breathing increased.

"I know when someone is panicking, Jake. I should, because I had—have flashbacks."

"What?" He blinked a couple of times, willing the visions away.

"I see my mother sometimes." Her voice was flat and cold. She turned away from him again, and he heard the sound of water running, then she was back with a glass in her hand. "Drink this slowly; I find it helps sometimes."

He did and was disgusted to see his hands were shaking. She placed hers over his on the glass and lifted it to his lips again when he lowered it.

"Thanks."

Lowering the glass, she picked up his coffee and wrapped his hands around it.

"Talk to me, Jake, it may help."

"Did it help you?"

She shrugged and remained silent.

Could he talk about it? Maybe, since she'd suffered too, in some small way she would understand.

"I was in Iraq and a school was bombed. We were first on the scene and there were kids lying dead or wounded everywhere. I worked for hours and hours...until Ethan walked in and threw me over his shoulder and took me out of there."

"He's obviously got some issues related to rescuing people. The other day, he saved me from humiliation in the supermarket when I didn't need saving."

The images were disappearing as he talked and focused on Branna's face, so he kept talking. "After I'd slept, I woke, realizing I couldn't do this anymore. I served the rest of my time there, and then when I came home, I told them I was leaving the army. They tried to talk me out of it, but it was Ethan who supported me and told me I was doing the right thing, because he had been the one who got me through those months until I could come home."

"Are they getting further apart? The flashbacks?"

Putting down his cup, Jake suddenly didn't want to be this close to her and not touch her; wrapping his fingers around her wrist, he pulled her into his body. Resting his chin on top of her head, he closed his eyes and held her.

"Yeah, they are, but they still come when I least expect them."

"I know what that's like. I'd see my mother lying broken and bloodied against the steering wheel and hear my father's words in my head. He was crying, the sound heartbreaking, as he begged her not to leave him."

"Christ…that must be hard. At least I didn't know these people."

"It's a bit easier, now that I'm older."

They stood in silence, holding each other, and Jake felt his memories slowly recede as he focused on the woman in his arms.

"And you hate doctors, needles, and the other crap that comes with the entire medical profession because of the time you spent in the hospital?"

"Something like that," she mumbled the words into his chest, and Jake decided to leave that conversation for another day.

"Thank you for telling me, Rosebud."

"Thank you for telling me, McBride."

"Will you tell me about your father now?" Jake asked her.

"No. Have you told your parents about that? What happened and why you gave up medicine?"

Jake closed his eyes and breathed her in. Her hair was soft against his cheek and he wanted her again, wanted to lose himself in her body.

"No, let's go to bed."

She didn't protest as he took her hand; she just used the other one to switch off the coffee and lights as she went. Soon, he had her naked again, and his mind was consumed with her... everything else was gone.

He woke alone again. Lying there in silence, he listened to the birds, and then he heard her voice floating up from downstairs.

"The thing is, I didn't ask you to stay, you just sort of appeared, and that's okay, if you need a place to stay, but I sure as hell wish I knew your name."

Jake got out of bed and pulled on his shorts.

"I mean, it's the least you can give me, considering I brought you food and set up that nice soft pillow for you."

He made his way down the stairs and out the front door. Branna was sitting in one of the two chairs, coffee in one hand and a large grey cat draped over her lap.

"New friend?" He bent to brush her lips, because touching her was beginning to be just about as important to Jake as a chicken and vegetable pie.

"He arrived on my second day here, just wandered into the house and sat down on my chair, then started to clean himself. He's been here ever since."

Her eyes were still sleepy and her hair mussed, and those long legs were bare under that silky robe, and Jake felt something inside him that wasn't indigestion.

"What's his name?"

"Cat."

"Suits him, for some reason. You got more of that?" he pointed at her coffee.

"Sure, I made a pot."

He fixed his coffee, then took the chair beside hers, and they sat in silence as around them the day came to life. It was peaceful and right and Jake had a sinking feeling which made him get back out of his chair. He didn't need peaceful in his life at the moment, not when his head was still screwed up. Hell, he could hardly function himself, without worrying about a woman.

"I've got to go." He went back up the stairs and found the rest of his clothes, then ran back down and out the door.

"See you 'round, McBride."

"Sure." He took a step off the porch, then retraced it. Grabbing her chin, he lifted it and kissed her hard. Without saying another word, he then walked down the driveway, and cut back up through the track that would lead to his home. Around him, the redwoods stood silently on guard as he ran home as fast as his legs would carry him, hoping the exercise would dislodge the disturbing thoughts that a night spent with Branna O'Donnell had created inside him. He didn't rate his chances very high.

CHAPTER TEN

Branna spent the day doing things she'd put off since arriving in Howling. She unpacked the last of her things and tried not to think about Jake. Tidied cupboards, dusted every inch, and tried to push the feel of his body pressed against hers from her head. She baked an apple cake and some vanilla cookies, and refused to imagine him leaning on her cabinets eating.

She wrote for two hours and hoped the words were useable and saw his face change as it had last night, saw the memories that rode him hard fill his dark eyes. His hands had been shaking, his jaw clenched, and Branna knew what he was feeling, had felt his pain. The man was suffering and had been for some time. Did his family realize? Who did he talk to when he was hurting? Branna thought maybe Buster and obviously the Texan, as he was the one who'd saved him.

She'd look differently at the big smooth talking Texan now. She'd see the man who'd gotten Jake to safety.

So many secrets and so much pain. Branna had always known that other people were hurting, and she'd comforted a few in her time, but her pain was hers, or had been until she'd met Georgie, Belle, and now Jake. They were the only three people who knew what had made her who she was today, and one of them was suffering right alongside her.

"God, what a mess." Sighing, she went upstairs to take a shower. Jake had left in a hurry this morning, almost like being here with her had panicked him; it had certainly panicked her to feel the rightness of it, the comfort of having him in her home.

Branna washed and pulled on a fitted dress in a soft fabric that reached her knees with a little ruffled hem. It was lemon with thin shoulder straps, and she'd last worn it to visit her agent. Adding raspberry colored sandals that gave her extra height, she slipped on a matching bangle. Pulling her hair up, she twisted it and clipped it into a messy knot. The mirror told her she looked ready to visit the school. She would arrive as school ended, and hoped to catch the woman before she left for the day; if not, she'd make time to come back.

Another beautiful day and the heat was easing up slightly as she drove towards the town. Howling Elementary, Belle had told her, was a small building with a small attendance, but it had good teachers, one of whom was hopefully Miss. Todd. Pulling into a parking space, she collected her bag. It was one level, with two wings; the main reception was through a set of glass doors. The cool air was nice as she walked up to the desk to where a grey-haired lady was typing.

"Good afternoon."

The woman lifted her head and smiled.

"Hello, Branna."

"Mrs. Huxley?"

"Yes, I transferred here, dear, from the high school. Closer to home, you understand."

Mrs. Huxley was tall, rail thin, and her hair was now grey, but still cut in the bob she'd always worn. She'd been one of the administrators at the high school Branna attended. She was kind and sweet-natured and capable of being a lioness when necessary. Fortunately, Branna had never crossed her, but she'd seen students who had and it never worked out pretty for them.

"I've read all your father's books, dear. He's something of a celebrity here in Howling, and we've claimed him I'm afraid, seeing as he lived here for a while."

"I'm sure he'll be happy about that." Branna wished people didn't continually need to mention her father.

"Be sure you tell him, dear, and when he comes to visit, perhaps you could get something autographed for me."

"He's pretty busy right now, Mrs. Huxley, but I'll see what I can do." When hell freezes over, Branna added silently.

She didn't want to see her father any more than he wanted to see her. When she'd told him she was leaving Howling after high school, he'd tried to argue with her, but Branna had seen the relief in his eyes, so she'd simply packed up and gone and left him here. He'd left too, not long after her, gone back to Ireland for a time; from there, she'd lost track of his movements. He'd contacted her regularly, but eventually even that had died off, as she'd always cut his calls short because it hurt too much to hear his voice. And with distance came a small measure of peace. If she didn't see him, she didn't hurt quite as much. Then they'd had their fight, and she knew now there would be nothing further between them.

"Mrs. Huxley, I wondered if it was possible to see Miss Todd."

"You know Ellen, Branna?" She could see the question in the woman's eyes, and wondered how much to say.

"No, but I know one of her students, and I thought I could help him out a bit with his homework."

"Well, now, that's nice of you, dear, and I'm sure Ellen would appreciate it. You just stay there, and I'll see if she's still here."

Branna wandered about, looking at photos of children who had yet to grow into their bodies. Knobby knees, missing teeth…they were all represented here.

"Come this way, Branna; Ellen's in her classroom."

She followed the straight back of Mrs. Huxley, then entered the room she indicated. A woman, who Branna guessed was a few years older than her, was seated at a desk. Straight blonde hair hung to her shoulders and she wore a pretty floral dress and sandals.

"Ellen, this is Branna O'Donnell," Mrs. Huxley said before leaving the room.

They shook hands and Branna took the seat across from Miss Todd's. The room was small, and filled with books and shelves; a whiteboard was covered in scribbles, which she was sure made sense to someone.

"How can I help you, Miss O'Donnell?"

"I wanted to talk with you about Michael Tucker, Miss Todd."

"Oh, dear, what trouble is he in now?" The woman sighed as she put down her pen and then rubbed the bridge of her nose. Branna empathized; she remembered how that felt, the endless paperwork, continual parent phone calls, rude students, and thankless days. Of course, like a lot of teachers, she'd loved every minute, but she loved her writing more.

"No trouble, in fact I wondered if you realized just how intelligent Michael Tucker is, Miss Todd?"

The tawny colored eyes of Miss Todd suddenly chilled. "He is a bright boy, Miss O'Donnell; however, no brighter than any of my other students, and indeed a lot more trouble."

Branna opened her handbag silently and found the papers she'd put in there, laying them on the desk facing the teacher; she then spoke.

"I met Michael Tucker a few days after returning to Howling. He came to see me because the woman who had bequeathed me her house upon her death was a friend, who supported and comforted Michael, which to me would suggest he was not receiving that in his own home," Branna said slowly.

"I have no reason to believe that. In fact, his mother is a very nice woman, and calls to see me when she can. Michael tends to lie when provoked, Miss O'Donnell." Miss Todd's hackles were now well and truly up.

"These," Branna said, holding onto her temper, because much as she'd like to let it loose, she would achieve nothing by doing so. "Are the after school work I have been doing with Michael. Mr. Hope tested the boy and found his IQ to be one hundred twenty-eight, which I'm sure is stated in his records, if you have taken the time to read them." Branna held the other woman's rapidly widening gaze. "I think they prove just what Michael Tucker is capable of, don't you?"

There was silence while the teacher studied Michael's work. There were mathematical workings and written work.

"H-he did these?"

"Yes."

"Well, they certainly show he's capable of doing a great deal more than the tasks he's currently being given, if indeed he did these, but they do not show me his IQ is quite what you state," Miss Todd said.

"Perhaps you should read his file then?" Branna snapped, rising to her feet. "And for the record, I would never lie about something as important as this. Especially as I was once in his shoes and have the same IQ. Believe me when I say it is a lonely and unenviable position for a ten year old boy to be in when your sole focus is on fitting in with your peers."

"I'm not sure what you are accusing me of, Miss O'Donnell?"

Branna braced both hands on the desk. "Look, Miss Todd, I'm not accusing you of anything, nor am I judging. I was a teacher also, and understand the pressures you face every day. A child who doesn't fit into the model you have written presents more work—"

"Which I have no problem with, as my students' welfare is important to me," the teacher said defensively.

"Excellent, then can I suggest you read his file thoroughly before you make any further judgments about his behavior?" She didn't stay to hear any further replies from the teacher; instead, she pushed off the desk and left the room. Waving at Mrs. Huxley, she then climbed into her van and drove out of the school gates. Lowering the window, Branna inhaled a deep calming breath.

For now, she'd done all she could, but she'd be back if she thought it was needed. Mikey would not suffer because he had smarts; she'd see to that.

Driving into town, Branna pulled up in front of the drugstore; minutes later, she was looking on the shelves for her favorite brand of moisturizer. When the door opened, she didn't look up, too busy reading labels, which was a bad pastime she had, but one that she had all the same. It always surprised Branna what actually went into things, and she usually tried to purchase things with ingredients that she at least recognized.

"You still suffering with that stomach upset, Macy?"

Branna wasn't visible to the people at the counter, which was a relief; she had no wish to get into it with Macy Reynolds again.

"I'll have this made up for you in a few minutes, Macy."

"Thanks, Mr. Pike."

Holding her breath, Branna eased along the shelf so she was tucked in the corner out of sight. Macy came into her view as she walked behind a set of shelves further down the aisle. She didn't look Branna's way, instead lowering her head into her hands as her shoulders started to shake. She then bent double, almost as if whatever hurt inside her was making it impossible to stay upright.

Branna was so shocked she couldn't stop staring. The woman was crying silently into her hands. What the hell should she do now? If she moved, it would alert Macy, but then maybe Branna should ask if she could help? The hand Macy moved from her face as she straightened shook as it reached out to grab the side of the shelf, her fingers clenching so hard the knuckles were white.

"Nearly ready, Macy!"

"Thanks, Mr. Pike, be right there."

Branna watched Macy shake her hands a few times, and then haul in a deep breath, and then she was gone.

What the hell was that about? Branna didn't want to feel sorry for Macy Reynolds-Delray, but right at that moment, the woman she had seen commanded her to do so. Whatever was behind Macy's pain, it was the kind of hurt that you felt through your entire body. When the door signaled she had left, Branna grabbed her selections, paid for them, and also made her way outside.

"Good, I was just going to call you, but now that you're here, we can just go straight to the Howler."

Belle was coming towards her, long legs eating the distance in seconds. Her friend was dressed in fitted jeans, high-heeled pink stilettos and a white shirt, under which she wore a pink silk camisole, the exact color of her heels. Her hair was pulled back on the sides and she looked beautiful and sexy.

"Wow, you look hot!"

"I was just going to say those exact words to you, Bran."

They both laughed.

"Come on, let's get a drink."

Why not, Branna thought. "Add food to that drink, and I'll agree."

"Done."

***

The Howler was fundamentally the same establishment it had been when Jake had first stepped foot inside it ten years ago.

The Harris family had owned it forever and it was now run by the twins, Faith and Noah, who were a year older than him.

It was an extension of the nature outside its door, the colors neutral, with a large open fireplace that during the winter months roared, wood paneling and a circular bar that was wrapped in beige stone. Soft lighting invited you in and the music and company made you stay. On one side was the bar and dance floor, the other a restaurant.

The walls were a shrine to the Packers, a team the Harris family had supported forever, along with the rest of Howling.

Walking towards the bar, Jake did a sweep of the room and found Branna and Annabelle seated at a table with Buster, Newman, and one other guy he didn't know.

"That woman makes me itch," Ethan said.

Dragging his eyes from Branna, who was smiling at something Newman was saying, Jake looked at him. "Branna?"

"Annabelle Smith," he glared across the room.

"Don't tell me there's a woman who can resist your charms, stud?"

"She has an attitude that drives me crazy."

Jake made himself turn and walk to the bar. The foreign emotion called jealousy was chorusing through his body, and all Branna was doing was smiling at his friend.

"She also happens to be an outstanding nurse and loyal friend."

Tex lounged on the bar beside him while they waited to be served.

"She's hot."

"Yeah, she is, but more like a sister, so it just feels plain wrong to call her hot, so instead I'll say pretty," Jake said, thinking about the brief look he'd gotten of Branna. She'd appeared happy, which should make him feel good, but instead made him angry that she wasn't being happy with him. Hell, he was screwed up.

"You better get over there, McBride, that guy with the blond hair is moving in on your girl."

"She's not my girl." *But if anyone touches her, they're dead.*

"Okay, just so I'm clear. You don't care that the man now has his hand on her arm, her bare arm," Ethan clarified. "And that she's laughing up at him, all flashing teeth and sparkling eyes."

Jake didn't turn even as his gut clenched.

"That shit only worked on me in college. I'm a big grown up now and Branna can talk and interact with whoever she wishes."

"Bullshit," Ethan whispered.

"'Hey, Jake, what you after?'"

"Faith," Jake acknowledged the woman who stood before him. She had the Harris dark skin and hair and fine delicate features. "Two beers, thanks, for me and the idiot."

"Ethan Gelderman," Ethan stuck out his hand and gave his patented smile, which Jake was pleased to see Faith ignored and turned back to him, after giving his friend's hand a good hard pump.

"Your mum and dad were in here earlier, they said Katie's coming home for a few days."

"Holidays are soon, so she's going to spend them here with us."

"Be good to see her." Faith walked away, then Ethan sighed. "What's your problem now?" Jake asked him.

"The women in this town are way too pretty and they all seem to have attitude."

"You mean they all seem immune to the patented Ethan Gelderman brand of charm."

"There's no lying, it's a strange thing, McBride. Like some kind of parallel universe where I'm invisible."

Jake laughed as he paid Faith for the beers. "Faith, give this man a compliment, will you? He's feeling insecure."

"You have good teeth." Faith Harris then walked away, leaving a devastated Texan at his side.

"Teeth! All she could come up with was my teeth are nice. I'm a broken man, McBride, my pride lying in shredded remnants at my feet."

"Well, step over the mess, buddy, we got beers to drink."

They walked to where the others had gathered, and Jake seated himself beside Buster, next to him was Branna, then Newman and the man he didn't know, then Annabelle. Ethan took the space beside her.

"Evening all." Jake smiled around the table, not letting his eyes rest on Branna for any longer than the others.

"This is Oliver Rendell; he's visiting from England," Newman made the introductions. "Jake McBride and Ethan Gelderman the 5th."

Ethan rolled his eyes as he shook the man's hand. His name was a constant source of amusement to Buster and Newman.

Jake sat back as he took a mouthful of beer, his eyes settling on Branna. She was talking to Annabelle. Her lemon dress had two thin little shoulder straps and a fitted top that sat low on her breasts exposing soft, slender shoulders and a cleavage that he'd had his mouth all over last night. The rest of her wasn't visible, as it was under the table, but what he saw was enough to heat him up. She'd pulled her hair into a messy knot on her head, and it exposed the delicate line of her neck and curve of her jaw.

"Are you fortunate enough to live in this town also, Jake?" Jake's mother had made him watch Jane Austen movies when she'd had no other sucker to do so, and this guy could have stepped right out of one.

"Yes, I was born and raised here."

"How wonderful, and are you a woodsman too?"

"Too?" Jake looked from the Englishman to Buster, who lowered his eyes.

"Buster and Newman told me they are log rollers, and I must say it sounds a dangerous occupation, and that to do it well one must have perfect coordination."

Jake leveled his friends a look. Last time they had told a group of tourists they were fire jumpers. This time he was going to teach them a lesson. Sending a silent apology to loggers everywhere, he said, "Unfortunately, no, I failed the log rolling course. You see, to be really good at it, you have to stand in ice cold water for long periods of time, and that does things to your…" Jake looked down at his groin briefly before continuing. "Over time, things fail to work as well as they once did, and eventually you're unable to rise to any challenge, Oliver. Loggers have even lost their, ah drive permanently. So, you see, it takes a devoted and dedicated man to give that up."

Jake shot Branna a look; she was staring into her glass of wine with her top lip clamped firmly between her teeth.

"Well, I must say, you are to be commended for such dedication, gentlemen," Oliver said politely.

"Yeah, dedicated is what we are," Buster scowled at Jake.

"I'm real proud of them, Oliver, it has to be said." Jake lifted his beer to salute his friends. Newman flipped him the bird, seen by everyone but Oliver.

"So, how about a dance to show off those fast moving feet, Newman?" Annabelle got to hers and held out one hand. "After all, you were crowned log rolling champion in these here parts for the last two years; you should be up for the challenge."

"Aww, shucks," Newman muttered. "There's no need to go on about that, Annabelle, you know how it upsets Buster that he came in second."

Jake watched Annabelle laugh as Newman led her to the floor.

Buster grabbed Branna before Jake could, and by the smug look on his face, it was payback.

"I can't line dance, Buster." She tried to stop him, but he simply picked her up and placed her on her feet, then tugged her behind him.

"You ever danced in a line, Oliver?"

"I haven't, Ethan, no."

The Englishman was looking at the dance floor as the lines formed. Jake watched Buster grab Branna's hips and push her into the space between him and Newman. She was nervous, her body stiff, as she listened to Buster explain the moves. She took a step to the right and turned back as Buster instructed her to do, and the hem of her skirt lifted, showing Jake, and anyone else watching, the lower half of her thighs. It was a dress that caressed her curves just like his hands had last night, a dress that he wanted to remove slowly and then kiss everything he uncovered. She had on heels, high enough to give her a few more inches, the color of raspberries; they did amazing things to her already amazing legs.

"Right, so let's find some partners, Oliver, and attempt to teach you a few things before you return to your homeland. Off your ass, McBride, and get us some women, seeing as you know every one of them in this room."

He did as Ethan asked, because he wanted to get onto the dance floor. Minutes later, he'd asked three women he knew, and soon they were all in a line. Jake could hear Branna's laughter as she got the steps wrong, often going the wrong way. Buster was patient, just placing a hand on her back and pointing her back the right way.

"You getting it, Rosebud?" Jake grabbed her hand as the song finished and she started to walk off the floor.

"No, in fact it's fair to say I'm hopeless."

Her skin glowed under the soft lights, and her eyes were alive, and he wanted her in his arms. "Come and dance with me and I'll give you some more lessons."

Branna looked into the black eyes of Jake McBride and fought the shiver of longing that raced through her. He was dressed in jeans and a white fitted T-shirt, and while she'd only had two glasses of wine, which for her was one too many, he looked so sexy her body was actually tingling being this close to him.

"I don't think I should embarrass myself anymore, Jake, I have to live here, after all."

"Just one dance, Branna."

She took the hand he held out to her and let him lead her back into the line.

"Think about the basic pattern, Branna. Right heel to the ground, then left. That's it."

He stood behind her, hands on her hips, leading her through the steps, and she began to see the pattern as he explained it to her. Pushing aside the feel of him so close, his breath on her cheek, hands on her hips, she concentrated and soon had the rhythm.

"I'm doing it!"

He came to stand beside her. "Clever girl."

She bumped into him a few times and his hands steadied her, then usually caressed whatever part of her body they touched before removing them. It was like some kind of bizarre mating ritual that was heating her up faster than a hot tub. His hip bumped hers, his eyes, when she was foolish enough to look up, would wander over her face and down to her breasts. Branna needed to get off this dance floor before she gave into the urge to jump him.

When the music finished, she thanked him, and then started back to where the others sat with Jake on her heels.

"My pleasure, now let me take you home and you can show me just how grateful you are."

Branna stopped at those growled words, turning, she looked up at him. His smile was soft and only for her, filled with sensual promise of just what the night would hold if she let him take her to bed.

"That's not a good idea, Jake, not after you running scared this morning."

"Sure it is." He stepped closer, crowding her with his big hot body. "And I wasn't running scared I had work to do."

"No," she took a step backwards, "it's not, and you didn't" Branna said, turning away from him and continuing on to the table, where she said good night to everyone as she retrieved her bag. Giving Oliver a friendly wave and telling him to come back soon, she then left before Jake could lay a hand on her, because she knew that if he did, she'd be lost.

Branna woke to sunshine again, her sleep had been deep, and luckily she couldn't remember her dreams, as they were almost certainly about Jake. Climbing out of bed, she hurried through her shower.

Mikey and Belle were coming to help her in the garden, and she'd promised to cook them breakfast as payment. After she'd prepared the batter for the waffles and started the coffee, she wandered outside. This place was changing her; she could feel it. Softening her edges, making her feel like she hadn't for years, and Branna wasn't sure how she felt about that. For so long, she'd managed not to care. But now she had a house, friends, and Jake, whatever that meant.

Walking around the side of the house, she came to a stop before the garden. It was totally destroyed. Plants had been uprooted, others stomped on, and the ones she'd brought, that had sat waiting to be planted, had been destroyed. Dropping to her knees, she looked at the mess. Why would someone do this to her?

The sound of a vehicle had her regaining her feet. She didn't want Mikey or Belle to see the mess. She'd take them out; tell them she hadn't managed to get the plants, take them to The Hoot for breakfast.

"We're here!"

She was too late; they were both coming around the house towards her. Belle saw the garden first and grabbed Mikey, but it was too late, he'd seen it too.

"What's happened, Branna?" He ran to the garden and looked at the plants, bending to pick up petals and broken plants.

"I didn't hear them doing it, Belle, I just saw it before you drove up." Branna felt the anger begin to simmer inside her.

"Bastards," Belle hissed. "Low life fucking bastards," she said, so the boy couldn't hear.

"Who would do this?" Mikey's little face was tight with worry as he looked from Belle to Branna.

"Some dickhead, with shit for brains is who, Mikey. Now, don't you worry about it, we'll get to the bottom of it. You just get mad and that'll make you mean, which is what we women need about now," Belle added. "Go get my camera from the car; I want to take some pictures of this."

"I can do mean." He bared his teeth and Branna managed to laugh. He hugged her then, before running to Belle's car.

"Jesus, Branna, why would someone do this to you?" Branna let her friend wrap an arm around her neck and pull her close.

Normally, she didn't like being touched or hugged, but that too seemed to have changed since she'd come to Howling.

"We should tell Cubby."

"Why? It's a garden, Belle, some kids probably got high and did it."

"This is Howling, Branna, not Washington. Kids may get high here, but it's behind closed doors where no one can see. People here know people; kids wouldn't risk doing this, not so close to the house. You could have woken anytime and seen them."

"But who else would want to and why? I've made no enemies since coming here, and I don't think even Macy hates me that much that she'd get dirt under nails."

They stood looking at the mess until Mikey came back and handed Belle the camera. She started snapping pictures as they watched.

"You should let Jake know, Branna."

"What is it with you and him?" Branna said, poking the boy in the stomach, which made him squirm. "He got a big S on his chest or something?"

"He'd make a fine superman, though, you know it's the truth," Belle muttered from behind her camera.

"I'm going inside and this conversation is at an end." Branna made her way back into the house and sagged against the door when she was out of sight. Who had done this to her garden and why? It terrified her to think that someone this angry had stood and destroyed her garden while she slept just above. Making her way to the kitchen, she started cooking the waffles, and wondered how the hell she was going to get any sleep tonight.

The day was spent cleaning the garden up, and by the time Belle and Mikey had gone, she'd just about convinced herself that it was a random attack...just about. When she finally climbed into bed, exhausted, she closed her eyes and willed herself to sleep.

CHAPTER ELEVEN

Something woke Branna; lying still in the dark, she tried to identify what. The faint whisper of voices and then the sound of breaking glass drifted up from below her. Someone was inside, and anyone who entered a home uninvited in the middle of the night was not paying a social call. Fear momentarily rooted her to the bed, and her heart thumped so hard it hurt.

Move!

Edging the covers aside, she forced herself to get up. Finding her shorts on the chair where she'd left them, Branna quickly pulled them up her legs under the large T-shirt she slept in. Moving silently towards the door, she eased it open, then listened. Something was ripping, and then there was more glass breaking, followed by a muffled curse. Shaking her head to clear it, she hurried to the window and opened it, then swinging a leg over the sill, Branna climbed out and rested on the small ledge. There was a ladder here somewhere, because Georgie had said that Dan had it fitted to the side of the house in case of fire; she just needed to work out how to lower it.

Feeling along the boards, she found it, and then fumbled with the latches until she had them opened. Hoping it didn't make too much noise, she slowly lowered it to the ground.

Branna turned and stepped onto the ladder, and then worked her way down as fast as she could without falling. Fear made her clumsy; occasionally missing a step, she was reduced to clutching the sides of the ladder to stop herself from falling. She hoped whoever was inside the house stayed downstairs while she escaped, because if they came outside now, they'd find her before she had a chance to run, and Branna didn't want to think about what they would do to her then.

When she finally reached it, the ground was cold on her bare feet. Running to the garden, she found the old boots she'd left there earlier and pulled them on, then sprinted to the driveway. The moon was high and showed her the way, but would also show anyone else who was looking. Running down the road, Branna searched for the entrance to the trail that would lead her to Jake. She needed to get off the road, because if they came looking for her, she'd be easily spotted in their headlights.

Her eyes began to adjust and she saw the opening in the trees. Running up it, she tripped on a root and landed on her knees; thankfully, she hadn't put her injured wrist out to stop her fall. Regaining her feet, she started again, this time more slowly.

Don't panic, Branna, it won't help you. Her father had often used those words when he had been in her life and still loved her enough to care. She'd always been a panicker. Things used to unsettle her easily, small things that really didn't justify her jitters, so he'd taught her to say that, *courage is resistance to fear, mastery of fear—not absence of fear*, and it had often worked enough to calm her down, help focus her attention elsewhere.

I need it now, Dad.

The big trees towered over her, and she knew they weren't dangerous. She knew she was the only person out here, but still the fear nearly choked her. It was hard to walk without knowing what was ahead, but she took it slow and stumbled a few times, but didn't fall again. Every noise and rustle made her flinch and fear made her imagine that at any second someone would spring out of the dark and grab her and she would never be seen again. She'd never used this track, but Branna knew Jake's house was close, because she'd run past it a few times.

It felt like she'd been walking for hours when she saw it, the long low house bathed in moonlight. Running off of the path as quickly as her shaky legs would let her, she made for the front door. She'd never seen his house, but this had to be it. Hammering on the wood door seconds later, she hoped he was there. Branna battled to subdue the sting of tears as a light came on through the windows. The door opened and revealed a bare-chested Jake, clad in shorts.

"Branna?"

"I-I need your help, Jake."

"What's happened?"

Her body shook as the adrenalin that had coursed through her and kept her moving drained away. She was suddenly weak and fighting the hopeless tears that wanted to fall as she scrambled to find her voice.

"I-I need to use your phone, please."

He gently pulled her inside, then led her to a chair, which he lowered her into. Are you hurt?" He crouched in front of her.

"No."

"You're frozen," his big hands rubbed her arms. Did you walk here?"

"I just need to use your phone, please, Jake."

"Branna, it's three in the morning, honey, tell me what's going on?"

"Men, Jake, there were men in my house."

His fingers bit into her skin briefly before they unclenched.

"Tell me what happened, Branna."

His hair stood on end, and his skin would be warm from the sleep she had dragged him from, and she desperately wanted to fall into his arms, needed to so badly she had to restrain herself by gripping the arms of the chair. She wasn't weak, and wouldn't fall apart now that she was safe.

"Something woke me and I heard them, the sound of footsteps downstairs. I listened, and I-I th-think they were trashing my house."

His body had gone still, alert, as he listened and watched.

"I d-didn't wait around, just climbed out the window and lowered the ladder that Georgie—"

"I know about the ladder, Branna."

"I didn't stop; just kept climbing down, and then when I reached the bottom, I found my boots and ran here. I remembered that Belle said the path led to you, so I was sure I was going in the right direction. I didn't think I'd make it to town and was worried they'd see me if I tried." She hadn't even thought of running into town. He'd been the safety she wanted, and so she'd run to him, not that she'd ever tell him that.

"Christ!"

She was slammed into his chest and two strong arms banded around her as he held her so tight she thought her ribs would crack. It was bliss.

"You stay here, and I'll go and check your house."

"No!" Branna grabbed his arms as he released her. "You won't go there and be hurt; I won't let you."

"I'll be okay, Branna. I'll be armed."

"No, I won't be responsible for you getting hurt; I can't go through that again."

"Hey, shhh, it's okay." He pulled her into his arms again. She wouldn't lose another person she cared about because of something she'd done. The vision of Jake broken and lifeless slipped into her head. "Promise me you'll stay here."

"I promise, but I have to call Cubby Hawker."

"Okay."

Jake's first reaction was to go to Branna's house anyway, and see if they were still there, then shoot them. Of course, he couldn't do that, but looking at her, huddled and scared in his chair, made anger twist in his gut. The scenarios of what could have happened to her were making him feel sick. Even now she could be broken and bloody, some man could be…no, don't go there Jake, she's here safe with you, and he'd make sure she stayed that way. Suddenly, all the reasons why he'd walked away from her the morning after they'd made love had disappeared. He wanted her here in his house, safe from whoever was intent on harming her. He'd wanted to follow her last night, after she left the Howler, but something had stopped him; now, for the life of him, he couldn't remember what.

Her eyes were wide and dry, but he knew she was battling tears. Branna O'Donnell's composure had deserted her, and she was scrambling hard to regain it.

No, I won't be responsible for you getting hurt; I can't go through that again. Jake knew that when the shock had passed, Branna would hate herself for saying those words, showing weakness.

He took one of her hands, warming the icy fingers in his. He didn't want to think about her running along that dark trail through the trees to reach him, or the terror that must have gripped her while he'd been lying warm and safe in his bed.

"I need to get my phone, Rosebud."

"Okay."

"Just a few seconds, baby, that's all and I'll be back." He ran a hand over her head before he stood.

"I'm okay, Jake, really." She nodded, her green eyes huge in her pale face, and he didn't believe her words; she was far from okay.

Running to the bedroom, Jake found his phone, then pulled a blanket from the bed and ran back. Wrapping the blanket around her body, he then took off her boots and tucked it around her feet. She huddled into it, looking so tiny and vulnerable he swore his heart just sighed.

"It's all right now." He kissed her softly, brushing those chilled lips again as he reassured her once more.

"I'm not hurt; it was just a shock."

"It's okay to admit you were scared, Rosebud. Okay to cry about something that no sane person wouldn't feel traumatized about."

"I don't like to cry."

He lowered himself onto the arm of her chair, then called Cubby. Her hand stole into his while he waited, and the gesture was telling. Branna O'Donnell didn't reach for people, she was insular and contained, but she'd reached for him.

"Cubby, its Jake. Branna's just run here along the trail because she heard someone in her house and she thinks they were trashing it. Yeah, okay, see you soon."

"So, why don't you like crying?" he asked, pocketing his phone.

"Crying doesn't help anything."

Jake lifted her hand to his lips and kissed the cold knuckles as he thought about that.

"Sure it does, it's like releasing the water after a bath, let's all that excess emotion spill down the drain. Keeping all that pent up inside you isn't healthy, Rosebud."

She was tense and nervous and her eyes still took up far too much space in her face. He knew about shock, knew how it worked, so he gave her hand one more kiss before he regained his feet.

"I'm going to make some hot chocolate." He couldn't stop touching her; his hands pushed the hair back from her forehead.

"Yes, I'd like some of that please."

So polite, Jake thought, moving to his kitchen. Big and open plan, his living, kitchen and dining areas all opened onto each other.

"I like your home."

"Thanks, my dad, some friends, and I built it."

It was a man's place; he knew that. Not much decoration, just a few paintings and rugs and the prerequisite pillows on the large sofas that his mother had insisted on supplying. But there was a big TV and a view of the lake, and it was his. For months after his return, it had been his haven…the bolt hole where he licked his wounds.

Shooting her a look, he saw Branna was resting her head on the back of the chair watching him. Leaving the milk to heat, he dropped down in front of her again. Touching her reassured him that she was here and safe.

"You okay?"

"Yes."

"You're not much of liar."

"I was a pretty nervous child, used to get panicked easily, and my dad taught me to say, courage is resistance to fear, mastery of fear—not absence of fear, over and over in my head when I felt it coming on."

"Mark Twain."

"Yes," she nodded, her eyes focused on his. "I said it over and over again on the way to you, Jake."

"I'm glad you ran to me, Branna."

"I-I," she frowned, as if the words confused her. "I didn't think about it. I just ran."

"And here I am."

"Here you are." She placed a hand on his chest, as if to check that he really was there. Who had she run to before he came into her life? Were there times when she needed someone, but no one was there because she'd shut everyone out?

"I thought about my father as I ran, and suddenly I missed him, which is strange, because I thought I'd gotten past that."

How did a person ever get past missing a parent? Jake wondered. Slipping a hand beneath the blanket, he then ran it up her leg, stroking the cold skin, soothing and reassuring both himself and her.

"I'm not sure why I'm talking about this now."

She looked genuinely confused, but he knew that she was reacting to what had happened, wasn't really back in control yet, as much as she wanted to believe she was.

"Where is he now?" Jake rose and finished making the hot chocolate. Then, bringing a large mug back, he placed it on the table beside her; she didn't resist when he lifted her up and sat with her on his lap. Picking up the mug, he then handed it to her.

She drank slowly, taking small sips, letting the chocolate slide down her throat, and then handed it back to him.

"Thank you, that tastes good."

"Of course it's good. I made it."

Her snuffle fell way short of a laugh.

"Do you know where your father is?"

"No, we lost touch."

Jake couldn't fathom that because, even when he'd been in another country, he'd known where his parents and sister were and how soon he could reach them if he needed to.

"What happened?"

She turned and rested her cheek against his chest, and Jake wondered if she would answer his question, but it seemed that fear had loosened her tongue.

"He couldn't forgive me for killing the only woman he had ever loved."

Jake didn't buy that, but he also didn't know enough about the situation to make a call. However, he had a hunch that somewhere along the line, Branna and her dad had driven each other away in their grief.

"You didn't kill her."

"He believed so, and didn't love me enough to forgive me."

He didn't believe that either. He listened as she talked about her father, about the life they'd had before her mother's death, and contrary to what Branna believed, he formed the picture of a man who loved his daughter, a man who helped to do projects, and went on school trips, and even made her a tutu when his wife had to work. That was not a cold-hearted man; it was a man who loved his daughter.

The flash of light through the windows told him Cubby had arrived. He lifted her off his lap and went to open the door to his old friend, who appeared looking rumpled and sleep mussed.

"Evening, Jake."

"Cubby." Leading him to where Branna sat, Jake went to make coffee for the sheriff.

"Hey there, Miss O'Donnell, remember me from school?"

"Of course, and thank you for coming here at such an hour. Please, call me Branna."

She sounded like the teacher she'd once been, polite and distant, and Jake wondered when she'd let the tears he knew had to be inside her, fall.

Pulling up another chair, the sheriff dropped into it and took the mug Jake handed him.

"Jake said you had some trouble, Branna, so I called by your house to check things over. I'm sorry to say, they've made a mess over there, and destroyed some of your property."

She lowered her head, letting her hair hide her face. Jake saw her shoulders rise and fall as she drew in several deep breaths before looking at Cubby again.

"I-I th-thought that's what was happening. I heard the sound of glass breaking and something tearing."

"I'm sorry for it, and will say that this is not something common for Howling, Branna. I hope you know that."

She managed a smile for Cubby. "It's not your fault."

"Would you mind telling me about it, and start from the beginning with anything you can remember. I'll make notes, if that's all right with you?"

After handing Branna her chocolate again, Jake sat on the arm of the chair as she began her story. He'd heard it, but hearing it the second time made him angrier, probably because he'd had time to think about the what ifs.

"You heard no voices?" Cubby questioned.

"Whispers, but no loud voices. Whatever was happening down there, they did not want me to wake up and witness it."

Jake touched her shoulder, then ran his fingers over the skin the loose neck of her shirt exposed. Cubby was scratching away in his notebook as she talked.

The childhood friend he and Buster had was now a man. Solid, with a shock of red hair, Cubby was a man the citizens of Howling had come to depend upon and often did.

"Now, Branna, I know you haven't been back in town long, but have you had any altercations with anyone? Been threatened in any way?"

Jake felt her twitch, the gesture was small, but her body jerked in response to Cubby's question.

"I need to know everything, Branna, no matter how small the detail is."

She shot Jake a look, then turned back to Cubby.

"Yesterday morning, I went out to inspect my garden, and found someone had destroyed it."

"Destroyed it how?" Jake demanded.

"Jake," Cubby warned, hearing the anger in his voice.

"Totally destroyed it. Tore out all the plants, stripped off leaves and flowers, uprooted everything and stomped all over it. Even my new plants were ruined."

"Why the hell didn't you tell me, Branna?" Jake questioned.

"Why would I tell you?" She looked genuinely confused as she looked up at him.

"Because I care what happens to you…because I could have helped clean it up."

"Sit, Jake, now." Cubby's voice was calm, and Jake hadn't even realized he'd risen until that moment.

"Okay, Branna, you tell me everything now. Every detail, and don't leave anything out because you think that big bastard seated beside you is going to get angry. I can handle him."

"You sure?" She shot him a quick look.

"I decked him once...he dropped like a rag doll. Believe me, he's not as tough as he appears."

"Six, Cubby, we were six, and I wasn't looking." Jake forced himself to relax.

"Still took you, bud."

Jake bared his teeth, but said nothing further.

"You can start now, Branna. He's subdued."

"There's not much else to say. The garden was ruined; Belle took pictures and then she, Mikey, and I fixed it up."

"All right, Branna, that will do for now. Tomorrow, I want to question you further, just to see if there's anything else you remember. I have my deputies at your place now, fingerprinting and taking photos."

"They're taking photos now, at this time of night?" Branna asked. Cubby nodded. "Needs to be done now."

Jake rose along with Cubby. "I'll be back soon, Branna," he said, managing a smile for her before following the sheriff outside.

"Spit it out, Cubby. I know something's on your mind," Jake said, when they reached his cruiser. The night settled around them, the absolute quiet that he loved, but tonight it didn't calm him as it normally did.

"This is a nasty business, Jake, and the truth of it is, I think someone's targeting that little lady. First the garden and now this, it smacks of someone trying to frighten her, but for the life of me I can't figure out why."

"Why her? She's been away for years and hasn't been back long enough to make trouble; it doesn't make any sense, Cubby."

"I've been to the house, Jake, it's not good. In fact, it's downright nasty. Tomorrow we'll all go there with her, because she's going to need the support. But before I leave, I need to ask you to look out for her, because I don't have enough deputies to do it. If this isn't random, which I can't see my way to thinking it is, then she needs watching, and if I've read the situation correctly, she's tugging at your heart strings."

She was, Jake couldn't deny it, although it scared him spitless.

Jake watched Cubby's taillights leave his drive minutes later, then with a final look to the stars, he headed back to Branna.

CHAPTER TWELVE

Branna watched him walk inside, his big body coiled so tight she could see the muscles in his chest clenching. She couldn't take her eyes off of him, the memory of his anger playing over and over again in her head.

"Are you all right, Branna? Can I get you anything?" He headed for the kitchen.

"It's been so long since someone cared about me, Jake; thank you for saying the words."

He stopped and turned at her words, then leaned back on the wall to look at her.

"What words?"

"That you cared enough to want to help me."

"You're a very special lady, Rosebud; I can't imagine anyone not wanting to protect you."

"I'm not special, but you make me feel that way." Branna held his eyes. "I-it felt so good to have you angry on my behalf, which is probably wrong on many levels, but right now it makes me feel warm."

"I want to find out who did these things to you and rip them apart."

The anger inside him hadn't lessened, and she marveled again that it was there because of her.

"I'm sorry that I didn't tell you about the garden; it's just that I'm not used to doing that…sharing with anyone. I always fight my own battles, and you seemed to leave pretty quickly that day after we…" She waved her hand about. "Then, last night you wanted to…" more hand waving, "and I walked away from you."

"How sorry?"

"Pardon?"

"How sorry are you, Rosebud?" His eyes had changed, something else was there, and she felt her bones turn to liquid as she realized it was lust.

"I-I ah, don't understand."

"The only reason I'm not looking at twenty to life right now, after going to your house and beating the tar out of whoever was in there trashing the place, is because I promised you, so I need something else to take the edge of my anger. Neither of us are criers, but we're both wired. So I'll say it again, how sorry are you?"

He may be lounging on that wall, but he was tense. Legs braced, arms folded. His shorts hung low on his hips and she saw the ridges of muscle on each side of his stomach disappearing below the waistband. He was sexy, pure and simple, and he should be hanging on a dozen walls for woman to ogle. But he wasn't; he was here and so was she. Messy hair, broad chest, it was a package that would make any woman melt.

"Something happened to your tongue, sweetheart?"

She wanted to run it all over him, starting with the band of hair that rose from his shorts. Heat suddenly pulsed through her veins and her breasts felt heavy as she rose from the seat and dropped the blanket. Branna had never been a femme fatale, never incited a man to unbridled lust, but she wanted Jake to be the first. The aftermath of fear had left her body pulsing with need and, like him, it needed an outlet.

"Those shorts can go first." His voice was a deep purr of pure sin.

Branna undid the button and slid them slowly down her thighs, then pushed them to the floor and stepped out of them. The long T-shirt hid her white lace panties.

"Shirt now." The rasp in his voice made her legs turn to liquid. Reaching for the hem, Branna lifted it slowly up her body, amazed at her daring, then pulled it over her head. Throwing it aside, she stood before him in her panties.

"Ah, baby, you are one sexy woman. Now come here and climb all over me."

She did and all the time his eyes ran over her, hunger in their dark depths. Branna kept walking until her body was pressed to his. She felt how rigid he was holding himself; felt the hard length of him pressed against her stomach. Lifting one hand, she grabbed a handful of his hair and tugged until his mouth met hers.

It was hungry and carnal, and Branna wanted it all; the savage heat and driving need inside him was matched by her own. It drove away thoughts of what those men had done to her house, and what they may have done to her.

"I don't want to hurt you." He cupped her face.

"Never, you could never hurt me."

Branna ran her lips over his jaw and down his neck. Her hands kept busy, trailing over his stomach then lower to release the button on his shorts and push them and his underwear down his body. His hands were in her hair and anywhere else he could reach, and she was on fire; her body wet and aching for him. Wrapping her hands around his hot hard length, she stroked him.

"That feels too good." Closing his eyes as she caressed him, his breathing grew harsh. "I want you so badly right now, Branna. I'm not sure I can wait."

"Don't wait, please, Jake, I need you inside me."

He lifted her into his arms and she wrapped her legs around his waist as he carried her to his room. Laying her on the bed, he stripped off her panties, then lifted her hips and sank deep inside her. It was hard and fast, and Branna cried out as ecstasy rolled through her in waves. He let out a long soft moan as she clenched tight around him.

"Last night, I watched you in that flirty little dress and thought about doing this."

The pressure inside her built as his hand slid to cup one breast, the fingers rolling her nipple.

"I had a long cold shower when I got home, but even that didn't help."

He pushed deeper, and Branna arched her back as the ecstasy built.

"Let go, Branna."

And she did, the pleasure almost too much to bear as it crashed over her, her cries loud and long. He answered after one more thrust, his shout as loud as hers.

Branna fell onto the bed and he followed, his big body blanketing hers as he pressed her into the covers. The only sound in the room was the deep rasps of their breathing. He eased to the side, pulling her back to his front.

Her body felt limp, limbs weak, as she struggled to draw in a deep breath.

"You okay?"

"Da, no." Branna seemed to have lost the ability to speak.

He snorted into her hair, and then maneuvered them around until they were under the covers. "Sleep now, Rosebud, the morning is soon enough to think about the rest."

"I lost my ability to think ten minutes ago."

"Tell me it was longer than ten." His words tickled her ear.

"Eleven then."

"My job is done."

He followed the words with a kiss as he pulled her closer to his naked body.

"I'm a job?"

His hand did a sweep of her front, brushing her nipples and the curve of her hip.

"Your body work is certainly in good shape; I'm just tuning you up a bit."

"I'm writing you into my next book, and you won't be the hero." Branna laced her fingers through the ones he rested on her stomach.

"I'm thinking I missed something under your hood...you seem to be misfiring, not purring like you were minutes ago."

Branna found herself flipped onto her back and his mouth was on her breasts. He then proceeded to kiss every inch of her, then took her to slow steady heights before he slipped inside her and drove her over the edge once more.

"I can't feel my limbs," she sighed when she could form a thought.

"I'll carry you everywhere from now on."

She sighed as sleep began to pull her down.

"Sleep now, baby."

And she did.

Jake was on the phone with his sister when Branna walked into the kitchen the following morning. She wore one of his shirts and he had to admit she filled it out a whole lot better than him. Her hair was damp from the shower and those beautiful bare legs glided towards him.

"All right, Katie, I'll see you when you come home, yeah you too." Putting the phone on the bench, he reached for her as she hesitated, pulling her between his thighs; he then proceeded to kiss her thoroughly.

"Morning."

Her lashes fluttered open inches from his face, he looked into those green gems, and felt the large organ in his chest shift and resettle.

"Was that your sister?" Her words brushed his face.

"Yeah, she's away at the police academy learning to fight bad guys."

"I envied her in school. She was really athletic, and I remember thinking she was one of those people no one would ever kick around."

"Anyone ever kick you round, Rosebud?"

"No, I'm pretty tough too. Plus, my father made me learn self-defense. When I was twelve, I broke a boy's nose."

A nose fracture is a break in the bone or cartilage over the bridge, or in the sidewall or septum (structure that divides the nostrils) of the nose.

"Okay, tough girl," he kissed her nose. "What can I feed you?" Lifting the hair from her shoulder, Jake burrowed into her neck, breathing in the delicious scent of woman still warm from the shower. She'd used his deodorant and it smelled way better on her than him.

"I'll just grab my clothes and then go home, Jake. I need see what they did; besides, neither of us is the morning after kind of person."

"You're not entering that house without me," Jake said.

The worry was back as she tried to pull out of his arms, but he held her close.

"Food first, then we'll go there together and fix what needs fixing, Rosebud."

"You don't—"

"Yes, I do, and you'll piss me off if you say otherwise."

"Jake, you ran from my house the other morning, and now I'm returning the favor. Really, it's okay, this is the way we both want things to be."

"Just be quiet and sit down, Branna. Please." Standing, he lifted her onto the barstool he'd just vacated, then began to fix them both breakfast. She watched him, unmoving, and Jake knew thoughts were churning 'round and 'round inside her head as she tried to reclaim the ground she'd lost last night. Tried to shore up her defenses and sink back into her shell.

"Thank you for last night."

"Which part?" He finished slicing the toast and dropped it into the toaster. "Because I'm pretty thankful too about now."

She glanced down at the hands he now braced on the counter across from her before looking at him again.

"I came here, and you didn't get angry or annoyed with me; you helped me and called Cubby. I want to thank you for that."

"Did you expect me the shut the door in your face, Rosebud?" He wasn't angry, just sad that she'd even thought he might.

"No, even with the changes in you, I knew you'd help."

"I'd have been pretty pissed if you hadn't come to me, if you didn't in the future as well."

"I can take care of myself, Jake, and have been doing so for many years."

"I know that, Rosebud, but sometimes you need help, and I look after the people I care about." The words felt right to Jake. He felt something for this woman, and a few days ago he'd tried to fight it, but no more. He was sick of running from his feelings, sick of living in the cold.

"What?" The words were a whisper as she shook her head. "Y-you can't care for me; I haven't been back long enough."

"There's a time limit on caring?"

"Caring leads to other things, and neither of us wants that." She was standing now, hands clenched.

He walked around the counter and took them in his.

"Too late."

"I don't want this, didn't come here for this." She tried to back away, but he held her still and then pulled her towards him until she was in his arms again.

"Why don't you want me to care about you, sweetheart?"

"Because I'm not the type that people care for."

It was so ridiculous, he laughed. Hurt, she tried to pull away from him.

"Don't laugh at me!"

"I'm sorry. Branna, stop fighting me," he gave her a shake. "I wasn't laughing at you, I was laughing at that ridiculous statement."

"I don't want to care about you," she said the words to his chest.

"But you do."

"Oh, God."

He didn't laugh out loud, but his smile would have really pissed her off if she saw it. She was upset and he was happy that she felt something for him, just as he did for her. It was too early to prod the emotion and define it. It was new and raw, and both of them had been in the dark for so long that it needed to be coaxed out, but for now, Jake felt warmer and lighter than he had in months.

"It's all right," he said the words solemnly. "We'll take it slow, Rosebud. But, for now, let's eat and then go and take a look at your house, okay?"

He let her go and she sat on the stool again. He left her to think in silence and watched the emotions play across her face as that big brain of hers tried to work a way out of what she had discovered.

Not this time, Rosebud; we're in this together from this moment on.

CHAPTER THIRTEEN

The house was a mess, and he wanted to shield her from it and the obscene words some asshole had sprayed on the walls, but she wouldn't let him. Her mother's picture had a big red X painted on it, which just pissed her off instead of making her cry. The sofas had been slashed, and it would all take some sorting, but she was unhurt and that, to Jake's mind, was all that mattered. He'd thought he had his anger under control, but it was back with a vengeance.

He watched her walk around the room, shoulders straight, chin raised, as she took in the mess that they'd made of her home.

"I'm not a violent person, Jake, but if whoever did this was standing before me right now—"

"You'd be administering a bit of ass kicking?" he added.

"Yes."

"I'm sorry you had to go through this." He gave her a hard hug before going to inspect the kitchen. "It's really only this room," he said, returning minutes later. There are a few things spilled and overturned, but this is the room worst hit."

"Because they knew this is the one I would see first."

Jake had thought of that too and wasn't surprised she'd arrived at the same conclusion.

"It was to scare me. All this," she swept a hand around the room. "It was meant to frighten me off, Jake, and that surely means it is tied into my garden being destroyed."

"It's the logical conclusion, Rosebud, but we need to let Cubby do his work before we know for definite."

A car pulled up the drive minutes later. Cubby and his mother, Maureen, walked in through the door. She was carrying a dish, which she thrust at Jake before grabbing Branna and hugging her hard.

"Well now, my dear, this is a nasty business. I heard Cubby's cruiser leaving this morning and knew there'd been trouble, so I woke him early to find out what."

Maureen Hawker was a smaller, more slender version of her son, although now her red hair was streaked with grey.

"Th-thank you for coming, Mrs. Hawker."

Branna looked at Jake, who smiled but said nothing, as he knew others would be arriving soon, and she'd be really unsettled by the end of the day. She didn't collect people, or lean on them, but that didn't wash here in Howling.

"My name's Maureen, dear, now I'll just get to the kitchen and start the coffee brewing before the others arrive."

Branna followed Maureen with her eyes, then looked from Cubby to Jake.

"Others?"

The second car pulled in then. Buster strolled in with a box under one arm. He grunted something to Cubby, who replied in the same language, then nodded to Jake before making for

Branna. Wrapping an arm around her neck, he pulled her in for a hug, then rubbed his chin over her head. "You doing okay, sweet cheeks?"

"I-I, yes, thank you, Buster."

"Good girl." He then handed her the box before turning to Cubby, where he proceeded to question him in detail about who could have done this.

Jake's parents arrived with Mikey's bike in the trunk. Jake was in sight of the door, scrubbing the walls, so he saw the boy start running for the house. His legs and arms pumped as he flew onto the porch and into the house.

"Brace yourself, Rosebud."

Mikey ran through the doorway as she straightened, and she just had time to drop the glass in her hands onto the chair before he lunged at her. Wrapping his arms around her waist, Mikey held her tight.

"Hey, I'm okay, Mikey, promise."

His parents appeared as she lowered her head to Mikey's and held the little boy close. Jake wondered why she thought she was unlovable when all around her people were telling her differently.

Doctor McBride went to comfort the boy, and Branna and his father came to stand beside him, the look in his eyes as he saw the mess mirroring Jake's.

"Cubby have any ideas what sort of scum is capable of doing something like this?"

"Not a one."

"This kind of thing doesn't happen in our town, Jake, makes you question things when it does."

"It'll be okay, Dad; Cubby will find them, he just needs time."

"It'll rock a few people."

"I know." And it would, the people of Howling didn't deal with a lot of crime. There were the usual things, but nothing this vicious, nothing to shake people's foundations. Jake had seen worse, many times over during the years he'd spent away from here, but some of Howling's inhabitants had never left here and change didn't sit well with them, good or bad.

"That girl is getting a hug from me," Jake's father nodded to where Branna stood with Mikey and his wife. "Then, you give me a job."

Jake organized things while Branna looked on bemused, and it was when he had issued the last instruction that Annabelle, Penny, and Newman arrived. Her car sped up the driveway and ground to a halt behind Jake's parents' car. She leapt out before it had stopped, and like Mikey, ran inside, leaving her passengers to gather whatever was in the back seat and follow. She stood in the doorway, her eyes looking around the room until she found Branna, then she was on the move again.

"Holy shit, Bran!" She grabbed her friend and Branna didn't resist; in fact, he saw her arms wrap around Annabelle's waist, and then he heard the first sob, and soon they were both howling loudly. She needed that, to finally let go of the tears that were backed up inside her. Maureen came out of the kitchen clucking, and ushered them, along with Penny who was patting Branna's back, out of the room.

"Tackle me if I even step in that direction," Buster said, as he and Newman came to stand beside Jake, and then by silent consent, they headed out the front door to where Cubby stood once again writing in his book.

"She ran up the trail in the dark to get to you?" Buster's eyes looked at the end of the driveway, picturing how it must have looked last night. "In the dark," he added.

"She did."

"You in love, bud?"

"Let's call it care for now, so both parties don't take flight."

"Good."

Newman grunted his consent, and that was how men did it, Jake thought, as he and Buster went back inside.

Branna was worn out. She'd not gotten much sleep last night, and seeing all these people here in her house, helping her clean the mess was making her emotional. She'd cried all over Belle, Penny, and Cubby's mother, and that had only added to her fatigue.

People seemed to be continually touching her. A hug here, the brush of a hand on her shoulder there. It was exhausting. Branna was a loner, but suddenly she was surrounded by people, and she couldn't seem to get her head around the fact that they were here to help her.

For a person who liked to be in control and shared her life with no one but her computer, this was almost too much. Yet, inside her there was a warm spot that was growing. She felt herself being sucked into all this, especially when she looked at Jake. He cared about her, and somehow she'd told him she felt the same, and that terrified her.

Slipping out the back door, she made her way to the shed. Branna wasn't running away; she was just looking for some breathing room. Opening the door, she took the key out of her pocket and slipped it into Geraldine' lock. Pulling the back door wide, she got in, closing it behind her, and then she lay on the back seat so she wasn't seen by anyone if they were looking.

It wasn't like she didn't like all those people who were currently redecorating her house; it was just hard to work out why they were here. Of course, Jake was part of the reason. They all loved him and as he seemed to like her, they had come. But how did they know he liked her when she'd only found out this morning? Closing her eyes, she let the cool quiet of the car's interior settle around her.

"Dan lent me this car to propose to the doc, Branna."

Her eyes sprang open as Mr. McBride settled himself in the driver's seat. "Don't get up." He lifted a hand as she attempted to do just that. "You've had a hard time of it, and I'm sorry it happened in our town."

"It's not your fault, Mr. McBride."

"I'm sorry just the same, and the name's Patrick. Mr. McBride was my father."

She lay there listening as he talked. He sounded so much like Jake she smiled. He told her all the town news, and about the night carnival that was happening in a few days, his lovely voice calming her nerves and lulling her as he spoke.

"Where did you drive Geraldine to propose, Patrick?"

"Well, I picked up Nancy from her parents' house…she wore this soft pink dress and was standing on the porch when I pulled up. Do you know what I thought when I saw her, Branna?"

"What did you think?"

"That she was the most beautiful woman ever created, and that if I was lucky enough to have her say yes to me that night, then I'd spend my life making sure she never once doubted that decision."

"Oh, that's so lovely," Branna sighed.

"We started with dinner in the next town. There was no way only the good folk of Howling were seeing me in Geraldine, with Nancy seated beside me. I wanted to show them off to as many people as I could." His laugh was a low rumble. "Then we drove back here and I headed for the lake. There's a place past my boy's driveway that has the best view, so I parked there."

When he'd said, my boy, Branna had heard the pride in those two simple words. She wondered if there'd been a time when her father had said "my girl," sounding just like that.

"I was so nervous when we got out of the car I had to wipe my hands on my pants a few times before I took her hand. Nancy, being with woman she is, just smiled at me and said yes."

"She said yes before you even asked her?"

He laughed again. "She did, and said that she could see how nervous I was, so she'd thought to make it easy on me."

"It must have been a special moment."

"Even thirty years later, I remember it as if it was yesterday."

"That's lovely, Patrick. My parents had me young, so I don't think they had a courtship." *Why had she told him that?* This town was loosening her tongue.

"And they loved you so much they stayed together because you made that love they share stronger, Branna."

"Do you think so?"

"Yes."

"They certainly seemed happy before my mother died," Branna said, remembering the times she had watched her parents together. "They were always touching each other and fooling around."

"There you go, then."

She heard Patrick open his door again, and suddenly Mikey's face appeared, looking over the front seat.

"You tired?"

"A bit," Branna said, lifting a hand to tweak his chin.

"Well, it's lunch time now, and we can't start eating Maureen said, until we find you and Mr. McBride."

"Well, how lucky are you that you found us both in one place?" Branna sat upright. She felt rested and less confused. Her quiet time with Patrick had calmed her down, and she felt ready to face the people out there again.

"There'd better be chicken pie, Mikey, or I'm getting angry."

"There is, Mr. McBride, and cake with chocolate frosting."

"I always say that everything seems a lot brighter when there's chocolate frosting around," Patrick McBride said.

Branna followed as Patrick teased Mikey. She let Jake's father put an arm around her shoulders, just like he did to the boy, and together they went inside, and she thought how lucky Jake was to have this man in his life.

They ate and talked, and Branna listened as the people of Howling made her feel loved. They painted off the rude signs in her lounge, and she laughed at Buster and Newman's bad jokes, and by the end of the day her house looked better than it had before it had been trashed.

"Pack some things, Rosebud, and we'll head off."

"Why?" She looked at Jake, who was sitting on her porch waving off the last car, while she stood doing the same.

"Because, firstly, you're not staying here alone, and secondly we can't stay here with the paint fumes."

"I'll be fine."

He rose as she spoke and Branna had the urge to take a big backwards step as he closed the distance between them, but digging her toes into her boots stopped her.

"Here's the way it's going to be, sweetheart. I'm staying with you until Cubby figures out what happened and who was responsible, so it would be in your best interest to get your head around that."

Suddenly, the man who had laughed and teased everyone today was gone, and in his place was the one who had hard edges again, the man she'd met when she first came back to Howling.

She'd seen people shooting him looks today, his parents mainly, and knew they were enjoying seeing their son smile. Branna in no way wanted to analyze why he had changed, or if she had a hand in it, for now she just wanted to stand her ground.

"And if you don't come with me, then I'll carry you."

"You don't get to make decisions for me, McBride."

"Wrong answer, want to try again?"

They battled wills silently for several long drawn out seconds, his eyes steady on hers until Branna sighed, knowing she was beat.

"Fine, but we're taking Geraldine. I'm not having those bastards come back here and go for her next time, because that would hurt just as much as the house."

"It'll be a hardship seeing that damned rust bucket in my barn, but I'll just throw a cover over it so I don't have to look at it." He was teasing her now, and she wanted to laugh, but managed to swallow it down.

"I'm driving and you can take that big green beast of yours," Branna added.

He grabbed her before she'd reached the doorway and spun her into his arms, then kissed her senseless. It was long and steamy, and Branna wanted to rip his clothes off. She'd spent the day watching him and his big athletic body, and she'd lusted after him, and it was disturbing because she couldn't remember ever feeling that way about any man before.

"Get your clothes now, and I'll get Geraldine, and then we're taking a shower."

Branna watched him get the key, then jump off the top step and jog to the shed. Smiling, she hurried upstairs, her body humming with every step she took.

Chapter Fourteen

In the four days since her house had been trashed, Branna had stayed at Jake's or he'd stayed at her house. Cubby had no leads, which was really pissing him off, as in a small town crimes were usually not that hard to solve. Branna didn't want to get used to cohabitating with Jake, but she had to admit she was. She enjoyed waking in his arms, going for a run, cooking for him, but most of all she loved talking to him. They didn't get into the deep heavy stuff of their past, they just talked about the years since she'd left Howling.

She could write there too, sitting on his front deck with the lake shimmering before her; she'd managed to get her first draft near to completion. Her agent would be pleased.

Jake had told her after their second night together that sometimes he had nightmares, and last night he'd had one. Heart pounding, Branna had woken when he yelled. He'd been lying on his side, fists clenched, arms curled around himself. She'd soothed him, wrapped her arms around him from behind, and he'd slowly begun to relax, and eventually he settled back into sleep.

"If you want to sleep in another room tonight, it's okay with me."

He was driving them into Howling; it was the Night Carnival, an annual event that Branna vaguely remembered from her years here.

"Its okay, Jake, I have nightmares too; so as long as you don't take to lashing out at me, I can cope."

He took a hand off the wheel and ran it down her arm, the contact making her skin tingle. They'd made love often, and each time she felt as if he was pulling her deeper under his spell. Every time he was inside her, she melted her body his to command.

"Thanks, and I'll look after you if you look after me," his smile was soft.

"Deal."

They didn't talk about emotions; the L word had never been mentioned, and for that Branna was grateful, as it scared the hell out of her.

They parked on a side street just out of town, as there were cars everywhere, and walked towards the main street. The sound of voices grew steadily louder as they drew nearer, and Branna could see the blaze of lights from shop windows, as around them the day began to slip into night. The main street was hung with banners and decorations, and citizens of Howling were all out for the Night Carnival; they mingled with the outsiders who had bussed in for the occasion. Pretty colored lights had been strung up all over the place and that, combined with the delicious scents coming from some of the stalls, and the amazing and colorful variety of things people were selling, made the atmosphere almost magical.

Jake and Branna walked along the main street, looking at the displays and chatting with people they knew.

"I remember thinking this was pretty cool when I was living here," Branna said.

"I can mark my age by this event," Jake said, taking her hand. "I had my first kiss behind that tent." Branna followed his hand to a large candy striped tent, where inside, children were having their faces painted by clowns.

"Who'd you kiss?"

"Annabelle."

"Hussy."

"What can I say? Even then, I had it."

"And there's that ego I remember."

"Over there, I got drunk for the first time and my father tried to look angry in front of the townsfolk when I puked up all over the place. But when we got in the car, he laughed the entire journey home."

"I like your father." Branna looked to the stage at the top of the main street where Jake was pointing. The band was playing country music and a few people were dancing.

"Me too."

They fell silent as they contemplated their fathers, and Branna felt that pain she always did with the memory of hers.

"You want some fudge?" He pulled her towards another tent. "Gussie Neeps makes the best fudge in town."

"That's an unusual name."

"Gussie or Neeps?"

"Both," Branna tried to dig her heels in as he dragged her, but he just tugged harder.

"Augustus Neeperman is a legend around here; she can trace her family back to the beginning of Howling, but if you don't have a spare hour or two, don't go there."

"Your teeth will fall out if you eat too much of that stuff." Branna nodded towards the confectionary laden table they were approaching.

"Will you still like me then?"

"Maybe, although, I'd hate to have to eat soft food all the time."

"And I couldn't use my teeth all over your body, and that would just be a downright shame," Jake said the words into her ear.

Branna shivered. She'd never thought of herself as a sexual person, but it seemed she was. Jake had ripped away any inhibitions she may have been harboring, and now he just had to give her one of his steamy glances and she was mush. A few little words and her body ignited.

"I like to tug on your—"

"Stop!"

His laugh was dirty, but he shut up.

They didn't talk about her father or Jake leaving the medical profession; she knew that would come, but for now they were just getting to know each other, and Branna could feel herself changing. Some of her hard edges were softening too; she was beginning to believe that maybe she was loveable enough to begin a relationship with this man. God knew she was so deep in like with him now, she wasn't sure she could pull back.

"Thanks, Gussie." Jake paid the large woman with no front teeth for the fudge, then placed a piece in her mouth, then his. He hummed his appreciation before swallowing.

"You didn't answer my question, Branna O'Donnell, which leads me to believe that you won't still like me if I lose all my teeth from eating this fudge, which in turn leads me to believe you're shallow." After these words, he ate another piece, making the same noise in the back of his throat.

"I'll probably toss you over for Ethan, Buster, or Newman, depending on which one has all theirs."

His smile was wide and showed off his sparkling white collection, all set off in a handsome tanned face. He'd dressed up tonight, his words, in jeans that had worn patches in all the right place and fitted him perfectly. His shirt was black and long sleeved, with buttons up the front, and he'd rolled the sleeves up so she could see his forearms. The man was a walking fantasy.

"What?"

"What?" She questioned him right back.

"You sighed."

"You've probably heard this a million times, but in all honesty, I'm not sure I can cope with your handsomeness."

"Handsomeness?"

Branna waved to Belle, who was debating something with Newman beside a stall, before she looked back at Jake. Surprisingly, he was embarrassed, which was a revelation to her. She'd never seen him flustered before.

"You know you're handsome, right?"

"Cut it out." Taking her hand, he tried to start them moving again, but she stopped in front of him.

"My God, you're embarrassed, and there I was thinking nothing had the power to do that to you." Branna hooted with laughter. "You own a mirror, right?"

He looked uncomfortable; his eyes checking to make sure no one could hear their conversation.

"Most women have a silly smile on their faces whenever they see you, McBride. It's lucky I'm not the jealous kind, because my insides would be twisted by now."

"Will you quit it!"

Oh, this was just too much fun. He was really uncomfortable now, his eyes looking everywhere but at her.

"And don't get me started on your body." Branna hummed her appreciation. I overheard that Ellie Putt, saying you should pose nude because it was just a downright sin to cover all that delicious flesh up."

"You having fun?"

"Totally." Branna gave him a big smile, which made him growl. "The fact that you don't know what a dreamboat you are is cute."

"Totally," he mimicked, and then wrapped a hand around her neck. "So, you think I'm a dreamboat?"

"Ellie thinks you are," Branna corrected.

"And what about you, Rosebud, do you know how hot you are?"

"Don't try and change the subject."

"Fair's fair. I have to walk around with the hottest woman in Howling, watch all the men ogling her, and pretend it doesn't bother me, and don't get me started on your body."

He pulled her closer so no one could see the hand that cupped her breast, which was devastatingly accurate, or the thumb he rubbed over her hard nipple that made her knees go weak.

"I yield."

His breath was uneven as he planted a smacking kiss on her lips, before he pushed a piece of fudge in there.

"Just so you know, I only have to see you to want you. One touch and I'm so hard it hurts, and—"

"Jake, we are in the middle of the entire town of Howling," Branna whispered.

"All the more reason to make you understand what you do to me. In fact, I'm thinking this whole Carnival thing is overrated and we should just head home."

"Stop that," Branna laughed, as he turned to leave. "We can't leave; we've only just arrived."

"You better make it up to me later then," he said, giving her a sexy smile that made her heart skip a beat.

"Branna, Delray and Macy are just ahead of us, you want to head in the other direction?"

She looked up and saw Macy, who, as usual, looked beautiful and immaculate. But this time, Branna looked closer, after what she'd seen that day in the drugstore, and really saw the look in the woman's eyes.

"Damn," she muttered.

"What?"

"I saw Macy in the drugstore one day; she didn't know I was there because I was hiding behind one of the displays."

"Why were you hiding behind the displays?"

"Never mind that, it's what I saw when I was hiding that matters," Branna added. "Macy walked around the display, so no one could see her, then put her head in her hands and sobbed. Honestly, Jake, she looked broken, and I could feel her despair from where I stood."

"Macy?" Jake looked at the couple who were walking toward them. "That Macy?"

"I overhead Mr. Pike saying she had a sore stomach, but to me it seemed to be much more than that, and that's silly, right? I mean, how could I know that with one look?"

"It's called instinct, Rosebud."

"It made my eyes itch to see her, Jake, which has to tell you how bad it was, because she's not one of my favorite people, as you know."

"No secret there."

"But now, I feel sorry for her, which is a real piss off, because I hate when that happens, as I'll have to be nice to her."

"You? The girl who doesn't collect people? The emotional void, the—"

"I get the idea, McBride, you don't need to belabor the point."

He cupped the back of her neck and gave a gentle squeeze before he took her hand again, and they walked to where Brian Delray was talking loudly to a group of people.

"Hey, Macy."

"Jake, Branna," her words were cold.

The woman was dressed as if she'd just walked down Hollywood Boulevard. Hair perfect, face coated in a fine layer of makeup, clothes fitted to show off her body, and tottering on six-inch heels.

Macy's smile didn't reach her eyes, but her husband's did. He pumped Jake's hand and grinned at her.

"I-I'm sorry to hear about your house." Macy said the words slowly, almost as if she was thinking about each one as she said it.

"Thanks. You still need help with the reunion?"

Surprise made those long fake lashes rise.

"Yes."

"Well, here's my card; you just email me with what you need done, and I'll see what I can do."

Fingers tipped with long pink nails took the rectangle of white.

"There you go, honey, told you it would all work out fine." Brian Delray wrapped a hand around his wife's waist and pulled her close. To Branna's eye, Macy looked as stiff as a board, and not too happy about the embrace. "She's working so hard on the reunion that she's not sleeping. Last night, I found her pacing the hallway muttering about banners."

Macy didn't laugh with her husband; instead, she had a blank expression on her face.

"You need me for anything, Macy, you just let me know." As someone who'd been desperately unhappy in her life, she recognized it in another person, and Macy Reynolds-Delray was unhappy.

"Thank you, Branna, I'll let you know."

"Same goes for me, Macy, minus the emcee duties."

"Thank you, Jake."

"Well, hell, if they're volunteering, I guess I should, Macy. You got any jobs you want me to do for the reunion?" Buster came to stand on Branna's left, his mouth full of the same fudge that Jake was just about to put in his.

"Th-thanks, Buster, I'll let you know."

Jake studied Mrs. Reynolds-Delray as she spoke to Buster. Branna was right, something was off with her. He'd never looked at her long enough to see the emptiness in her eyes or the blank expression on her face. She was just always smiling her silly smile and covered in makeup. Always perfect, her hair styled, clothes designer.

"I told you they'd rally, Macy. And thanks so much, everyone, for offering to help. I'm doing the best I can, but business is busy right now, so I can't do much."

Brian Delray was relaxed, unlike his wife. He smiled his nice guy smile, the same one he'd always used since the day he moved into Howling and wooed Macy. He'd then stepped into her father's shoes and into the people's hearts, and taken over the Reynolds Real Estate business. Jake hadn't had a lot to do with the man, just in passing, but he'd always figured he and Macy were happy, not that he'd given the matter much thought. They'd not had a family yet, but there was still plenty of time for that, although now that he thought about it, that was strange too. Macy had told anyone who'd listen when she'd first married Brian that they were going to settle down and raise kids. Maybe they couldn't have them?

"Macy and I need to catch up with a few people, so see you all later," Brian said.

Jake lifted a hand to the Reynolds-Delrays; Macy didn't return the gesture, just let her husband lead her away.

"Something's not right there, Jake." Branna was still watching them walk away as she spoke. Worry drew a line down her forehead.

"Think you could be onto something, Rosebud."

"What?"

"Macy, Buster, something's off with her."

His friend was looking at the backs of Macy and Brian, his forehead also now creased.

"Off how?"

"She's unhappy, I noticed it a few days ago, and looks... frozen."

Buster looked at Branna when she finished talking. "What the hell does that mean?"

Jake stayed silent as she tried to enlighten Buster as to her concerns about Macy. The hand he didn't hold waved about as she spoke. He liked anchoring her to him, liked that she wanted it too. Her hair hung in a long plait that he wanted to wrap around his hand to draw her in for a kiss, then he'd remove that short scrap of material she called a dress from her lovely body. The color of her eyes, it hung in a simple straight line down her curves and there was nothing simple or straight about how it looked on her. It clung to the soft swell of her breasts, and stopped high on her thighs, which left those long shapely legs free for him to lust after. She was understated in what she wore, not much makeup that he could see or jewelry, just a small gold bangle and necklace, and she was the sexiest woman he'd ever known.

She'd tied him in so many knots, he'd forgotten where he began and ended. His dark places were getting lighter, and suddenly, he wanted to get out of bed in the morning. Not strictly speaking true, as he wanted to stay in there with her, but in general life had suddenly become worth living.

"It's been brought to my attention that the members of our award-winning high school band of 2004 are all here in Howling tonight."

Branna spun to look at the stage, where Mr. Hope now stood at the microphone.

"Is th-hat Mr. Hope?"

Jake felt Branna's fingers grip his tightly as she spoke.

"Yup, since he retired from teaching, he's become the unofficial emcee in Howling," Buster said. Unlike Jake, he hadn't made the connection to Branna and the band of 2004.

"Don't be shy now, you people," Mr. Hope's voice continued to boom into the microphone. Jake eased Branna's nails out of his flesh as they dug in. "I taught each and every one of you, in class and in band practice," Mr. Hope added. "I know how good you are."

"Hide me." Branna's voice was desperate.

"What's the problem here, Branna?" Buster asked.

"She was in that band," Jake replied.

"Well, shit."

He and Buster looked around for the nearest escape route.

"Anybody see our band members?" Mr. Hope yelled so loudly that Jake winced. "Annabelle Smith and Branna O'Donnell, I know you're out there."

"I'm going kill Mr. Hope. I don't care if he gave me an A in music." Annabelle appeared before them. Unlike Branna who was literally shocked into a statue, she was fuming. "Springing this kind of shit when neither of us have touched an instrument or played together for years. This could be a disaster. Still, at least that would ensure it never happened again."

"I'm not going up there." Branna found her voice.

"Where you planning to run to, O'Donnell? Your path is blocked, and these people can be mean when they don't get what they want."

Jake watched Branna look around her at Annabelle's words. It was crowded, but if she really wanted to leave, he'd have her out in seconds.

"Suck it up, Bran, and let's get it over with, then I'll buy you a beer." Annabelle grabbed Branna's hand.

"I hate beer and I'm not singing," she gripped Jake's hand as Annabelle tried to get her moving towards the stage.

"I thought you Irish were meant to be tough," Jake cupped her cheek, running his thumb over the soft flushed skin. "Where's that fighting backbone your countrymen are known for?" Jake gave Annabelle a look, and she dropped Branna's hand.

"I can't do this, Jake."

He pulled her into his arms, ignoring the people around him, and whispered into her ear. "I heard you sing once, and I remember thinking that I'd never heard anyone sound like you before. Every hair on my body stood up, and I thought that one day I'd be listening to you on the radio, Rosebud. You have the voice a million musicians would die for. If you don't want to sing because it scares you, fine, I'll get you out of here, but if it's because you don't believe you can, then I'm here to tell you that's bull."

She sighed, her breath brushing his neck, then lifting her head, she gave him a wobbly smile.

"I hate that you always know just the right thing to say all the time. I hated it in school and I have to say it still bugs me." Her words made him smile.

"What can I say? Life sucks."

She kissed him, which surprised the hell out of Jake, because she wasn't one for demonstrative gestures, especially not in front of the entire town of Howling, and then let Annabelle lead her through the throng of people towards the stage. He lost sight of her briefly, and then she was taking the stairs.

"I'm thinking a mystery muffin might have to be made in her honor for this. I've never seen a woman turn white that fast," Buster said, as he and Jake watched the girls walk up the steps.

"You know how anything that crawls turns you into a weeping, sniveling infant? Well, this kind of thing does that to her…without the weeping and sniveling."

Buster whistled, not at all put out by Jake's explanation.

"She's scared to death then."

"And then some," Jake added, watching Branna say something to Mr. Hope that made him laugh. She talked to the other guitarist, drummer, and Annabelle, and after a discussion they all took a few seconds doing things with their instruments, and then Branna stepped up to the microphone and Jake held his breath.

Come on, baby, you can do this.

"I'll be expecting you all to dance, seeing as you dragged us up here." Nerves made her accent thicker. A ripple of laughter swept through the crowd after she spoke.

"There will be two songs, as Mr. Hope won't let up after just one, so if you don't like what you hear, stick your fingers in your ears."

Beside him, Buster snorted, and Jake felt a smile on his lips. She looked so sexy standing up there, and she was his.

Her voice was still amazing, that deep husky purr that ran up and down his spine, and accompanied by Annabelle's backup vocals and nimble fingers on the keyboard, they sounded as if they'd been playing together for years. They played two well-known rock ballads that had everyone dancing, like Branna had asked them to. She'd gone up there terrified and delivered an amazing performance; he was so proud of her his chest hurt.

"She's good."

Jake didn't answer Buster; his eyes never moved from Branna.

He thought about what she'd endured and overcome to be the smart, funny, sexy woman he knew today. She'd fought her battles alone, as far as he could see, but she'd come out the other side. Jake knew she had baggage, most people had some, but she'd gone on living her life, being who she wanted to be.

"So, you know how I said I'd stand aside and give you a clear run with her, McBride?"

"She's mine, Tex, go find your own woman," Jake said, as Ethan moved to his other side.

"The little lady can sing, McBride; can't believe she doesn't do it for a living."

"I thought you liked her books?"

"I do, they're awesome, but hell, this is talent."

"It is at that," Jake agreed.

"Annabelle's got some talent going on there too, shame she's such a she-devil."

Buster joined in the conversation by saying. "You're just pissed she turned you down when you asked her on a date."

"Shut up, bakery boy, when I want your opinion I'll ask for it," Ethan said.

"Make me that appointment when you fly home tomorrow, Ethan."

Ethan looked surprised at Jake's words, because he'd been after him for months to go see the shrink he knew.

"I'll do that, McBride, and come pick you up when it's time."

"Appreciate it."

Jake was grateful Ethan didn't ask why now, he just picked up where he started with Buster and they continued abusing each other, while Jake watched his girl.

She was his now, and she deserved him to be whole. Deserved that he at least try and make sense of the nightmare that was inside his head. He might or might not be a doctor again, but he needed to at least try, and he needed to do it for both of them.

Her voice was a thing of beauty and one song turned into three, and he never moved, just drank in the sight of her body swaying to the music. By the time she sang the last note, she had the entire crowd in the palm of her hand, sitting right alongside where he'd been since she'd arrived in Howling.

"Good night, everyone, and don't expect a repeat performance next year."

Everyone applauded as Branna spoke, and then kept clapping until they'd left the stage. People touched her shoulder as she walked, and she smiled and spoke a few words, and then she was there in front of him.

"Hey, you." He was so full of pride he could hardly get the words out.

"Hey, you." Her smile was real, but some of it was relief, Jake was pretty sure.

"You were amazing." Wrapping a hand around her neck, he pulled her into him briefly. Inhaling her, he kissed her cheek, then let her go.

"I hate to admit it, Bran, but that was fun. Maybe we could just do a bit of jamming when we get time?"

Branna literally glowed as she turned to Annabelle. "I guess we could use the shed now that Geraldine's at Jake's."

"Will you guys play at a party I'm organizing?"

"I suppose you think that's funny, rich boy?" Annabelle rounded on Ethan as he spoke.

"What?" He looked confused. "I was serious."

Jake looked over the heads of the people milling, as Branna and Annabelle talked to Ethan...correction...they talked at Ethan...loudly. He saw the tall dark-haired man walking towards them. People seemed to naturally move to one side as he wove his way through them, and there was something familiar about that face. Dressed in a blue shirt and jeans, he should have fit right in here, but didn't; he stood out. Even his walk was different; he seemed to glide, long legs moving with ease as he covered the distance, and then it clicked into place. He knew another person who walked like that.

"Branna."

She turned as he spoke, hearing the urgency in his voice.

"There's—"

"Hello, Branna."

He was too late; D.J. O'Donnell had arrived in Howling.

CHAPTER FIFTEEN

The smile fell from Branna's face as she looked at her father. Her fingers clenched around Jake's before she released his hand and took a step backwards.

"What are you doing here?" Her words were hoarse.

"I came to see my daughter. I heard you sing. You were amazing."

He spoke with the same soft burr that she did, and those eyes were Branna's too. The deep green pools that had sucked Jake in from the first glance he'd taken of her.

"Why would you want to be my father now?"

"Branna, love, let me—"

"You'll leave here now; I have no need for you."

"Branna—" Jake tried to stop her from walking away, but it was too late. She was running through the crowds, and was soon swallowed up.

"We'll go after her, you take him," Buster said, preparing to follow with Annabelle and Ethan.

Jake was torn. He wanted to comfort Branna, because she was his first concern, but he didn't want Declan O'Donnell to leave until he'd spoken to him about a few things, which was what he appeared to be doing. His tall figure was making its way back through the crowds, back the way he had come.

"Stay with her till I get there." Jake ran after O'Donnell, finding him with one hand braced on the wall of The Hoot. His head was lowered, and his breath was rushing in and out of his body.

"Did you expect that to go any differently?" Jake said, coming to a halt behind him. "It was never in the cards that she'd fall into your arms crying, 'Daddy, I've missed you.'"

The man straightened to his full height and tried to glare at Jake, which was ruined by the devastation on his face.

"Who the hell are you and why were you holding my daughter's hand?"

"I'm the man who she told that her father never forgave her for killing the only woman he'd ever loved. The man who held her when she said she was responsible for the death of her mother."

If he'd hit Declan O'Donnell, the pain would have hurt him less. His shoulders slumped, and even in the growing dark, Jake could see the pallor of his cheeks.

"Someone broke into her house a few nights ago, while she was sleeping, but she woke and ran to me, and do you know what she said to herself while she ran frightened and alone?" Jake continued talking at the man, needing him to know what he'd done to his only child. His anger was simmering, but he had it under control.

"Courage is resistance to fear, mastery of fear—not absence of fear."

"The very words, Mr. O'Donnell, and do you know what has become of your daughter because you turned your back on her?"

"No," he was broken, a defeated man as Jake struck yet another blow. "I didn't turn my back on her."

"She's locked herself away," Jake said, ignoring his words. "Away from any emotional entanglements, and I would lay most of the blame for that at your feet."

This man had failed in his duty as a parent. Failed to provide love when his daughter wanted it most, and because in his own life he'd had that in abundance, Jake could only imagine what it was like to have none. "Jake?"

His father and mother appeared at his side.

"You remember Declan O'Donnell?" He nodded to the man before him. Manners having been drummed into him from birth, he then made the introductions. "Mr. O'Donnell, these are my parents, Patrick and Nancy McBride." Jake watched his father shake the man's hand.

"I remember you both from my time here," Declan O'Donnell said in a tired voice.

"Are you staying in Howling for a while, Mr. O'Donnell?"

"I had hoped to, but am uncertain at this stage."

"You can stay with us."

Both Jake and his father looked at Nancy McBride with raised eyebrows.

"We have that spare room downstairs with a bathroom attached; he can settle in there."

"Mom, I don't think—"

"Jake, I don't know what has happened between Branna and her father, but to my mind, they need some time to fix it."

"I'm not sure it's fixable, Mom."

"Shouldn't we help them at least try?"

"I'm sure he can stay in town at the Howler," Jake added.

"It's booked fully at this time, especially with the carnival on tonight," Nancy McBride added.

She was right, Jake knew that; he just didn't know how Branna would feel about her father staying with his parents.

"Do you have a car, Mr. O'Donnell?"

"I do, but I can just as easily find a place out of Howling to stay, Mr. McBride."

"Howling counts your daughter as one of theirs, and as you're famous, we've claimed you too, so if word gets out you're staying in another town, it won't be pretty. My advice is to just follow along with my wife's wishes, Mr. O'Donnell."

"Very well."

Before Jake could protest, his parents had gathered up the man, and his father was driving his car back to their house. Jake said he'd follow soon, but first he needed to check on Branna.

Fifteen minutes later, after a text from Buster, he walked into his friend's house. It had been his parents' first, until they'd decided to retire and travel around the world. Beige weatherboard with a stone front, it had a tidy front lawn with a large green leafy tree and a nice little fence that said it should be a family home, which was exactly what it had been for years. Now it was the home of single man who was a slob.

"Annabelle, I'm not baking her a mystery muffin now just because she's upset."

Jake heard Buster's frustration as he walked in through the front door. Vaulted ceilings and plank floors led him towards the voices. Stepping over shoes, books, boxes, and baking stuff, he found Buster, Tex, and Annabelle in the only immaculate room in the entire house, the kitchen; of Branna, there was no sign.

"Where is she?"

"In the bathroom," Ethan said. "And she hasn't spoken a word, or cried a tear. Just sat in the car, still as a bloody statue, staring out the windshield. I tell you, Jake, it was sadder than seeing her break down. We tried to talk to her, Annabelle, Buster and I, and she responded, but only one syllable answers. She didn't resist or protest, just let us bring her here, walked inside and straight into the bathroom, after asking Buster politely where it was."

He saw the worry in their faces. They cared for Branna now, she was one of theirs, and it hurt that she was in pain and they couldn't help her.

"This business with her dad is pretty messy." Jake ran a hand through his hair. "Mom and Dad have taken him to their house."

Tex whistled and Annabelle swore loudly.

"Yeah, not ideal, and I'm not sure how she'll cope with that news."

"Go find out, Jake. She's been in there a while now," Buster said.

He did, climbing the stairs to the bathroom Buster had directed her to...the guest one that was probably still clean.

"Branna, it's me, Jake."

"I'll be out soon." Her words were muffled through the wood.

"Open the door, Rosebud."

"Go away, Jake, I just need a minute."

"Now, Branna."

"No."

"Yes, or I'll break it down and Buster will be pissed."

"You wouldn't!"

He didn't answer, instead waiting silently. Seconds later, he heard the lock click, then the door opened.

She'd left off her shoes, and stood before him looking lost and alone, and so small it made him hurt. "Hey, you." She bit her bottom lip and fought the tears, so he pushed harder. "Want a hug?"

"W-we're, not huggers, you and m-me."

"Sure we are. Why, just tonight I gave you one before you went up on that big scary stage. How about we give it another try?"

"I-I just want to be alone, Jake, please." The sniff was loud in an effort to keep the tears at bay.

"That's not how this relationship thing works, sweetheart."

"We're n-not in a relationship." Her knuckles were white on the door.

He reached for her before she had a chance to close it. Pulling her into the hallway, he wrapped his arms around her and held tight. "It's a relationship, Rosebud, pure and simple." The words felt right, so Jake stopped fighting and held his woman. She kept herself rigid, but he just held her tighter, until she slumped into him, resting her head on his chest.

"Why is he here, Jake?"

"To see you, Branna, his daughter."

"He didn't want me before. Why now?"

This was a minefield that needed careful navigation. "Branna, he's not going anywhere till he talks to you, and right now my mother's settling him into their house."

"What?" She tried to pull away, but he wouldn't let her.

"My mother saw me talking to your dad, and she stepped in; next thing, they're driving off."

"I don't want him there."

"It's done, sweetheart, changing my mother's mind is not something you'd want to take on; believe me, I've tried many times with little success."

She lifted her head to look at him, her eyes sad. "It just about kills me to see that look in your eyes."

"I'm okay; it was just a surprise after all this time to see him again."

He kissed her, soft and sweet, and her lips clung to his and told him she was anything but okay.

"How long's it been since you saw him?"

"Five years. We had a fight and then he went away for good and I don't want him here, Jake. The last time we spoke we both said horrible things, nasty hurtful things, a-and I can't do that again."

If Declan O'Donnell walked into Buster's house right at that moment, he'd take him apart, no questions asked, no explanations given; he'd destroy him for the pain he'd caused the woman in his arms. She'd arrived in Howling to make a home, and her garden and house had been trashed, and now her father had arrived. She was tough, but everyone had a breaking point.

"Annabelle's trying to convince Buster to bake you a mystery muffin, and he's resisting, but my money's on her."

She huffed out a breath, but didn't move.

"I don't want this, Jake. I came here to rebuild my life and find some peace. I want to write and nothing else."

"The sex is good, though, you have to admit?"

"Average."

"I need to put a bit more effort in, obviously."

"Make him go away, Jake." She sounded defeated.

"Let me know when you're done being pathetic, and we'll head down for coffee."

She rested against him for a few more minutes, and then with another sigh, she pulled out of his arms. "I'm done."

"That's my girl." Jake gave her another kiss, then took her hand and they headed back down the stairs.

"Buster's house is really cluttered, considering The Hoot is so pristine."

"His mother said he was born with slothful tendencies, but when he's in the kitchen, he becomes a domestic goddess; it's one of life's little mysteries."

Buster was muttering and putting a tray into the oven, while Annabelle made coffee when they entered. Tex had flicked on the T.V. and had his feet up on the coffee table.

"Fifteen minutes, Branna, and you better eat them." Buster shut the oven and threw down the oven mitt. "And, no, you can't have the recipe."

"You ever thought of hiring a cleaner?" Annabelle stepped over a pile of what appeared to be aprons.

"It's my home; if you don't like it, leave."

Jake pulled out a bar stool for Branna, and took the one beside her. Together, they listened to Buster and Annabelle bicker, with Jake tossing in the occasional comment, and all the while he knew she was thinking, that sharp little brain of hers working out how she could avoid all contact with her father.

Jake woke the following morning and reached for Branna. It was something he did instinctively before opening his eyes. Feeling her body still soft from sleep, running his hands over it and hearing her sigh was a thing of wonder. However, this morning the space beside him was cold and empty.

Climbing out of bed, he found a pair of shorts and pulled them on, then made for the bathroom, where he washed and brushed his teeth. The kitchen, which incidentally was empty of women, smelled of coffee. Filling a mug, he walked through the rooms and still there was no sign of her. Opening the door, he headed outside and around the house towards the barn. If she'd gone for a run without him, he'd throw around a few weights before fixing breakfast.

He heard the radio as he entered, and found her under the hood of Geraldine. She wore one of his T-shirts, which had ridden up, and a pair of panties, and he wished he had a camera because he'd make a shit load of money with that one single shot. Not that he'd sell it; it'd be for his eyes only.

"Rosebud, you know how most mornings I wake ready for anything?"

She straightened at his words. Hair a mess, smudge of grease on her chin, a wrench in one hand.

"What?"

"Seeing you like that is not helping my condition."

Her eyes went to his crotch, then shot back up to the smile he now had on his face. Very slowly, she put the wrench down, and lowered the hood of the car.

"I was just checking her over. Dan, Georgie's husband, taught me to do a service on her, so I was," she licked her lips as he started towards her. "Doing the service."

"Need any help with that...service?"

"Ha, that was cheesy, even from you." She started backing away, moving around the car as he stalked her.

"Hot woman dressed in nothing but a T-shirt and panties, with a wrench in her hand and grease on her chin. Tell me any man who hasn't fantasized about that?"

She kept walking around the car and he followed every step.

"I couldn't sleep and didn't want to wake you, so I came out here. I-I like tinkering with Geraldine, always did."

"How about tinkering with me instead?"

"Will you stop that? You sound like you're making a bad porn movie."

She was backing herself into a corner, between the workbench and the back wall of the barn, but hadn't worked that out yet.

"Now how does a good little Irish girl know about that kind of thing?"

It was good to see the worry gone from her eyes, if only for a while. The green depths were definitely heating as he drew closer, and Jake was so hard, each step was uncomfortable. She bumped into the workbench and turned to see what she'd hit, and he made his move, caging her in with his arms and body.

"What are you doing, Jake?"

The pulse in her neck was racing, so he put his lips there.

"Well now, sweetheart, I'd hoped after all the practice we've had, you'd know what it was."

Jake slipped his hands under the shirt and eased them upwards, taking the shirt with him.

"S-someone might come in."

"I'm hoping they won't stay long." Pulling it over her head, he gripped her waist and boosted her onto the bench.

"Don't suppose you'd stay there while I got my camera?"

"Will you stop talking!" She grabbed a handful of his hair and tugged, bringing him closer.

The kiss was deep and their tongues danced as he eased her hips forward. Her hands held his head as they took and gave whatever the other had to give. They were both struggling for breath when he broke the kiss.

"Behind you, there's the back of the bench, grip it tight, baby." She did as he asked and Jake began a slow torturous journey over every inch of her chest, his mouth caressing the slopes of her breasts and circling the nipples that were hard and ready for his mouth. He teased her by touching everywhere but the dark circles.

"Jake!" his laugh blew heat over one nipple as he finally gave her what she wanted and sucked the aching bud deep into his mouth. She arched into him, her legs clamping around his hips.

"Don't let go, baby."

She was panting, little breaths of need as he pulled her legs from his waist, then slowly removed her panties.

"I need you now, Jake."

"Soon, Rosebud, you got to let me fulfill my fantasy."

He cruised his lips over the smooth skin of her stomach and through the thatch of black hair to where she needed him most. Her scent drove him crazy, as did the taste of her. He licked the soft pink folds and the tight bud and she jerked upwards.

"Now."

"Don't let go, Branna." He teased the damp flesh, stroked and nibbled and the tension inside her rose as she began to make those sweet little noises that drove him crazy.

"You bastard, McBride, I said now!"

He laughed as he pulled off his shorts and then grabbing her hips, he thrust inside that wet tight heat. He rode her hard, and she met each thrust, urging him on until she screamed loud and long in his ear as he grunted in hers. He fell face-first into her lap, and she slumped backwards, both breathing heavily.

When they could both breathe and think again, he lifted her down, holding her against his chest.

"You okay?"

She managed a dry laugh.

"I don't think I need a run this morning."

They showered, ate, and then he said he had some errands to do in town.

"I need to head home, Jake, I have work to do."

That suited him just fine, as he had something he needed to do to, and not having her with him would make it easier. He walked into his parents' house an hour later.

"Son." His dad was sitting at the table drinking coffee with O'Donnell.

"Dad," Jake poured himself a cup and took the seat next to him. "Mr. O'Donnell."

He looked about as approachable as his daughter, and in the daylight he saw the resemblance was even stronger than he'd originally thought. On Branna, those looks combined to make her the knockout she was; on him, they made up a man with sharp edges to his face and cold eyes beneath lowered brows.

"Declan is my name."

"I know."

"And you hate me because I hurt Branna."

"About sums it up."

"Hear him out, son."

One thing Patrick McBride had always been good at, was judging people, but Jake wasn't inclined to agree in this situation.

"Branna told me you shut her out of your life after your wife was killed. Is she lying?"

Declan closed his eyes briefly, like his daughter did when she was gripped by emotion; Jake didn't like seeing the similarity. He didn't want to feel a damned thing for this man…ever.

"I should have this conversation with my daughter, not you."

"You could, but then I'd have to tell you where to find her, and I'm not inclined to do that yet, especially as she asked me to make you go away."

The man flinched and the hand that reached for his coffee shook.

"I thought she'd speak to me, thought she'd at least do that."

Jake understood the power of silence, so he said nothing and waited; his father took his lead and did the same.

The room they sat in was on the second floor, and looked out over the yard of the Munro family next door. Oscar had been his age, and they'd been able to shoot arrows from his toy bow, right from that yard into this room. Jake remembered his mother shrieking at him when one had landed in the fish tank. His parents' house was home and always would be, no matter where he settled. He loved the wood paneling, and the chart that marked his and Katie's growth. Occasionally, there was another name, usually one of his ten cousins that were scattered around the U.S. and had come to visit. But the real heart of this place, the reason it felt as it did, were the two people that lived in it. He couldn't imagine growing up without them, or having their love ripped away like Branna had when the man before him had turned his back on her.

"When Rose died, the devastation of losing her stole my will to live. We'd been together since she was thirteen; she was, quite simply, my life. I didn't know how to cope. I kept seeing her lying there, hearing her screams, and I couldn't help her." The words were spoken in his soft Irish burr, and the sadness was evident in each one.

"Did you know that Branna blames herself? That, and I quote, 'My behavior killed my mother and drove my father and I apart.'"

"No! I never wanted her to believe that."

It was the truth. Jake could see it on his face. The man was shocked.

"She also said that you didn't love her enough to forgive her for killing the only woman you'd ever love."

"Dear God!" Declan started shaking, his hands gripping the cup before him, and he looked nothing like the man Jake had seen in those interviews he'd found on the internet.

"I-I never knew she felt like that. I-I just thought…Christ, I don't know what I thought. When Rose died, I turned in on myself for a while. I tried to be there for Branna, tried to give her the support she needed while she grieved, but I was so devastated I didn't know how to comfort her, and when I did try she'd push me away, saying she was all right. I believed her, so I didn't try harder. We existed for two years, going through the motions. Me providing food and shelter, working in the same school she was at. Then I was advised to take a break by my colleagues…they said that I was stressed and soon something would give. I spoke with a psychiatrist, who told me to move somewhere quiet, out of the city and into a smaller town, so I saw the ad for a position at the local high school here, and took it, hoping the change of pace would help us both."

"Branna seemed okay, she was young, elevated two years due to her intelligence, but she was coping, so her teachers said. So, life just passed us by, until she graduated and came to me the next day and told me she was leaving for Washington, that she'd been offered a place at WSU. I was stunned, hadn't seen it coming, hadn't even known she was thinking of teaching. I tried to talk to her, tell her I'd relocate with her, but she said there was no need, she had a dorm placement and everything was settled. I asked about money, I'd give her some, but she said she had been given a scholarship and would work for the rest.

Jake could see her saying these things. That cold controlled face she sometimes used on him, explaining things precisely with no emotion.

"I hadn't known what she was doing. Not once did she ask my advice or tell me what she had planned; she just did it. She even forged my signature on some papers she needed signed."

"She said you tried to stay in touch with her a few times, but the last time you had a fight, and she hasn't seen you since," Jake said.

Declan ran a hand through his hair, sending the thick waves in every direction.

"For what it's worth, I've always known where she was. In the beginning, I made sure she was settled, then made friends online with a few of the lecturers and they keep me up to date with what was happening with her. I then returned to Ireland and started writing, which luckily became a successful career for me."

He was modest like his daughter too.

"When I'd earned enough money, I hired someone to keep a watch over her for me, because she'd let me know quite clearly that she wanted no further contact with me. I was to be told if she was in danger, or needed anything. Then one day, I decided enough was enough; I wanted my daughter back in my life, and so I went to the university and met with her, but it did not go the way I had planned."

"Too much water under the bridge?" Jake asked.

"We both have tempers, I'm afraid, and they were unleashed that day. Suddenly, all the pent up emotion and despair came out and we hurled vicious hateful words at each other. We're both wordsmiths, so there was no lack of resourcefulness, and when it was over, we both walked away broken and bleeding."

"Why are you here now, Mr. O'Donnell?"

"I love my daughter, Jake, and I'm sick of living without her. I'll stay for as long as it takes to get her to talk to me, and then I'll take it from there."

"So, if you've had her followed, you know what her career is now?"

"I do, and she's an outstanding writer; better than I could ever hope to be."

He was proud of her...the pride a parent showed in a child; in Declan O'Donnell's case, however, it may be too late.

"I have no idea if she'll speak to you, Mr. O'Donnell. Furthermore, if she does and you hurt her, then you'll be leaving this time for good," Jake added.

"I understand that."

"I will talk to her, but I'm not pushing her; the ultimate decision is Branna's."

"They're bound to run into each other, Jake. Howling is a small town," Patrick McBride said.

"I guess so, and Branna will have to deal with that if it arises." But he wouldn't let this man hurt her again; he didn't care if he was her father. Jake didn't want her hurting any more. As far as he was concerned, she'd already suffered more in her life than she should have.

After leaving his house, he went home and worked on a few cars, which was hell, because every time he looked at the bench where they'd made love this morning Jake went hard, so he had to avoid that area.

He heard Ethan's big bird overhead a few hours later, the loud whop, whop, whop of the Rota blades echoing around the barn. Minutes later, the Texan strolled in.

"You wanna throw a ball round down at the park? The domestic goddess heard me land and sent a text. Seems he wants to test his arm against the champ."

"Who just happens to be me," Jake said, starting to put his tools away. He could do with some physical exercise about now. Then he'd go talk with Branna, and hopefully she'd be rational when he brought up her father, but he didn't hold out much hope.

CHAPTER SIXTEEN

Branna worked on the book and tried to push thoughts of her father aside. She wanted him gone, wanted him out of Howling, so she never saw his face again. The shock of him suddenly appearing before her had not lessoned in the day since it had happened. Their last conversation in Washington had been fueled by suppressed emotions and rage, and she'd told him then she never wanted to see him again.

Memories of how she'd spent the morning with Jake also filled her head…naked and seated on his work bench while he kissed every inch of her body. There was nothing comfortable about what was happening between them, but she didn't want to change that, she wanted to embrace it.

An email popped into her inbox; the sender was Macy Reynolds-Delray. It was short and detailed, explaining exactly what she wanted Branna to do. None of it was overly difficult, but would take a bit of her time, but she would do it because she'd seen Macy hurting that day, and if there was one thing she understood it was pain.

"Hello!"

Getting out of her office chair, Branna made her way to the front door to see who had called out, and found Elizabeth Heath there. Just like the first day Branna had arrived in Howling, Mrs. Heath was dressed immaculately, although today's cap was green.

"Here is the paperwork, dear, read it through and the meeting is at my house on Thursday this week. All the details are in there for you, so go over them thoroughly and any questions just contact me, my number is in there too."

"This is for the Book Club?" Branna took the large envelope.

"Yes, we have a nomination process for members. Another cannot enter unless a member dies or moves from Howling. When you come to your first meeting, you bring a sealed envelope with the name of your successor in it; it's placed in a locked box with the others."

Was this woman serious, a locked box? Forms to read through and fill out, and all for a book club? Branna had never belonged to one, it had to be noted, but she was certain all that was required was a book and maybe a plate of food.

"I'm not sure I'll have the time to join your club, Mrs. Heath."

"It was Georgie's wish, Branna, and while there are some who are displeased about the prospect of someone so young joining, others are excited about it. I think it important also for you to understand just how many people want to join this club, dear. It's a highly sought after group; however, the laws about membership are governed strictly and have been in place from the first meeting by our forbearers many, many years ago."

"I've never attended a book club before." She had to try and get the woman to see reason, yet Branna knew even as the words left her mouth, she was going to fail.

"All you need to know is in there." Elizabeth Heath flicked her wrist in a surprisingly elegant gesture towards the envelope. "And, of course, Georgie always brought her Peach and Cornmeal Upside down cake, and as I'm sure she left the recipe here, you'll be able to carry on the tradition."

"I—"

"Can't stop, dear; we're hiking in thirty minutes," Elizabeth Heath stated, turning from Branna and stepping off her porch to stride back to her shiny silver sedan.

"Do you hike, Branna?" The woman opened her car door then turned to look at her.

"I'm sorry, no, I don't." She wasn't sure why she felt the need to apologize, but she did all the same.

"That can be remedied," Elizabeth Heath said, and then she was gone, her shiny car disappearing down Branna's drive.

"What the hell just happened?" Branna said the words to Cat, who was weaving through her legs. Mrs. Heath had said the answers were in the envelope, so she made coffee and took it back to her office. Opening it, she found some papers and a book. "You're kidding me." Whistling between her teeth, Branna read the title. It was gritty, raunchy, and several other words that evaded her right now. The Howling Book Club was reading this?

She'd imagined lots of literary books and poetry, not this. Placing it to one side, she looked at the papers. Headed on top of each were the words, "Please do not share these details with anyone," written in capitals. Intrigued, Branna read the first page, which was just a form that needed her personal details. Then there was a hobbies sheet, which made her smile, as she had no real hobbies besides writing, which was her job. The third and last was a schedule, which included the homes the meetings would take place in, she noted it was every three weeks, and hers was there in blue, in a month's time.

She heard another email arrive and saw it was Macy again. Deciding that no one knew Howling better than the homecoming queen, on an impulse, Branna told her about the visit from Elizabeth Heath and asked her about the Book Club. Macy replied instantly, starting with, "OMG, do you know how many woman in Howling have been dying to get into that club? It's been an institution here for years, and no one knows who is going to be called up next, just as no one knows what goes on at the meetings. There has been speculation about who would be Georgie's successor; now we know."

"So, from that email, I would say that I'm honored and that in no way can I refuse?" Branna typed back.

"Hell no! You'd be run out of town. In saying that, there are sure to be a few angry women about when they find out you've taken the spot, but I'm sure you can handle it; you do that *don't mess with me face* well."

Branna smiled at the screen. This was a side to Macy she had never seen before…the funny, smart woman.

"Me? I'm a pussy cat. Sweetest person ever."

What came back was a line of hahaha.

"How's the writing going?" was the next question.

"How do you know I'm a writer?" Branna replied, to which Macy added.

"Town grapevine."

Weirdly, she felt comfortable talking to Macy about one of her characters she was struggling to fit into the role Branna had mapped out for her. It was strange how the woman she had hated at school was so different to talk to by email. She even had some insightful comments about how the woman should react when a man threatened her. After she had said thanks to Macy for her advice and goodbye, Branna put on her headphones, and minutes later was deep into the book, and didn't come out for quite some time.

Looking at her cell, she noticed a text from Jake that simply said. Come to the park down beside the lake. Noting the time, she saw that she'd been writing for three hours, so she took off her head phones and shut her computer down after backing everything up. Changing into her running shorts and singlet, Branna then pulled on her shoes. She needed the exercise, needed to clear her head, and if she was running around the lake she wouldn't run into her father or hopefully think about him.

Where was he? Had he left town, or was he still staying with the McBride family?

Shaking the thought aside, Branna headed out the front door and stopped as she saw the pool of blood beneath the cat's tail that was nailed to the roof of the porch. Her scream was heard by no one. Fumbling for her cell, she rang Jake.

"It's Cat; you need to c-come quick."

He ran up her drive minutes later, his body tense, eyes alert.

"They killed Cat." She edged around the blood and leapt off the step and into his arms. They closed around her, and she felt the thud of his heart. He must have sprinted here. "I-it's not fair."

Branna gripped the front of his T-shirt and held it tight while she burrowed her head into his chest. He held her, stroking her hair, and she soaked up his strength until she regained control of herself again.

The sound of a car made her lift her head, and then she saw Jake's pickup arrive loaded with men. It stopped, and out jumped Ethan, Newman, and Buster. All were sweaty like Jake, and each looked serious.

"What the fuck?" Buster stomped up to the tail and glared at it. "This shit has to stop!"

"Go see if you can find Cat; I don't think it's him," Jake said, gripping her shoulders as he eased her from his arms. "Look at that tail, Branna, Cat has white circles in the ginger; that tail is lighter, and the stripes less distinguishable."

She turned, and Jake stepped up behind her, caging her inside his strength. Looking at the tail, she studied it. Was he right?

"I need to go look for him now, just to be sure." She stepped away from Jake, and Ethan kept pace with her as she ran around the house to where Cat sometimes slept in the sun. The relief at seeing him made her drop to her knees and pick him up.

"He's okay; it wasn't him."

"He may be okay, but he's now seriously pissed you woke him up, honey."

Branna laughed with relief at Ethan's words. Putting Cat back in his place, she regained her feet.

"I don't even like cats."

Ethan rubbed her back, but didn't reply, instead urging her back around the front to where Jake and Buster were examining the blood.

"Red food coloring and tomato sauce." Buster held his pinky finger up to examine the red on the end of it. "Not blood, Branna."

"Why is someone trying to scare me?" Now she wasn't shaking and scared, she was angry.

"That I don't know, but I'm sure as hell going to find out." Jake's words were a growl as he pulled out his phone. "Cubby, you need to get to Branna's place now." Pocketing it again, he said. "Get me the keys, Rosebud. Buster and I will take a quick look around the shed, just to make sure nothing else is off. You take the Texan inside with you; he can look around in there, and then he'll need feeding.

Branna looked at Ethan, who shrugged.

"He's right, I am hungry."

Jake was so angry he could spit fire. Someone was trying to frighten Branna and doing a good job.

"What the hell's going on, Jake? This is Howling, not downtown L.A.; this kind of crap doesn't happen here," Buster said.

Opening the shed, Jake entered with his friend on his heels. "It's got to have something to do with this place, Buster, because she wasn't here long enough to make enemies, and it's unlikely someone this nasty would have held a grudge for ten years."

"You think whoever's doing this is trying to scare her out of the house?"

"Just a hunch, but it makes more sense than anything else I've thought up," Jake added.

Buster whistled through his teeth, which was his answer for most things when he had no words.

They walked around the barn, but came up with nothing obviously out of place and no sign of forced entry. They were heading back to the house as Cubby pulled up in his cruiser.

"What's happened now?"

Jake pointed to the cat's tail and pool of fake blood as the sheriff approached. "Branna found this about thirty minutes ago. She'd been working inside with her head phones on for most of the day, so never heard anything."

"This is just getting plain weird, Cubby, you got any answers?" Buster watched the sheriff go back to his vehicle and pull out his camera and a bag.

"Coming around to a few, and they're not happy ones, I have to say, but the evidence is building." He snapped the pictures and then bagged the tail.

Jake unwound the hose and sprayed the deck to get rid of the mess, so Branna didn't have to see it when she came out the door again.

"So, you want to share these conclusions?" Jake said, when he'd put the hose away.

The sheriff gave him a steady look, which Jake ignored.

"She's freaking out, Cubby. Branna came here to make a home, and someone's trying to scare her away." Running a hand through his hair, Jake sucked in a breath. "We need to stop this before whoever is doing it decides to push her harder."

"I have to say, it's nice to see you lively again, Jake, even for this reason."

"He played ball today, Cub…the man is making strides, I'm telling you."

Jake snorted. "Shut up, Buster, in case it slipped your mind, my girl is under attack here."

Two sets of eyes swung to him.

"She's your girl now, big boy?" Buster said.

"Fuck you both!" Snarling something else under his breath, he made for the house.

"Sorry, it was hard to resist," Buster drew alongside him.

"It's only 'cuz we care, Jakey boy," Cubby added, sounding like his mother. "Seriously," he added. "I know you want this thing sorted, and I'm onto something, Jake, but I need to do this by the book, because if I'm right, then it's going to have repercussions."

Jake stopped before entering the house to look at Cubby.

"Is she in danger?"

"That I don't know, but I need to you to keep a real close eye on her now, Jake. Real close."

"Do you think this all has to do with Branna now being the owner of this house, Cubby?"

"I believe so."

"Ethan and I can help, and we know others who can dig deep and find whatever you need about anyone," Jake said.

Cubby thought about that for a couple of seconds. "That could be useful, because if it's who I suspect, then we need to keep it real quiet until I can bring them in."

Jake thought about the people he knew in Howling, and came up blank. None of them could do, to his mind, what had been done to Branna.

"Hell of a thing thinking it could be someone you swapped cookies with in school." Buster's thoughts were obviously running along the same lines as Jake's.

They said nothing further, and found Ethan in the small dining room. The Texan had his boots dangling over the edge of the table, chair balanced on two legs, and a large piece of cake in his hand.

"Comfortable?" Jake questioned, making his way past him and into the kitchen.

"Peachy."

Branna was making coffee and cutting more cake, her movements quick and jerky, shoulders rigid.

"You doing okay?"

She turned with the plate in her hand, face carefully blank.

"Of course. You take this in, and I'll bring the coffee." Her words were clipped, eyes avoiding his, and Jake knew now wasn't the time to get into this, so he took the plate and went back to the dining room.

They ate and talked, and Branna sat quietly and listened.

"I don't want to scare you, Branna, but you can't stay here alone anymore until I find who is responsible for this."

Her eyes shot to Cubby.

"That's not always easy, Cubby. Plus, I need to be here alone during the day to write."

The sheriff gave her gentle smile. "During the day should be okay, I guess, but no head phones, and maybe take your laptop onto the porch and write somewhere you can be visual."

"You can write in The Hoot," Buster said. "And bake this cake for my customers while you're there. What's the recipe?"

"I've repeatedly asked you for Mystery Muffin recipes, and you haven't come through, so forget it."

"Is it called Mystery Cake?"

She managed a smile at Buster's words. "Thanks for the offer of The Hoot, but I like to write alone with no distractions."

"I'll take care of it," Jake said, and then swallowed a mouthful of coffee as she frowned at him. He knew she was independent, even understood that she'd been on her own for years looking after every aspect of her life, but that was no excuse for stupidity.

"I can take care of myself."

"Sure you can, but I'm pretty sure you've never had someone threatening you like this before, so use that oversized brain of yours and understand that you need help until this is settled," Jake said calmly.

She didn't say anything, just got to her feet and began to collect up plates and cups, before stomping off to the kitchen.

"I'm out," Ethan got to his feet with the speed of a man who had dealt with an emotional woman before.

"Me too," Buster followed.

"I'll be in touch," Cubby patted Jake's shoulder and closed the door behind them.

He found her washing cups and plates and making more noise than she needed to.

"Ready for that run now?"

"You go on; I need to get a few things done."

"Not happening, Rosebud, so let's go."

She slapped a cup on the board before turning to face him. "Don't tell me what to do."

Jake saw she wasn't about to be reasonable. In fact, he thought that the cat's tail was about the last straw when you combined it with her father arriving and her house and garden being trashed.

"We going to have our first fight, sweet cheeks?"

"I don't need you protecting me or looking out for me. I can do all that by myself, McBride."

"Fine, you're a big girl, got it. Now, let's go." Jake had a temper too, and knew why she was striking at it, but it still pissed him off.

"No."

He picked her up, threw her over his shoulder, and left the house. She hammered at his back and cursed in a thick Irish accent until he put her down at the end of the drive. She took a swing at him, which connected with his chest, so he grunted to make her feel better.

"Fuck you to hell and back, McBride." Rage made her eyes bright, her fists were clenched and her breasts heaving under her singlet, and he wanted to strip her and bury himself inside her, right there on the side of the road.

"Yes, please."

She raised her eyes to the sky, and when they lowered again, he saw they were calmer.

"Now run, you Irish wench."

She did, and soon they had a steady rhythm going. No words, just his woman at his side and the countryside he loved around them. Jake let her set the pace as his mind went back to the cat's tail. It was another tactic to scare Branna, and Jake kept circling back to the reason being that someone wanted her gone from Georgie's property, but why?

"Someone wants to scare me into leaving the house, Jake."

"That's my thinking."

"But why?"

"That I don't know."

"I love that house."

"I know you do, and we'll get to the bottom of this; I promise, sweetheart."

She didn't saying anything else, and both were breathing heavily as they arrived back at the place they'd started.

"Let's swim." Jake took off his shirt and bent to remove his running shoes and socks.

"I don't swim."

"What, never?"

"It's not something I've ever enjoyed."

"Can you swim?" Her hesitation was brief, but it was there.

"Badly, so I'll see you back at the house."

"I'll look after you, Rosebud, now strip off and get in that water."

She put her hands on her hips and glared at him.

"Will you stop throwing orders about; it's getting tiresome."

His answer was to grab her and haul her into his body. Heat radiated off them both, heat and sweat. He kissed her thoroughly and then ran his hands all over her until she was arching towards him. Releasing her seconds later, he dove into the water.

"Wh-what was that about?" she said when he'd surfaced.

"Come in here and find out." He trod water, watching her. She was certainly easy on the eyes, especially in those running shorts.

"I'm not a teenager…that kind of talk doesn't work with me."

"Sure it does. You're horny just like me; I can see it in your body." He laughed as she looked at her nipples, which were hard and showing through her top.

"Teenagers get horny, big boy. Adults," she tapped her chest, "which I happen to be, feel lust."

"I've got lust, Rosebud, right between my legs, and if you'd don't get in here soon, I'm coming after you."

"Shouldn't you be," her hands flapped about before she bent to pull off her shoes. "Deflated from the cold."

"Just a quick lesson from the *Men's 101 Handbook*, sweetheart. We never want to hear the word deflated in relation to our most prized possession."

Her giggle was a sweet sound. Jake then watched as she tucked her socks neatly inside her shoes, then to his surprise, she dropped her shorts, pulled off her top, and dove in. He had a flash of small white cotton panties and a sports bra in pale blue, then she hit the water with a loud splash, belly first. Surfacing, she spluttered and started flapping her arms around. She went under before he could reach her, but he hauled her up, and she threw her arms around his neck and wrapped her legs around his waist.

"You weren't kidding about the swimming then?"

"Lust made me do it, now I want to get out, because I'm cold and no longer horny."

"Teenagers get horny, not adults."

"Take me back to the bank, Jake."

"I got you." He used his arms and legs to keep them afloat while she clung to him. "Try and relax."

"What's under us?"

"Water."

"What else?"

"More water, then maybe some dirt and a lake monster or two. But the last time it ate anyone was back in 2000, so we're sweet."

"Funny guy."

He felt her start to relax as he moved around slowly. He loved it here; no houses were visible, although a few were tucked up driveways like his. It was peaceful for the most part, and a reserve was situated further down the road, so he didn't hear the noise when someone took their kids there to play. Not that he minded, he liked children, although until lately he'd never thought about having any of his own.

"This is nice now; I could almost fall asleep."

"That's because I'm doing all the work."

"I have to go to the Book Club tomorrow night, Jake."

"Ah, so you're the one. The town's been a hotbed of speculation, wondering who Georgie had selected."

"Mrs. Heath dropped off the paperwork this morning."

"Paperwork?"

"I can't tell because all members are sworn to secrecy."

"You're not serious?"

"Totally, it's written on the top of the first page. Supposedly, I have to take an envelope with me tomorrow night with the name inside of the person I choose to take my place when I retire from the Book Club or die."

"Who you going to choose?" Jake asked.

"I can't tell you that."

Jake rolled his eyes. "The men of this town have been wondering about that group of women for ages. My mom's part of it."

"That makes me feel a bit better," Branna said.

"She won't spill, but you will, and then I can share the knowledge with the men folk."

"Told you, that's not happening. Seems I have to take a Peach and Cornmeal upside down cake too, like Georgie always brings." Branna wondered if she was even allowed to share that information with him.

"Do you have to read all those books with big words too?"

"Not so much," Branna said. "In fact, the titles are not what I expected."

They floated awhile, thinking about that.

"Now I'm going to give you your first lesson."

"In what?" Branna looked at him.

"Staying afloat."

"I'm not letting you go."

"And while those words would normally be music to my ears, I need to know if you're ever in the water again that you can stay on top of it."

"Jake, I don't need to learn to swim because I don't go in the water." She looked up at him, hair black as midnight and slicked back on her head, which meant he could study her delicate features. Her eyes seemed greener out here, cheekbones pronounced, lips pink. She had a face that anyone would love to photograph, but it was her mind he loved too. She was sharp and sassy, and didn't take any crap from him.

"How about if you're ever on a boat?"

"Don't like boats."

"Walking along a beach and a freak wave drags you out?"

"I don't like sand between my toes."

"Driving over a bridge and it collapses, your car fills with water, and then you open the window and have to swim out?"

"Ummm, I'll stay away from bridges."

Jake kissed her, then swam them back to the bank. Once there, he stood on the side, still submerged up to his waist.

"I'll hold your stomach while you practice."

Branna knew she wasn't getting out of this easily, and he was probably right, she did need to learn to at least float.

"All right, let's get it over with."

He looked good wet, his big body shimmering in the sun. Branna felt something move in the region of her heart, and convinced herself it was lust.

She squeaked as he flipped her onto her stomach, then the breath hissed from her throat when she felt Jake's fingers slip under the waist of her panties and stroke the top of her buttocks.

"Hey!"

"You have some lake monster slime on you."

Over the next twenty minutes, he patiently taught her to float, and by the end she could keep herself on top of the water if ever there came a time when she needed to.

"Okay, first lesson over, Rosebud," he hoisted her up onto the bank. "Now, about that lust."

"I'm cold and wet now; the lust seems to have disappeared." Branna gathered up her clothes.

"It'll come back," Jake said, pulling on his shoes, then throwing his T-shirt over one shoulder. "Hop on, and we'll head to the showers."

She watched Jake crouch in front of her with his back turned.

"The last time anyone piggy-backed me, I was in single digits."

"You have to lean to be more spontaneous, Rosebud. It's real tiring dating an older woman."

He was taunting her again, so clutching her clothes she climbed onto his back, and then he started jogging up his driveway.

"Two things I can honestly say I haven't done for a while would be this and swimming, and I did them both in one day," Branna said, enjoying the feel of all that power and strength under her. The man wasn't even breathing hard.

"Stick with me, sweet cheeks, and I'll show you a few more."

Branna snorted as Jake walked them into the house and straight for the bathroom. Once there, he lowered her down his back. Turning, he cupped her face and kissed her. It was a kiss of possession, a kiss that drove any thoughts of being cold or swimming lessons and lake monsters from her head.

"Let's get warm now," he released her to turn on the shower and Branna dropped her bundle of things, then took off her bra and panties. She stepped under the spray as Jake pulled off his shoes; seconds later, he joined her. But she was ready for him and as he reached for her, she placed one hand on his chest and pushed him against the shower wall.

"You have lake monster all over you, Jake; let me clean you up."

He gave her that slow smile.

Soaping her hands, she then started with his shoulders and began cleaning him slowly, running her hands in circles over his big solid body.

"You're being thorough there, Rosebud." Branna heard the hiss in his breath as she scraped her nails over his nipples.

"That slime is sticky." She ran her tongue along his lips, then bit the tip of his chin. She loved touching him, feeling all that leashed strength. Her own body was aroused, her breasts aching and full, and the ache between her legs needing release. Moving to his stomach, she stroked the flat planes as she leaned forward and took his nipple into her mouth. His body jerked forward.

"Jesusssss."

Smiling up at him, Branna moved lower. Getting on her knees, she took the long hard length of him in her mouth. Two hands gripped her head, fingers raking her scalp as she swirled her tongue around the soft silken head. Bracing her hands on his thighs, she took him deeper.

"I'm done," he rasped, lifting her to her feet seconds later; he then opened the door and walked out with her in his arms. Lowering her to the vanity, he spread her legs and slid inside her.

It was slow and achingly sweet. Steam swirled around them as Branna held on by digging her fingers into his shoulders. Her head hit the mirror as the pleasure exploded through her in a shuddering wave, as Jake emptied himself deep inside her.

He lifted her back into the shower seconds later, and Branna slumped against the wall as he washed himself and then her.

"I'll make us some food." He kissed her softly, and then she was alone…her body weak, mind swirling. He unbalanced her, stripped her raw with the need she felt for him.

Turning off the water, she stepped out and dried herself. Pulling on her damp panties, she gathered up her running clothes, then wandered into his bedroom. Grabbing a T-shirt from the pile of neatly folded clothes on the end of his bed, she pulled it over her head. Then, using his hair brush, she attempted to untangle the knots in her hair.

The smell of coffee greeted her as she reached the kitchen and she smelled grilled cheese sandwiches and realized she was starving.

CHAPTER SEVENTEEN

"Smell good?" Jake watched Branna drop her stuff by the door, then walk around his breakfast bar and sit on one of the stools.

"It does, and makes me realize that it's been way too long since I ate anything."

"All that exercise has to tire you out."

She didn't answer, just took the coffee he handed her.

"You have to see him sometime, Branna."

The cup had been halfway to her mouth, but she lowered it, placing it carefully on the bench before her.

"No, I don't."

Jake hated that particular expression of hers. The blank one that told him nothing of what she was feeling. He realized that he knew most of her expressions now.

"He's not going anywhere, Rosebud. He'll stay until you do."

"As long as he keeps away from me, I don't care."

"Now, that's a lie; he's your father, you care." Taking a sandwich out of the pan, he put it on a plate, then slid it in front of her. "This thing between you is not going away."

"I don't want to talk about it."

"I do."

"Leave it, Jake." Her face was shuttered.

"Come on, Branna, the man is living with my parents, so every time I go there I see him, and he talks to me. Tells me about you and what you mean to him. Give him a chance to at least tell you his side of the story."

"I didn't ask your parents to take him in, nor did I ask Declan O'Donnell to come here, so don't tell me what I have to do, Jake. I'm an adult and can make my own decisions."

"So what, you're just going to avoid him? Stay out of Howling until he hopefully leaves?"

"Don't talk to me about avoidance, McBride." She tore the crust off the sandwich and then began to shred it between her fingers. "You spent years learning to heal with those hands," she pointed to the one he held a spatula in. "Don't you think it's about time you faced up to why you walked away from that?"

"We're not talking about me." Jake put another sandwich into the pan, because he needed to do something.

"So, it's okay for you to poke at my raw spots, but I can't do the same? Or are your demons more important than mine?"

"You know what happened and my reasons why I walked away, Branna."

"And that's it?" She was angry now, her body rigid, eyes flashing. "You were traumatized, so case closed. You're just giving up on what you love? You going to stay hidden here, Jake, tucked away from the world and the career that you dedicated years and years of your life to?"

He was back there again, with the blood and screams of the children. Their eyes pleading with him to take away their pain, live or die, they didn't care; they just wanted to be free of it.

"You know nothing about it." Jake tended to get ugly when people made him face the fact that he no longer did what he was born to do.

"And you know nothing about me either." She was standing now, hands clenched into tight fists.

"He's your father, Branna. The man raised you, and from what I can tell, he's not a bad guy. He deserves at least a chance to talk to you." Jake tried to sound calm and reasonable, but his words were cold and clipped. His palms had begun to sweat and his head was filled with visions, but no one looking at him would know what was going on inside. Just like Branna, he'd learned to hide.

"I deserved more from him!" she cried. "I deserved his love and comfort, but he gave me nothing, turned his back and forgot me. I don't have to forgive him anything."

"I understand what you're saying, Branna," Jake put the spatula down and moved to face her across the bench. But I think it will help you if you at least just talk to him, and if you can't find a way forward, then you will have given it a shot, and he can leave knowing he tried."

Her face was flushed and she was breathing fast. She was staring at him as if he'd betrayed her, and maybe in her eyes he had, because he was forcing her to face something she didn't want to face. He didn't want to acknowledge that she was trying to do the same with him.

"And, what about you, McBride? Are you going to find a way forward, or live in this town fixing cars, while your adoring public make excuses as to why one of their golden boys copped out on life?"

"I didn't cop out." Jake braced his hands on the bench. I just don't want to be a doctor anymore." His words were a low growl, which most people would realize meant he was angry, but not her, she simply growled back.

"If that is truly the case, then fine, but will that choice make you happy? Can you say that, Jake? Say you're really happy not doing what you love?"

"We are not talking about me, Branna, we're talking about you," Jake said slowly, keeping his words even, when inside his body was furnace of seething emotion.

She placed her hands before his and leaned forward, their eyes now level. Hers shot green sparks at him, little lasers of hurt and anger.

"You can't say it because you're not; in fact, you're miserable. I see the sadness in your eyes, the sorrow that grips you when you don't think I'm looking. It hurts that you're not practicing medicine anymore, hurts way down deep that you're not helping people."

"You have no fucking idea what you're talking about." But she did, because she was the only one to have ever spoken to him this way, the only one who made Jake face how hard it would be to give up medicine for the rest of his life.

"Oh, I know all right. I know you're scared and that you're hurting," she said, backing away from him. "Because I've been scared and hurt too, Jake, but I don't need you or my father, because I've survived without you both, and I will do so again."

Before he could reach her, she'd left, slamming the door behind her, and Jake stood rooted to the spot replaying her words in his head.

"If that is truly the case, then fine, but will that choice make you happy? Can you say that, Jake? Say you're really happy not doing what you love?"

He stood at that sink as his sandwich went cold, and didn't fight the memories as they filled his head.

The day he left here to go to medical school, the day he graduated. It all came back. And then he was there in Iraq, standing in what had once been a school. The bomb had ripped through the place, killing and maiming, and he'd done what he could for days until he could do no more. His mind had gone blank as he worked, and then Ethan had come and taken him back to base. When he woke after two days of sleeping, his head was filled with what he had witnessed. After the first consult, he'd refused help; no shrink was getting into his head, and he'd come home to heal. But he hadn't. Instead, he'd placed a temporary bandage over his pain, and then locked it all away and just existed.

Branna was right, he had been surly and punished those closest to him, and the people he cared about had accepted his behavior because, unlike him, they believed in him and that one day he would once again be a doctor.

Picking up the phone, he rang Ethan.

"I need that appointment now, today or tomorrow." He listened to Ethan tell him that he'd make a call and get back to him. Minutes later, his cell rang, and it was the Texan telling him to be ready as he was flying over to pick him up.

After that, Jake called his father and told him to keep an eye on Branna, then Annabelle to ask her to stay with Branna at night.

"None of your business, Annabelle, just stay with her till I get back." Disconnecting the call as she asked another question, Jake then called Buster.

"I'm going to be out of town with Ethan for a few days, Buster, watch over Branna for me."

His friend didn't ask questions, just said he would, and Jake knew she'd be safe until he returned to straighten out the mess he'd just made with her.

He was ready when he heard the thunder of Ethan's helicopter approach. Picking up his cell phone, he sent a text to Branna, telling her he was going to be out of town for a few days, and that he would see her as soon as he got back. He finished with the word "sorry," because in all honesty he didn't know what else to say. Picking up his duffle, he walked out the back door to the paddock Ethan was landing in. Ducking under the blades, he opened the door and climbed in. Strapping himself in, he put on his headphones and then they were in the air again.

Branna stood at the window and watched Ethan's helicopter rise in the air and disappear. She'd gotten Jake's text, but didn't reply, because she had no idea what to say. Her eyes were raw from crying and acid had formed in her stomach at the thought of the words they'd said to each other. Where was he going and why had he left? She missed him already, and that annoyed her, because it meant she cared…which she already knew, but now she really cared because the pain was bad.

"And that, you idiot, is why you don't form attachments to people," Branna muttered as she finished dressing.

Heading downstairs, she grabbed her keys and handbag and left the house. Her father had kept her out of Howling, and Jake was right about one thing, he wasn't keeping her away any longer. She needed supplies, and if she saw him, she'd nod her head and walk away. Declan O'Donnell wasn't the kind of man to make a fuss any more than she would. He wouldn't force a confrontation between them, so she was safe there.

She thought about the argument she and Jake had. They'd struck at each other in their most vulnerable places, the places that because of their growing closeness were bound to eventually be exposed. They'd both been hiding with no wish to come out, and because of this they had hurt each other. Maybe they were best apart? Her heart ached at the thought of not seeing him again or feeling his body close to hers.

"Damn, I love him" The realization had her pulling off the road while she recovered from the shock. How the hell had that happened?

Shaking her head, she restarted the car and slowly drove into town. She could hide her feelings, he need never know, or maybe she would tell him? *What? Are you crazy, O'Donnell?* Love made you vulnerable; she knew that, so why the hell would she contemplate exposing herself to that again?

Because he'd made her feel again, made her remember what it was like to be part of someone and not just a cold emotional shell that went through the routine of day to day life, convincing herself she was happy.

Branna found a parking spot on the main street, and for once the quaint beauty of the town didn't make her smile. Climbing out of the car, she walked slowly down the street, nodding and acknowledging people as thoughts tumbled around inside her head. Could she put herself back together if Jake was no longer in her life? How would she cope if another person she loved turned away from her?

When was he coming back?

Pushing open the door to the drugstore, she went inside.

"Hey, Branna, we got some more of that lotion you like in for you."

"Oh, hi, Mr. Pike, and thanks, I'm just about out." Picking up a few things, she paid for them and the lotion before leaving.

The thing was, Branna was starting to feel like she belonged here. The big cities she lived in were not good for a person who kept to herself, but like her home town in Ireland, Howling embraced people.

"I'm finished with my cookies, Branna."

"I'll get to it, Jilly," Branna said, as she made her way into the grocery store. "Or you could try and bake some for yourself."

"I can't cook."

This was what happened in small towns, you got involved or you didn't, which sounded simple, but if you didn't you were a hermit who everyone talked about.

"Why can't you cook?" Picking up some bread, Branna put it in her basket before looking at the girl. Today, her hair was spiked blood red.

"Mom's just not big on baking."

"You want me to teach you?" Branna said, before she could stop herself. She had a book to finish by deadline and then revisions, plus several other things that needed her attention, and let's not mention the fact that she was meant to be the reclusive type.

Jake had done this to her, he'd made her *open* up like a bloody flower, and now she was having a hell of time closing.

You better come back soon, McBride.

She headed to The Hoot after making arrangements with Jilly for her first cooking lesson. She's wasn't feeling social, but then Buster wasn't big on talk either, so she'd just slip out back, and sit and watch the scenery, eat her muffin, then go home and think some more.

"You bring that face in here and you'll scare away my customers, O'Donnell."

Branna forced her lips upwards. "Sorry, just thinking, Buster. How you doing?"

"I'm good. You want a muffin and coffee?"

"Thanks, I'll just go sit out back if that's okay?"

Buster's lips tilted, which Branna knew was a smile. "You a paying customer or planning on doing a runner?"

"Paying."

"Well, you get to sit then."

She found a table that looked out the big window, and Branna refused to acknowledge that maybe she would see Ethan's helicopter come back into town if she sat here long enough. She was halfway through her muffin, which she was sure had pineapple in it, but Buster refused to confirm or deny that ingredient, when she heard his voice. The deep Irish rumble.

She'd gone to sleep many nights lying on her father's chest while he'd read her stories, and sat at his feet as he sang her songs. It was a voice she still heard in head, no matter how much she'd tried to remove it.

Looking out the window, Branna willed him away before he saw her. He was talking with Buster, asking about the pies and complimenting the cook. Her father had always been good with people; he could subdue the angry, and make anyone smile… it had been his gift. The gift of trust. It was instinctive. He'd charmed her teachers and made every man feel as if they were friends, but like her, all that had changed with the death of his wife.

She looked at the hills in the distance, counted the rises and dips, and knew he was coming towards her even before she heard the sound of his steps.

"Branna, will you let me talk to you?"

"We have nothing to say to each other." She kept her eyes on the window.

"I think we do, daughter."

He'd brought her up to respect her elders, and even though she had no wish to look at him, manners dictated to her from birth said she must, so she turned, keeping all expression from her face.

"If we talk, then will you leave Howling?"

"If that's your wish."

He stood a few feet from her, dressed in worn jeans and a shirt that had a missing button. He'd always had no idea of the appeal he had to women, and she and her mother had often laughed at the surprise on his face when they'd pointed out a woman looking at him.

But why would I care when the only women I want to look at me are my own.

He was only eighteen years her senior, and had aged well, despite the grief he had suffered. His black hair was peppered with more grey now and in need of a cut, and she saw a few lines on his face that had not been there when last they had met, but his green eyes were still clear and bright. He was tall, about Jake's height, and his body lean. Branna knew he did nothing to keep it that way, but like her, did not put on weight easily.

"I will talk with you, but have no wish for anyone to over hear us. I have to live in this town; you don't." Branna was pleased her voice sounded calm.

"Then I will speak quietly, and if anyone comes in, I shall discuss the weather."

She didn't smile as he teased her, instead nodding as he took the seat across from her. She felt his eyes on her as she looked down at her muffin. If she ate any more, the beautiful flavors would now blend together in her mouth and taste like dust.

"Firstly, I want to start with an apology, though God alone knows why you would forgive me. Were I in your stead, I certainly would not." His accent, like hers, was thicker when he was emotional.

"I turned from you, my only child, at a time when you most needed me. My grief was so consuming I could see nothing beyond it."

Branna relaxed the fist she'd formed around the muffin, and put her hands in her lap. She didn't want to relive those days again, dredge up the pain and misery, but she said nothing. Head lowered, she let him talk, then she'd get up and walk away and never have to see him again.

"I have no excuse for shutting myself away from you, Branna, only that I did not know how to go on without your mother. It was as if the light had suddenly gone from my life, and I lived only in darkness."

I should have been your light too.

"I went through the motions of making your lunch, and cooking and clothing you, but I could do nothing else. The psychiatrist the school made me see said I was suffering from clinical depression, and that a change would be the best thing for us. I spoke to your teachers before deciding to come here, and they said you were a quiet but studious girl, who seemed to be coping quite well with the loss of your mother."

She'd become very good at hiding.

"So, we came here and I watched as you apparently settled into your new school. You didn't ask me for anything besides the necessities, and you did your homework and made no demands on me, and I thought that meant you were doing okay, which left me time to grieve and wallow in my pain. I gave you no time until the day I found a flyer you'd left in your room. It said you were part of a band that was singing at lunchtime that day, so I went along to watch, and it was that day I realized I'd lost you, because the child who had once told me everything had kept this from me."

Please stop.

Branna wanted to put her hands over her ears to shut out his voice. She couldn't breathe; his words were thrusting her back into that place filled with pain.

"I brought more coffee." The hand Buster put on her shoulder, was large and warm and she felt the support that came with it. Sucking in a breath, she slowly exhaled.

"Thanks, Buster."

"You let me know if you need anything else."

"We will," she said, giving him a quick look before lowering her eyes to the table once more.

"You have friends here."

"Yes."

Declan O'Donnell sighed at her tone before he resumed his story.

"That day, as I stood at the back of that auditorium and watched you sing, I knew what I had become and how I had let you down. I went home and began to make changes. I took you out for dinner that night, and other than please and thank you, you said nothing to me, no matter how many questions I asked you."

Because I knew you blamed me for killing her.

"I continued to try, but you seemed to grow more distant, and then after your graduation you came home and told me you were leaving for WSU. Showed me the paperwork and that you had organized a place to stay. You calmly told me how you'd forged my signature, and that the only thing you would need from me was some money to get there, as you had been given a scholarship and would get a job."

"I tried to talk to you, tell you I'd take you there, but you said in that cold calm way you had adopted that you needed nothing further from me. I stood and watched the bus take you away from me, my sixteen year old daughter who was a mere child, and felt my heart break all over again."

"No!" Branna jumped to her feet and looked down at her father. "Don't speak to me of love, not now, not when I don't need or want it anymore."

"Branna—"

"No," she sliced a hand through the air. "You had your say, now I get mine."

"Sit then."

"I don't want to sit. I want to talk, and then I want to leave." She sucked in another breath. "You blamed me for her death and turned your back on me when I had no one else to turn to. I was broken inside; I hurt so bad that just breathing seemed to take too much effort. I heard your words that day, heard you say there was nothing left for you now that she was gone."

"No, Branna, I never meant them that way." His green eyes were filled with anguish, but she didn't care; she wanted to hurt him like he had her.

"You couldn't even stand to look at me. I was a constant reminder of her death. So, I tried to be as quiet as I could, tried to keep out of your sight, and then we moved here to Howling."

He was pale now; all color had left his face.

"The other students had friends…a small community like this, everyone had grown up together, and there I was, an outsider who talked funny. So, one day I woke up and went through the house and found every pill I could, then I hid them in my room." Branna fought the tears; she wouldn't cry yet, not with him watching.

"No, Branna—"

He rose too, and reached a hand towards her, but she stepped back and it fell to his side.

"I went to school for the last time that day, deciding that I'd take them that night and then the pain would be gone, then you'd be rid of me...the constant reminder of what you had lost."

"Dear God, don't say it, Branna."

"And when I was huddled in that bathroom stall at lunchtime, like I had done every day since I started school there, waiting for it to be over so I could go home and find some peace, I heard a voice outside telling me to come out, and that was when I met Annabelle Smith. She's the only person who has ever really been there for me since the death of my m-mother, and it is because of her, only her, that I stand here before you today."

"You wouldn't have, I can't believe you would—"

"You know nothing about me," her hand slashed the air again. "Nor of what I was capable of. After all, I had always believed you'd be there if I needed you, and that all changed, didn't it?"

She walked away from him then and never looked back. It was done, over, he would leave Howling now, and she would once again attempt to pick up the pieces of her life.

"Branna, you want me to take you somewhere?" Buster appeared beside her as she reached the door, his face lined with worry.

"Thanks, but I just need a bit of time alone for now, Buster." Branna wasn't sure how she formed the words, when inside she was coming apart.

"I'm worried about you." The words came out so fast it took her a few seconds to unravel them.

"I'll be okay, Buster, really," she added, before pushing open the door and walking out of The Hoot.

Once she was clear of the window, she ran to her van. Fumbling for the keys, she got them in the ignition, backing out, she then pushed her foot down on the gas pedal and shot out of town.

Chapter Eighteen

Jake was exhausted. Ethan had arranged an appointment to see the psychiatrist for that day, so he'd flown into Brook and gone straight to see the man. He'd had more emotions wrung out of him in that sixty minute time slot than he'd experienced in years. Not quite years, Jake amended, thinking of the emotions Branna made him feel.

"How you doing, bud?"

Ethan folded himself into the chair opposite him. Picking up the beer Jake had brought him, he then took a long pull on it.

"I feel like someone's punching bag without the physical pain."

Ethan had lived in Brook for two years; it was the closest main town to Howling, two hours forty minutes by car, and twenty minutes by chopper. It had bars and cafes, shops, banks, businesses, and plenty of people.

Around them were the usual sounds of a night just starting, greetings, the clink of glasses, stories being recounted.

"It was always going to be tough, Jake. Besides me, no one else knows what you went through, and even I don't know everything." Ethan leaned back on the legs of his chair and let his eyes scan the room. Jake knew he was looking for women, because once he'd been the same way.

"Branna knows some of it."

"Yeah?" Ethan whistled. "Must be love."

"I guess it must." Jake said the words, testing how they sounded in his head. Did he love her? Was it love when you couldn't stop thinking about someone? Couldn't stop worrying about her, and recalled everything about her right down to the smell of her skin.

"I like her, if that helps."

Jake lifted his bottle in acknowledgement. "I live my life to please you, Tex, you know that."

Ethan laughed that deep rumble that made women go weak.

"Doctor Nigel wanted me to ask you if I said anything that day you pulled me out of that school, or what was left of it?" They'd never spoken of that day, so the surprise on his friend's face was real.

"Blood, Eth, so much blood." The words were softly spoken, each one slow and precise.

"Anything else?"

"I couldn't help them all."

Jake didn't remember much about the day, but he saw by his friend's expression that he did.

"It was like you were a zombie, Jake. You kept saying those words, blood Eth, so much blood, and I couldn't help them all, over and over again, and all I could do was tell you it would be all right now." Ethan took another long pull on his bottle. "I thought you were broken, that your mind had gone, and wasn't sure it'd come back. But after the long sleep and food, you were back, although then there was this blank look in your eyes, like you were just going through the motions of living."

"I was," Jake said. "I really was in the beginning. And then I got angry and belligerent; I hated the world and everyone in it."

"Except me and Buster."

"That's a given."

"And then you met Branna."

"And then I met Branna," Jake confirmed.

"And?" Ethan questioned, giving a shapely brunette a slow smile as she walked past their table.

"And she has as many issues as me, and the day I called you to make the appointment, we fought about them."

"Ah, now it makes sense."

"She deserves the best of me, Ethan, and I'm not sure whether that means I return to medicine or not. But right now, none of that matters, only getting the stuff inside here," Jake tapped his head, "right."

"What's between her and her father?"

"A whole ton of shit that they need to work through."

"Well, boy, you got another session tomorrow, so how about a steak and an early night?"

"What?" Jake looked at his friend. "You not on the prowl tonight?"

"Nah, I'm giving you my undivided."

Jake watched as Ethan rotated his left shoulder joint.

"What's up with that?"

"It's been giving me trouble for a few days; I need to get it checked out. Hurt it throwing a curveball at Debronskie. Struck him out, though."

Scapular dysfunction, neurovascular compression, and inherent structural pathology in the glenohumeral joint, including the rotator cuff, labrum, and capsule.

Jake didn't try to push the dialogue running inside his head aside this time. Instead, he tested the words and found they didn't created as much panic as they usually did.

"Have to say, I'm honored about having your undivided attention, Tex."

"As you should be."

They ate and talked, and then he found himself in Ethan's spare room staring into the dark as he thought about Branna. Was she thinking about him? Had she read his text? Would she talk to him when he got back? Did she love him? Closing his eyes, he let the questions come and go in his head until finally sleep claimed him.

***

Branna drove back into Howling at two in the morning. She pulled up her driveway and saw the lights on in her house and the blue sedan parked in front of her barn. Sitting in the van, she contemplated her next move. Would people intent on scaring her have left their car in plain sight and the outside porch light on? Who did she know that drove a car that color? Was she about to walk in to a mess, would there be other cat body parts pinned somewhere?

Too tired to care, she grabbed her bag, and the sack of luckily non-perishable groceries that had been in the back of her van all day, and stomped onto the porch and opened the front door.

"What are you doing here?"

Her father sat in the chair beneath her mother's photo facing the door. On his knees rested his laptop; he wore glasses perched on the end of his nose, and she saw in a glance how tired he looked. Not that she cared.

"I couldn't be anywhere else after what you said to me before you left today. I had to be here, waiting for you."

"No," she wasn't angry now, she was done with that; she'd spent the day getting rid of that emotion. She'd cried and yelled as she'd driven, and now she was just tired. "You don't need to be here, now please leave."

He put down his laptop and regained his feet.

"I went back to the McBrides' and packed my things and came here. I can't go back there now."

"You're not staying here, Declan."

He winced as she used his name. Once, she would have called him dad.

"I am because someone is trying to scare you; Buster told me about it today."

You're dead, Buster Griffin.

"And Jake's left town, so I'm staying here."

"I can call Belle." *Where had Jake gone and when was he coming back?*

"I told her I was staying with you when she called. It's two in the morning now, Branna, your other friends will be sleeping."

"Fine, do what you want, I'm going to bed." She walked past him and slapped the grocery sack down in the kitchen. Maybe all her anger wasn't gone. Then she walked upstairs and slammed the door to her room.

The shower didn't settle her, nor climbing into a cold lonely bed without Jake. How could she sleep when someone was in her house, her father, also settling in for the night? Once, she would have joined him, settled down on his bed to talk about the day, but not now, not ever again.

Sleep came because she was exhausted, and when she woke her eyes felt heavy and gritty, but she was determined to get through the day as if her life had not just been turned on its head. Jake had left Howling, and her father was in her house. So much for coming here to find peace.

After her shower, she pulled on a singlet and cut-offs, and contemplated using the ladder outside her window, but thought better of it. This was her house, not his; he could leave because she was staying.

He was sitting on the porch with a coffee in one hand when she walked outside clutching hers. His hair was wet and he wore an old shirt that she remembered from when it was new, and jeans with rips in the knees. His long bare feet were resting on the hand rail.

"Morning."

She didn't know what to say to that, so she grunted, then walked off the porch to inspect her garden.

Part of her was struggling with being rude to him...the irrational part that had always been respectful around the man who had raised her. Yes, they'd spoken hateful words to each other when last they'd met, but this was different, he was being nice now, and although she was justified in ignoring him or even in being cold, she didn't like it, which made no sense at all.

"You should put in herbs."

"I don't know about herbs."

"I do."

Aren't you the lucky one then.

"I got work to do." Branna felt his eyes on her as she walked back inside. Grabbing a cookie, she poured coffee and made for her office, shutting the door behind her. After checking her emails and social media sites, Branna lost herself in the world of her imagination. Two hours later, she came back to reality. She was done with her first draft and happy with the finished result so far. Hoping Declan O'Donnell was no longer lurking in her house, she made her way through it to the kitchen. Pulling a bottle of water from the fridge, Branna took off the cap and drank deeply.

He wasn't in here; did that mean he'd gone? Heading out the front door, she walked around the house, stopping when she heard his voice.

"The soil has to be rich for the herbs to grow well, Mikey, so you need to fertilize it. But Branna's soil is good to plant in already, which makes our job easier."

They had their heads together, looking over a long narrow box that had appeared along the back edge of her garden. Beside them were plants, herbs, Branna corrected, which she guessed were going into the planter box.

"Hey, Mikey, you had food?"

His smile was sweet. "Hi, Branna, I like your dad!" The boy jumped up and raced over to give her a hug, which he always did now whenever he saw her. "I'm hungry."

"Now, there's a surprise," Branna brushed a kiss over his head. "I'll make you something. Releasing him without acknowledging her father, she went back inside.

She made sandwiches, and because he was there and because that inner moral dilemma was still raging, Branna made Declan O'Donnell food too. Loading the tray with food and a pitcher of juice, she went back outside and placed it on the ground beside them.

"Eat," she said. Her father looked at her, but said nothing. Instead, he dusted off his hands and took the sandwich Mikey held out to him.

"You going to help us plant your herbs, Branna?"

"Do you mind if I go back inside, Mikey? I have heaps of work to get through and a cake to bake before I head out tonight."

"Will it be all right if I say out here then?" His face was eager, but Branna could see he didn't want to disappoint her. She squashed the small petty jealousy that welled up inside her. Declan O'Donnell would not hurt the boy. In fact, he was good with children…it was just her he hadn't wanted around.

Mikey would gain a different kind of knowledge out here, an important kind that included the basics of beginning to understand about nature and things that could turn you into a competent adult, just like she had at the hands of the man watching them.

"Sure it will, and we'll catch up on the homework I have for you another time."

"I can help him with learning." Declan O'Donnell gave her a smile that once would have had her responding. Instead, she nodded.

"He's got the same IQ as me. Not sure if you know what that is, but—"

"One hundred twenty-eight."

Surprised that he remembered, she looked away and bussed Mikey on this head, then went inside and began to bake her Peach and Cornmeal upside down cake. She'd make a macaroni and cheese too; like her, her father had to eat, even if she didn't want him in her house.

The recipe wasn't hard to find, as it was headed, Book Club Cake, and underlined in red, twice.

"Let's hope I don't buckle under the weight of expectation, Georgie," Branna muttered, as she melted the butter in the skillet.

She thought about Jake as she sprinkled the sugar into the butter, wondering when he would come back, and if he would want to see her when he did. She missed him…it was that simple. He was part of her life now, and she wanted him back in it.

Maybe that was one of the reasons she came back to Howling. Because she'd known that she wouldn't be able to maintain that distance here, and because, finally, she needed to belong to somewhere and to someone again.

She'd felt something different with Jake McBride from the first day she came back to Howling. He'd challenged those barricades she'd erected, and then smashed straight through them, and this time Branna feared that if he turned away from her, she would never be able to pick up the pieces of her heart again.

Opening the oven, she slipped the pan inside, and set the timer.

"One day at a time, Branna," was what Belle used to say to her when she thought she would simply fold in on herself and disappear under the weight of grief. "Small, tiny steps, Bran, and I'll be here to help you take each one."

She owed Belle Smith more than simple friendship; she owed her for saving her life.

"I have to go now, Branna."

"Okay, Mikey, you want me to run you home?" He'd come into the kitchen and was sniffing the air like a bloodhound.

"I can ride; it's still light," he said, looking through the oven window at the cake. "What you making?"

"Peach and Cornmeal Upside Down Cake, I'll make you one if it works out okay."

His smile was wide in his dirt-streaked face.

She blew him a kiss before he raced out the door, and then she started to clean up her mess.

"He's a nice lad."

"Yes." Declan O'Donnell now stood in her kitchen doorway, effectively penning her inside.

"How's your writing going?"

She turned from the sink, soap suds dripping of the end of the brush she was using to clean the dishes. "How do you know about my writing?"

"I had someone look out for you when I couldn't. They kept me up to date on anything you did."

Branna felt the brush slip through her fingers and fall to the floor at his words.

"You are my daughter and I have always loved you, contrary to what you believe. There was no way I was leaving you alone and unprotected when I was unable to settle near you, so I found someone I could trust to do it for me."

She'd always believed she was alone, always believed that no one knew what she did and when; now it seemed that was not true.

"Did you ever wonder why your rent was so reasonable, Branna?"

Gripping the sink behind her, she tried to focus on what he was saying, tried to make sense of his words, but her head was suddenly a swirling mass of emotion.

"Those textbooks that suddenly got handed to you one day by a fellow student? The trip to Paris that was funded by an anonymous benefactor?"

"Th-that was you?"

"Yes," his face was calm, words spoken slowly. "And I'm not telling you to buy your gratitude; I'm telling you so you understand that even though you thought I had walked away from you, in fact, I hadn't. I used everything I had at my disposal to make sure you never had to struggle, never had to know hardship. It was the only thing I could do as your father, seeing as you wanted nothing else from me."

He stood in her kitchen doorway, dirt under his nails, smudges on his face, and blew everything she had believed about her life apart.

"You are my daughter, Branna O'Donnell. We share bloodlines, and once we shared love, and while I understand why you feel as you do about me, I am telling you from the depths of my soul and with the strength of your mother's love inside us, that you have always been my blessing and the one thing I had a hand in creating that makes each day worthwhile."

"No." The word was wrenched from her chest, but he didn't stop...he kept on talking in that calm clear voice.

"Yes. You were an extension of the love I felt for your mother, daughter. Her death plunged me into a hell that I had no idea how to drag myself out of, but know this, had you succeeded in taking your life that day, then I would have followed you, because losing her nearly destroyed me, but you..." Branna watched as he closed his eyes. "Losing you would have simply taken my will to live."

Branna turned back to the sink and closed her eyes, gripping the sink hard; she waited until his footsteps started on the stairs before she let the first tears fall. All these years, she'd believed one thing...only to find another. He'd watched over her, made sure she never went without, and all the time she'd thought he had no idea what was happening in her life. She remembered the things that used to happen to her, the small random acts that she could never account for, and now she realized they were him.

The timer went off, and drying her hands, she took the cake out, surprised to see it actually looked good when she was crumbling inside. Branna set it on the rack to cool, then made her way upstairs. She had to pull herself together before going to the Book Club. Find a way to lock the emotions back up inside her like she had always been able to do. But now, she wondered if the box was even big enough to fit them all.

By the time she'd showered and dressed, she felt calmer, at least on the outside. She would shelve thoughts of what her father's declaration meant until tomorrow. For now, Branna had to go to her first Book Club meeting. A book club? Seriously, what was she thinking? Smoothing down the skirt she'd chosen, Branna wondered if it was the right outfit to wear to Elizabeth Heath's house.

Looking in the mirror, she wondered how she looked the same as she had this morning, the same as a week ago, when inside she felt so different. She felt a sharp tug of longing for Jake. She wanted his strength, needed to feel his arms around her.

"You can do this, Branna; you managed before."

Pulling her shoulders back, she studied herself. Rose-colored, the dress was slim fitting with small sleeves and finished just above her knees. She'd added black sandals with a small heel. Her hair was piled on top of her head and fixed with a large clip, and to give her courage, she wore her mother's thin gold bracelet and hoop earrings. Her makeup was minimal, with a touch of rose-colored lip gloss.

Going back down the stairs, she found her father sitting with his laptop in the lounge.

"I made mac and cheese," Branna said, collecting up the cake tin and her bag, inside of which was the envelope and book she had to take. "I-it's in the oven on low."

"Thank you, Branna. Have a good evening."

The great secret, Eliza, is not having bad manners or good manners or any other particular sort of manners, but having the same manner for all human souls: in short, behaving as if you were in heaven, where there are no third class carriages, and one soul is as good as another.

Her father had often quoted George Bernard Shaw to her, but why it now played through her head, she had no idea. Maybe she was finally succumbing to the hysteria that had been bubbling inside her for days.

"Good night, Declan."

She left then, climbing into her van and backing around his rental car, then pulling out of the drive.

CHAPTER NINETEEN

Elizabeth Heath lived in a house not dissimilar to Buster's and as most of the houses in Howling were grouped in this area, they were not too far away from each other. Mrs Heath's home was white with sky blue trim, and the lawn looked as if it had been manicured. Parking on the road, Branna got out and collected her things, just as a large beige Cadillac pulled out of the garage and began to back slowly down the driveway. She waited for it to pass, but it stopped beside her and the window lowered slowly.

"Well now, Branna O'Donnell, it's my hope you're ready for those old biddies."

Bending, she looked in the window.

"Walt Heath, girl, it's a pleasure to finally make your acquaintance."

Juggling her cake, Branna managed to stick her hand through the window and shake the one he extended towards her. He had thick white hair that Santa Claus would give his eye teeth for, and neatly trimmed matching eyebrows beneath which sat soft brown eyes.

"Pleasure to meet you, Mr. Heath."

"Walt, girl, you just call me Walt, and you remember, Branna, not to take any of their crap. They'll boss you about something fierce if you let them, seeing as even the youngest in there has fifteen years on you."

Fifteen? Branna had thought at least thirty.

"Thanks, I'll give it my best shot, Walt."

"And don't offer to do stuff. Make them ask you," he added. "And any of them give you grief, you tell me about it, and I'll sort it."

"You think they will?" Branna didn't like the sound of that.

His smile flashed a stunning row of white teeth, and she wasn't sure if they were real or not.

"Count on it, but from what I hear about you, little girl, you're more than up to the challenge. Those biddies know it's time for new blood, Branna, especially if it comes with youth."

"Okay, and thanks for the vote of confidence."

"Anytime, girl, now you get on inside and make sure to save me a piece of that cake. I'm heading out for a few hours of peace at the Howling with some friends."

The door opened behind her as she watched Walt Heath drive off slowly down the street.

"Don't loiter, girl; we don't do that kind of thing in this neighbourhood."

Branna turned to find Henrietta Roberts-Haigh on the doorstep glaring at her.

Mother of God, this woman had terrified her in high school. She used to sweep through the halls of school, like a battleship with a small flotilla in her wake, usually the headmaster and some hapless members who were on her board. The students used to say, "Run, HRH is on the move!"

"Good evening Mrs. Roberts-Haigh."

She was big and raw-boned with short steel grey curls and eyes that matched.

"Henry will do fine," the woman said, holding out a hand to Branna as she approached. "And I'm glad to have you here, Branna O'Donnell."

"H-Henry." Branna took the hand, reeling from the knowledge that HRH was now Henry to her. She couldn't wait to tell Jake that one.

They entered the house, where everything was as neat as she'd expected it to be, right down to the signs telling people to take off their shoes and place them here, an arrow indicated the spot.

Slipping off her sandals lowered Branna a few inches, which put her at a disadvantage to the woman leading her into the room.

She had glimpses of cream walls and neatly arranged vases, and then they approached a dining room table, around which sat five women, all looking at her...some friendly, others weary, and one openly hostile. Surprisingly, Ellen Todd was there, Mikey's teacher. They'd not exactly hit it off well, but the woman was giving her a smile, nonetheless.

"I'll tell you right off, I'm not happy to have you here, girl! You're an outsider to Howling, and Georgie should have nominated a local."

"Oh, shut up, Millie Lawrence, nobody wants to hear your opinion!" Henry followed those words up with a slash of her right hand through the air. "You leave this girl alone. I, for one, am glad we have someone young to liven things up; we may finally get that trip away organized."

Trip?

"Just letting her know where I stand."

Millie Lawrence wasn't familiar to Branna. She had cropped red hair, sharp features, and eyes that were shooting angry barbs at her.

"Millie Lawrence, you were an outsider ten years ago, and we took you in, so you leave Branna alone." Doctor Nancy McBride got to her feet with these words and glided across the floor. She was a seriously beautiful woman. Blonde hair was pulled back from her face, and she wore a crisp white shirt and black Capri pants, belted at the waist with a twist of red leather.

"Hi, Doctor McBride." Branna was hugged, and then kissed on the cheek by the woman whose son had stolen her heart.

"Hello, Branna, now you come and sit between Ellen and me…we're the only ones who don't bite."

Three hours later, Branna waved goodbye to Lizzy, as Mrs. Heath was known by everyone in the Book Club, and got into her van. Her head was spinning with what she had learned tonight. She now knew that the town of Howling wasn't run by the council; it was run by the Book Club. The meeting had started out by talking about the book they'd all read, and Branna had been shocked rigid when Henry had mentioned the word penis, and then Lizzie had started discussing orgasms as if she was exchanging recipes.

"It takes a while, but you get used to it." These words had come from Ellen Todd, who had told her that she'd read up on

Mikey, and was sorry she hadn't done so before, but was now making sure he had enough challenging work to occupy his mind.

After the book discussion came the general business discussion, where they talked about extending the library and, heaven forbid, putting a skate ramp in at the park. Henry wanted to lower the speed limit on the main street, but Nancy had been against that.

Branna had sat and listened as they talked. These women were intelligent, strong, and all were intent on making Howling a city that moved with the times, but it was also important to each that it retain the heritage and roots that had formed it and had made it what it was today.

Pulling out onto the main street, Branna lowered her windows to let the cool breeze waft through. Mindful of Henry's wishes, she dropped her speed and crawled past the shops. The last item on the Book Club's agenda tonight had been her. She'd had to tell them about herself and what she'd done with her life, and surprisingly, she had told them...not everything, but most, finishing with her writing name. Everyone but Milly knew who she was, and Branna had promised signed copies of her latest release.

"I'll be reading them, girl, and I'll let you know what I think," Milly Lawrence had declared, to which Branna had replied she was looking forward to the feedback.

She'd sat there with those women and realized that this was where she belonged now. No matter what happened with her father or Jake, Howling was her home. These people had made it so; they'd pulled her into their lives. Mikey, Buster, Penny and Belle. The list was long, and each was now dear to Branna.

She needed to settle things with her father. He was living in her house, and she couldn't avoid him or what hung over them forever. The thought made her stomach roll. Branna had so many angry feelings towards Declan O'Donnell, and after what she had shared with him that day in Buster's café, she knew that when they got down to talking, it would be long and emotional. At the end of it, she had no idea if she and her father would have a relationship, or if he would leave and never come back, but it had to be dealt with for her to move forward.

Jake was another that she needed to talk to, be honest with, especially if they were to have any future together. Where was he? Would he back soon?

Looking out the window, Branna saw a flash of white by the drugstore. Slowing more, she heard something whimpering. Pulling into a parking spot, she listened again. It was soft and pitiful, like an animal in pain or a child crying. Looking around, she could see no one else on the street, and no car lights approaching. Her cell phone said it was eleven o'clock, so it was getting late for anyone to be out here, so it must be an animal.

Being an only child meant Branna had been schooled repeatedly on the dangers of being out alone at dark, and told never to approach strangers. Finding Belle's number, she got it ready in case she needed back up, then opened her door and got out.

"My name's Branna, and I'm not sure what you are, but I'm coming to see if you need my help."

"G-go h-home."

The voice was female, which relaxed her slightly, although the words were slurred, which told her that maybe whoever it was could be drunk or high on something.

"I'm coming closer."

"N-no."

She kept walking, lifting her cell phone to light the way down the narrow space between the drugstore and Mr. and Mrs. Parson's craft shop. Unlike Jake, she didn't have the flashlight app, and now wished to hell she'd downloaded it like he'd told her to.

"Go away, Branna."

The words were slowly spaced, as if saying them was an effort. Whoever this woman was, she knew Branna. She saw her then, legs curled under her body, arms wrapped around her waist.

"Macy?" Dropping to her knees, she reached out a hand, but the woman winced.

"He'll come soon, and if he finds you, he'll hurt you," the words were a furious whisper.

Her eyes were wide, face wet with tears, a bruise was forming on her chin, and she was a mess. Her hair was everywhere and her makeup was smeared over her cheeks.

"You need me to take you to see Doctor McBride, Macy?"

"No!"

"Okay, no doctor then," Branna soothed, as Macy looked terrified. "But, you have to know I'm not leaving you here alone, don't you, Macy?"

"He'll c-come and find me s-soon."

"Then we need to get out of here before he does. Will you let me help you to my van?" Branna didn't wait for consent; instead, slipping an arm under Macy's shoulder, she helped her to her feet. "Can you walk?"

"I-I think so. But we have to h-hurry, and you can't tell anyone."

"All right, Macy, we'll do whatever you want," Branna soothed, as she half-carried the woman to her van, then opening the passenger side, she helped her in. Closing the door, she ran around the front and got in the driver's side.

"I-I'm going to hide on the fl-floor. Drive slow, and w-wave if you see anyone, like you're just going h-home."

"Okay," Branna heard Macy suck in a breath as she crouched on the floor so no one could see her. Her teeth were chattering, so Branna put on the heater.

What the hell was happening? Where was Brian? Surely he wasn't responsible for the state of his wife...was he?

"I s-see lights!"

"It's a white sedan, Macy." Branna lifted her hand and waved as the car passed her by. She didn't see who was driving it, because it was too dark and because she didn't want to make it obvious she was looking.

"Th-that's him."

"Brian?"

Macy didn't answer, just started sobbing softly into the edge of the seat she huddled against.

"Did he do this to you?"

"D-don't ask me...pl-please, Branna, just help me."

It was a cry for help, and just like Belle had done for her all those years ago, she would do it now for Macy.

***

Jake's cell beeped, and noting the caller ID, he put down the gaming control and answered it.

"Buster, you missing me?"

Jake listened as his friend spoke, the smile falling from his face as the conversation progressed. "You heard it all?"

Jake ran his hand through his hair as Buster confirmed the details of the conversation he'd overheard between Branna and her father.

"Did you believe she meant it, Buster, to take her life like that? Jesus," Jake felt sick as Buster confirmed that he thought Branna had been serious. "Why the hell did you let her leave town after she and Declan had talked?"

Ethan raised and lowered his hand to calm Jake down from his horizontal position on the sofa, gaming control in the other hand.

"Okay, so maybe you should have told me that she came back again first," Jake added, feeling the air rush back into his lungs. "He's what!" Jake roared into the phone seconds later. "He's moved into her house! The bastard, what he's playing at? I'm coming home at first light." Disconnecting the phone, Jake jammed it into his pocket.

"I'm picking up that all is not rosy in Oz, Dorothy?" Ethan put down the remote and got off the sofa to switch off the T.V.

"Branna and her father had it out in The Hoot, and Buster said he's still recovering, so he has no idea how she's feeling. He then said she left town, and when she came back, he'd moved in."

"Buster?"

"Declan O'Donnell, you idiot!"

"Gotcha. So I guess we're leaving at first light?"

"You okay with that? If not, I can hire a car or something, but I have to get back to her now; she'll be spinning out about this, Eth, having him there living with her."

"I'm off for a few days, what better place to spend it than in my second favorite town?"

Ethan wandered to the fridge in his apartment and pulled a couple of beers from it; handing one to Jake, he sat back down.

Jake could imagine the hell Branna was going through at the moment, and he felt like a selfish bastard for leaving her so suddenly now. A text was all he'd sent her, and he had owed her more, because she was the woman in his life, the woman he cared about…very much.

"Me or Buster for best man?"

Jake's smile was brief before he swallowed a mouthful of beer.

"Hard call to make, it has to be said. Buster has history on his side, and you…well, you saved my life."

Ethan looked at him briefly.

"I never really thanked you, Ethan, for what you did. I know what I was like and that you kept everyone away until I was ready. I know that you've stood by me when I probably deserved that you walk away."

"Jake, if we're gonna have this moment, let's make it brief, because I can feel the rash already forming. But if we're sharing shit, then I have to be honest and say it's me that owes you."

"How so?"

"I never had a real friend until you came along, and with you came the domestic goddess of Howling, who I count as my second best friend. Before that, I was pretty much a loner...now, not so much. I got you and the town of Howling. It's a win-win as far as I can tell."

Jake didn't know much about Ethan's past. He knew he had obscene amounts of money and three siblings. His parents lived in Kerrville, Texas, and that was about it.

"One day, you have tell me about you, Tex?" He saw something pass over his friend's face, and then it was gone.

"Maybe, when I've downed a bottle of something potent and sliced open a vein."

"That bad?"

"Worse."

"Okay then, well, my ears are yours when you need them, and FYI, Howling has adopted you, so it's too late to pull back."

"They can do that?"

"Can and will. Branna and her dad are in, but that's because they're famous, and we're pretty shallow when it comes to that kind of thing."

"It's gonna be hard to see them together. I'm not going to lie about it, McBride. They're both superstars in my book, and I have a serious case of hero worship going on."

Jake just rolled his eyes.

"Anyway, I'll try not to embarrass you by gushing, okay? I'll play it cool and stuff, now that we're all citizens of Howling, that is."

"The head doctor said I need to express my feelings more, let out the angst and let people see the real me," Jake said.

"Yeah, well don't go crying next, or I'm out, no matter who your girlfriend and future father-in-law are."

"Not my thing, all that emotional sharing stuff, but it has to be said that I need to be a bit more open with mum and dad, and definitely Branna, and maybe Buster. But, you know how he is, Ethan, the goddess never shuts up, hard to get a word in at the best of times."

"Well, fuck, Jake, the man bakes for a living, hardly surprising he's made of Jell-O, is it?"

"Who we kidding? Buster Griffin makes us look like Oprah. The man never uses two words when one will suffice," Jake said.

"There you go with those big words again, McBride."

"I'm going to call Branna," Jake pulled out his cell phone and punched in the numbers. He listened as it rang, and then he heard her voice on the answer phone.

"Branna, I'm coming home in the morning early…" *What the hell else should he say?* "I love you." Ending the call, he shoved it back in his pocket. Jake then got to his feet, ignoring the wide smile on Ethan's face, and headed for the bathroom. Once there, he washed up and cleaned his teeth and thought about Branna. He felt on edge suddenly, as if his hair was all standing on end and he had no idea why.

After the day he'd just had, it was possible this was just the after-effects of baring his soul, but something uneasy was settling in his stomach. Getting out his phone again, he called Branna, and there was still no answer. This time, he asked her to call him when she got the message, and made an apology for the way he'd left suddenly.

Saying goodnight to Ethan, he then got into his bed and lay there for long hours, staring into the dark. So much had changed since Branna had come to Howling, and there was still so much change to go. He knew that now, understood that he needed to continue seeing the psychiatrist to ensure he was whole again. Branna deserved the best of him, just as his family and friends did, just as he did.

When his eyes began to close, he tried Branna one last time, but still no answer. Sleep began to pull him under, and his last thought was for the woman he loved. The woman he would one day marry, if she'd have him, the woman whom God-willing he would have a family with. The soft smile on his lips was for her as sleep finally claimed him.

Chapter Twenty

Branna pulled the van as close to the house as she could. The lights were still on, which meant her father was up.

"Macy, my father's here, but he won't say anything to anyone; I promise. He-he's a good person, okay?"

"A-are we hidden here? Can any passing cars see us?" Macy slowly pulled herself back up on the seat, every movement causing her pain.

"No one can see the house or van from the road, Macy, I promise." Branna jumped out after these words and ran around to the passenger's door and opened it. "I'm going to help you out now; you lean on me as much as you need."

Macy yelped in pain as she swung her legs towards the ground, and Branna winced as she tried to slide off the seat.

"Branna?"

"Come quick, Dad! I need your help."

"What's happened, love?" He was at her side in seconds, his hand warm on her back.

"Sh-she's hurt. I know Macy from school, and I found her like this."

"You need to stand back now, Branna, and let me get her out of there. Can you do that for me?"

Branna moved to the side, still clenching Macy's hand.

"Macy, I'm Branna's father, Declan O'Donnell, and I'm going to get you inside so we can take a look at you, would that be all right?"

"I…I don't want you touching me," the words were whispered, but both Branna and her father heard them clearly.

"Macy, I know you have no reason to trust me, but I'm going to ask you to try," Declan O'Donnell said gently.

Macy was biting her lip hard, but she managed to nod. Branna watched then, as her father slipped his arms under her legs and lifted her. They both winced as Macy inhaled sharply in pain.

"Go clear the sofa of my things, Branna, so I can put her there for now," Declan O'Donnell said, as he moved slowly towards the house.

She tried to let go of Macy's hand, but the woman held onto it with a surprisingly strong grip.

"N-no phone calls to anyone, Branna. Promise me!" The hysteria was close, each word pitched with fear.

"I promise." Macy released her then, and Branna ran inside. Once Branna had moved everything off the sofa, her father arrived seconds later and lowered Macy onto the cushions, which made her moan again.

This was the first real look Branna had of Macy, and she had to swallow the instinctive cry that rose in her throat. Declan rose to his feet, and Branna took his place.

Macy's jaw was almost black now, the bruise vivid in her pale face, and there were others forming too, and a cut to her forehead that oozed blood. Her shirt was ripped and exposed the pink satin of her bra. She was shaking violently, her body almost convulsing with fear and pain. Pulling the throw off the back of the sofa, Branna quickly wrapped it around Macy and kept her arms there, holding the woman as close as her injuries allowed, giving whatever comfort she could.

"I'll make some tea, but first you tell me where the first aid kit is, daughter, and then I'll bring you some water to wash her."

"Under the sink, and bring more blankets and pillows."

He went then, and she was relieved to have him here. No matter what lay between them, he would help her care for Macy, because she hadn't lied, he was a good man, even in her angriest moments she'd known that.

"Br-Branna," the first sob was pitiful as Macy gripped the front of her dress, her hands clenching in the fabric as Branna held her. Belle had done this for her once, and she still remembered how it had felt, the relief that she wasn't alone, and that someone actually cared whether she lived or died.

"Shhh now, it's safe; you are here with us." Branna rested her hip beside Macy's and rested her head on her cheek. "We won't let anyone hurt you again."

Macy's cries were soft and heartfelt, and came from that place deep inside that was shattered. Branna felt her father's hand on her head, and then he placed another blanket over the shaking woman in her arms.

"I'll make the tea now."

Macy cried until her tears became sniffs, and then finally, on a deep shuddering breath, she stopped.

"She needs to drink this now, love," Declan said gently when he returned.

Branna eased back and used the edge of the blanket to wipe Macy's tears.

"Can you drink on your own, Macy?"

"Yes."

Declan handed her the cup, and she wrapped both hands around it and took a small sip. Branna knelt beside her and picked up her own drink, while Declan pulled a footstool close to her side. They all then sat and drank in silence, she and her father watching Macy. It was he who spoke first.

"My worry for you, lass, is that you're hurt and we can't see how badly. Will you tell us of your pain, so it will ease my mind?"

Macy lowered her cup and looked at them. "I shouldn't have come here. Th-this is my problem and one I can d-deal with alone. I can't involve you both."

"I fear tis too late for that, Macy, and more than time for you to stop whatever this is." Branna let her father talk, let his deep voice draw what needed to be drawn from Macy. One thing Branna knew was that she would never let her go back to whoever had done this to her. She had found her tonight, and while she had no idea what it was she was dealing with, she had the terrible feeling that Macy had been suffering quietly for a long time.

"I-I c-can't, don't you see? H-he'll kill me if he knows I'm here." Her face was white and fear filled her eyes. "He's crazy."

"He being, Brian, your husband?" Branna asked gently, trying to get her head around the fact that the mild mannered man they all knew had the entire town of Howling fooled.

Macy looked away from her. "H-he didn't mean it. He just g-gets angry and frustrated sometimes."

"I've always believed that a man who strikes a woman is not a man at all, Macy. He is a coward and a bully. That a man would touch a woman in anger, when his strength often is twice hers is, in my opinion, unforgivable."

Her face crumpled at the words Branna's father had spoken.

"It takes a strong brave woman to stand up against such a man, Macy, a strong brave woman with someone at her back. Will you allow Branna and me to have yours?"

"H-he tried to kill my b-baby."

"Dear God!" Branna felt her father's arm around her shoulders as she reached out to take Macy's hand.

"H-he's not the man you all know."

"And this baby you carry, Macy, does it deserve to live with such a man?"

Her eyes were big as she looked up at Declan O'Donnell. "No," she shook her head. "I want this one to live."

Branna must have made a noise, because she felt her father pull her close briefly and she accepted the comfort, too shocked to pull away. Macy had lost other babies at the hands of the monster she was married to. Dear God, she couldn't get her head around it. Why had no one noticed what was going on in this woman's life?

"I want you to take these now, Macy. They won't hurt the baby, but will help with the pain and sleep."

Like a small child, she did as he asked her, opening her mouth and swallowing the pills. Between them, she and her father then cleaned Macy and put a bandage on her cut. He then picked her up again and they went upstairs.

"I'll leave you to Branna's care now, Macy, but if you need me, just call and I shall hear."

She nodded and managed to whisper thank you, and then the door was closed, leaving Branna and Macy alone.

"H-he's a nice man."

"He is. Now, do you want a shower or just a wash before you get into bed?" Branna asked.

"Shower."

She walked like an old woman, but when Branna asked if she was in pain, she just said that her tummy was fine and that the baby was unharmed.

"Brian will be looking for me, Br-Branna. He'll get angry when he doesn't find me."

She was terrified, her fingers twisting into each other.

"Macy, he has no idea you are here with me. Furthermore, he thinks we hate each other, so why would you come here?" Turning on the taps, Branna made sure the temperature was right before she turned back to Macy. "Now, let's get your clothes off."

She didn't leave, because in all honesty, Branna feared Macy may faint and she wouldn't know. She unbuttoned the ripped cotton, and then eased if from her shoulders.

"Dear God, he did this to you?" Branna said, horrified, as she looked at the bruises, old and new she realized. They covered her body.

"I deserved s-some of them."

"No!" Macy flinched at Branna's anger. "You did nothing to deserve these, Macy Reynolds. Nothing, do you hear me?"

"You're sh-shouting; of course I can hear you."

Branna cried then, hot angry tears as she pulled the skirt and torn underwear from Macy's body.

"Don't cry for m-me, Branna. I'm not worth it." The sadness in the words made Branna cry harder.

"You are worth a million of that man, Macy, a million of me and everyone else I know. You're strong and beautiful. Do you know what?"

"What?"

"He's never getting his hands on you again."

"D-don't promise me that, Branna, not that, because I don't think he'll let me go."

"And neither will I." Branna sniffed loudly, and then helped her into the shower.

"We won't talk about it anymore tonight. Tomorrow is soon enough."

She stood there and waited for Macy to finish her shower, and what emerged was a woman she had never seen before. Without makeup, Macy was completely different, even with the bruises. She was so small. Branna had always thought of this woman as strong and larger than life, but she wasn't. In fact, she was tiny, and her features were delicate.

She helped to pat her dry gently, and then lowered a loose T-shirt over her head.

"Come on, let's get you into bed before you fall over and I have to pick you up."

Branna pulled the covers back and Macy slipped beneath.

"Branna?"

"Yes."

"W-would you stay with me for awhile?"

"Of course." Knowing the pride this woman had and how much those words had cost her, Branna climbed on the bed beside her and took one of her hands.

"Tell me about your book."

So she did, explaining the plot and telling her about scenes she'd created. She talked and talked until finally the fingers inside hers relaxed and Macy slept. Pulling the covers up to her chin, Branna looked down at the bruised and battered woman.

You will not touch her again, Brian Reynolds. It was a vow, and she would do whatever needed to be done to ensure she kept it.

Branna left the room, leaving the door ajar slightly, she washed in the bathroom and cleaned her teeth, and changed into one of the old T-shirts she slept in. Then, pulling on her robe, she made her way downstairs to the couch. "She sleeps?"

He was sitting in the chair, the cups and things now put away, blankets and pillows neatly folded on the sofa.

"Yes."

"You called me dad tonight."

"Did I?" Branna went to the sofa and unfolded the blankets.

"That was my shirt."

"Was it?" Branna was too tired to deny it.

"I'll sleep there, Branna, you take the other bed."

"I'm all right here." She went to lie down, but his hands stopped her.

"If you think I will leave you down here alone, with her husband out there somewhere looking for her, and with what has already happened to you, then think again, daughter.

"I don't need you protecting me."

"Now, that's just too bad, because I will."

Branna felt the anger inside her slip away to be replaced by a weariness that made her slump onto the sofa. It was all too much for a girl who, until recently, would have walked miles over hot coals to avoid any emotional entanglements. All these people dragging emotion from the block of ice that had, until recently, been her heart was getting to be more than she could handle.

"I can't take much more of this." Leaning back, she rested her head and closed her eyes.

"I'm sorry, love, sorry that I'm causing you this pain, but I'm not going away, neither I suspect is Jake, or for that matter, Macy. It's my belief that she will be around for awhile and need us both to hold her up."

"The bruises, Dad, they were all over her body, some old some new. He's been beating her for years, and no one knew. She just caked on her makeup, put on her high heels, and faced the world each day, knowing that when she shut herself back inside her house at night, she was once again in the hands of that monster."

"Do you want more tea?"

"Whisky, I think." Branna went to rise, but he placed a hand on her head.

"I'll get it; tell me where it is."

"Kitchen cupboard, top left."

Had she forgiven him? No, it would take time for that. Did she want him back in her life? Branna tested those words in her tired mind and realized she did. The door was open again, and she was letting people in. But forgiveness would take time.

"Here."

She took the glass he handed her and watched him drag the chair across the room and place it before her.

"Here's the thing, daughter." He sat and cradled the glass between his long fingers. "I'm not leaving you again, so you can live your life apart from mine, and I will respect that, but I will stay here, Branna, never doubt that. I know it's hard for you to forgive me, but if you will just try, love, please."

She looked down into the amber liquid as he spoke; she heard the pain in his words now that she allowed herself to. "I'm just scared because I don't want to ever hurt like that again, and now it's not just you that has that power over me, Dad; Jake does too."

"And you think we'll both hurt you?"

"No," she looked up at him, daring to hope. "I know he wouldn't, and I want to believe you won't again."

"Sweetheart," he lowered his glass to the floor and she noticed his hands shook. "I can only promise you again and again that I won't, but if you don't believe me, then I can do no more."

"What will we do for her, Dad? Macy is hurting, and I don't know how to go about fixing her, fixing the mess that is about to unfold around her."

He understood that she didn't want to talk about them anymore. Picking up his glass, he took another mouthful, sighing as the liquid burned its way down.

"We take it in small steps, love. When she wakes, we give her breakfast, and then we talk to her. She will have to tell someone she's safe, maybe her parents? But she doesn't have to give away her location if she doesn't want to, and we can keep that a secret, and for now we will just keep her here, out of the hands of that monster."

"Jake will know because I can't keep this from him." Branna wanted him so much right at the moment, needed his strength and his wisdom, but most of all, she wanted him to hold her.

"Go to sleep now, Branna, and I'll watch over us."

She struggled to her feet and let her father brush a kiss on her forehead before she stumbled up the stairs and fell into his bed.

CHAPTER
TWENTY ONE

Jake and Ethan arrived back in Howling as the sun rose. They covered his helicopter and made their way into the house.

"You going to Branna's now, Jake?"

"Yeah, I'll just wash and change, then head over."

"Pretty early, bud," the Texan said, as he put on the coffee.

"I need to see her." Was all Jake added, and twenty minutes later, he was walking out the door. Ethan had already disappeared into one of the spare rooms and would be asleep.

Jumping into his pickup, he made his way out the driveway and drove along the lake. This early, the sun was coloring the water as it rose, and all around him Jake could see the signs of a day about to begin. Pulling into Branna's drive a few minutes later, he stopped the pickup behind her van, which was parked close to the house. Relieved that she appeared to be here, along with her father, his rental was parked too, Jake then headed for the front door and knocked. He heard footsteps, then the door was opened, to reveal Declan O'Donnell.

"Jake."

"Mr. O'Donnell." He stepped inside when the man stepped back to allow him room. "Is Branna awake?"

"She's not, but I thought I heard her stirring. If you'll tell her breakfast will be ready soon, I'll put on some more for you."

What was Jake meant to say to that? He'd come here ready to have it out with this man, get him out of the house and away from Branna if she wanted him gone, and here he was telling Jake to go and get his daughter from her room, so they could all eat breakfast together.

"Ah, sure."

"She's in the spare room because we have a guest."

"You do?"

"I'll let Branna fill you in on the details."

Jake watched Declan O'Donnell make his way back to the kitchen before heading up the stairs. Knocking on the door, he then turned the handle. She was lying on her front, hands flat under the pillow on either side of her head. The covers had ridden to her waist and her shirt was tangled around her ribs, showing him the line of her vertebra that disappeared into her blue panties. He couldn't see her face, even though it was turned his way, as her hair was covering it. She slept deeply, her breathing even, body still. He just stood there, drinking in the sight of her. Jake felt the pain of longing in his chest, the need to hold her, press his lips to hers, trail his hands up her back and cup her neck. This woman was his future; she now controlled his happiness. With her, he wanted a family and roots of his own. The darkness that had settled over him for so long was lifting, and it was due to her, his prickly, belligerent Irish woman who was kind, honest, and had a beautiful soul.

"Hey, Rosebud." He reached out to brush aside her hair as she stirred. Bending, he then kissed her cheek as she came awake, her sleepy green eyes widening as she realized he stood beside her bed.

"Jake?"

"You been entertaining anyone else in here? Because, I have to say, that would really piss me off."

"Why are you in my room?" She pushed herself upright, rubbing her hands over her eyes. "What time is it?"

"Early." She didn't fight him when he pulled back the covers and picked her up. He carried her to the chair under the window. Sitting, he slipped one hand under the hem of her shirt, skimming the warm soft curves of her body as he kissed her.

"I'm sorry, baby; I never meant to hurt you."

"Me either, and I'm sorry too." She settled into him, her chin under his, one of her palms flat on his chest.

"I've been to Brook with Ethan to see a shrink. I've had two sessions, but I need more. He pulled stuff out of me that I didn't even know was in there." She listened as he spoke, her hand rubbing circles over his chest as he told her everything that needed to be said, and he felt calm for the first time since he'd left her.

"Do you feel better for talking to him?"

"Yeah, I think so, but I'm not sure I'm ready to practice medicine yet."

She tilted her head back, resting it on his shoulder, her green eyes studying him. "It wasn't about you being a doctor, Jake; it was about you making the decision not to be because you could, not based on what had happened to you."

"I think that makes sense." He kissed her again, soft and lingering.

"I wish your father wasn't downstairs."

"Me too," Branna sighed."

"How's that working for you?"

"He's talked at me for two days, and I've listened and tried to understand, and then last night everything changed."

"How?" Jake felt her tense, saw as she remembered something that she didn't want to.

"I went to the Book Club."

"How'd the cake go down?"

"Good," she waved a hand in his face. "It was weird and kind of cool, but I'll tell you about that some other time. Right now, I have to tell you something else."

"Okay."

"I need you to promise me you won't tell anyone else, Jake."

"Okay." Jake rubbed a finger down the line that had appeared between her eyes.

She told him the events of last night, finishing with the fact that Macy was now sleeping in her bedroom.

"Brian?" Jake couldn't get his head around that. "Brian Delray has been beating Macy for years. She's miscarried at his hands?"

"You don't believe me, do you?" She tried to get off him as he spoke, but Jake held her there.

"I'm not saying I don't believe you, Rosebud, but give me a minute here, all right? It's just going to take a bit to process something like that."

"I shouldn't have told you, but I thought you needed to know, and that you would help us keep her safe." He saw she was genuinely worried, and that just pissed him off...that she would think he was a threat to Macy.

"You think I would betray a woman who is being beaten, to the man who's responsible?"

"No!" Her reply was instant and made him happier. "I just don't know where to go from here, Jake. Brian is a popular man in Howling, and when it gets out what he's done, I'm sure there will be some people who won't believe Macy."

"Because she's never shown us what he's capable of until now?"

"Yes, but, Jake, if you could see the bruises on her that I saw last night, some old some new, you'd feel as bad as I did. I just stood there and cried, and do you know what she said?"

"What?" He had a really sick feeling in his stomach now, at the thought of Macy suffering and none of them realizing it.

"That she deserved some of them."

He whistled softly. "I'm going to have a little chat with Mr. Delray when the time comes, and explain how a lady should really be treated."

"You believe me then?"

"Of course. If you say it's true because you believe her, then it is." And it was that simple to him.

"Oh...oh dear." She pressed a hand to her mouth and tried to get off his lap again.

"You going to cry?" He wrapped his arms around her tight.

"No...maybe. It's all the emotion; I'm not used to it."

"Here's some more for you," he said to the top of her head. "I love you."

"What?"

"I'm sure you heard me."

"I love you too."

"You don't sound too happy about that, sweetheart."

She chewed her lip. "I am; it's just that I'm not used to it anymore."

"It, being love?"

"Love, friendship, emotion, they're very tiring. People always smiling at me or asking after me. Last night I made more friends, more relationships to juggle. Even Mr. Heath told me that I could go to him if the Book Club ladies gave me any angst."

He smiled into her hair. His town was folding her into their ranks slowly, molding her into one of them.

"Millie Lawrence doesn't like me, though."

"Millie Lawrence doesn't even like her own kids, Rosebud; don't take it to heart."

She sat upright and looked at him. "Okay, you all win; I give up. I'm now a Howler."

"That's the spirit."

"And if you ever just fly off in that helicopter without telling me where you are going or when you will return again, I will not be accountable for my actions, Jake McBride. You got that?"

"Got it."

She braced her hands on his chest and kissed him, soft and sweet and way too brief; he felt it to the edges of his heart.

"I never wanted to love someone so much that just seeing them walk into room makes something ache inside me. I didn't want to have my happiness reliant on another person ever again, but you've done that to me, McBride, and I'm sure I should be really pissed with you, but all I can think is that you're mine and I'm yours and I always want it to be that way."

"You must be a writer to have those words at your disposal." Jake slipped his hand under her hair. "And if I say ditto, will that be an okay response? Because there's no way in hell I can compete with you."

"Yes."

He held her and kissed her until he had to lift her off his body or take her back to bed.

"We need to go downstairs now, Rosebud, before your father comes looking for us."

"Okay."

Jake was happy that she sounded as frustrated as him. He watched as she pulled on a shirt of her father's that reached her knees, then rolled the sleeves five times.

"You're one sexy woman, Branna O'Donnell."

"Okay, sure, now let's get out of here before I jump you."

Jake's eyes crossed at the thought of her sitting on him. "Give me a minute here." Adjusting his jeans, he thought about his grandmother, who was at present sailing the med, and felt himself begin to calm.

"Right, get moving," patting her backside, he followed her out and down the stairs.

Declan, Branna, and Jake sat around the table drinking coffee and discussing Macy in hushed voices. They decided it was best to take things slow and work out what to do with her, instead of for her.

"She'll want to go back to him at first. He will have brainwashed her into making her believe that she's to blame, and that combined with the fear of both him and exposure to the town, will make her want to go back," Jake said.

"We can't let her go back."

"I know that, baby, but I'm telling you what she's going to say."

"It will be hard in a small town," Declan added.

Jake looked at him and nodded. "And she's going to need strength that she probably doesn't even know she has right now."

"Morning."

Jake stood as Macy appeared in the doorway. He hadn't seen her without makeup, six-inch heels and expensive clothes for years, and he'd forgotten how small she was...fine boned. She looked like a child standing there in Branna's robe. He took in the bruises on her face and the wounded expression in her eyes, and wondered why he hadn't looked closer over the years.

"Morning, Miss Macy," Jake said, forcing himself to smile at her, when inside he was angry as hell.

"Come sit down beside me, Macy, and I'll get you some coffee and toast." Branna pulled out a chair and motioned her into it. She hesitated, and then did as Branna asked.

"Would you be able to take me home soon, Branna? Brian will worry about me if I'm not there to make his breakfast."

"No, Macy, you're not going home."

"Why, Jake?" She looked genuinely confused at his words.

"Because Brian has been abusing you, and you're pregnant, and it's my understanding that you don't want to lose this child like you have the others."

Her face broke, she lowered it to Branna's shoulder and began to cry, silent tears that made her shoulders shake. Branna held her, speaking softly, and Jake and Declan stayed where they were, very aware that the last thing she wanted at the moment was support from a man.

They talked to Macy gently, asked questions until the story of her life at the hands of Brian Delray began to unfold. Declan was gentle; Jake was insistent, but gentle, and Branna was the rock Macy had tethered herself to.

He asked her questions about her pregnancy and the state her body was in. Was she experiencing pain anywhere? Did she have nausea, any bleeding? Jake's training came back as he questioned her, trying to work out what she would need from a medical standpoint. His mother needed to check her out, as he was sure she wouldn't want a man touching her, but that would come, just not today. He would get her something to help her sleep, because at the moment that was the best he could do for her and the baby.

It was Branna who told Macy that Cubby would need to be involved, and when she finally agreed, the sheriff arrived twenty minutes after Jake phoned him.

"You got a full house now, Branna?" Cubby wandered in, dressed in an old pair of shorts and a T-shirt. Jake had told him to come out of uniform and that they had Macy here and that Brian had been abusing her. He'd heard the hiss of his friend's breath down the line, but nothing more was added, only. "Be there soon."

"I'm a social sort of person, Cubby, you know that."

Branna was sitting with Macy at the table still, and Jake could see the stress in his girl. She was torn between rage and pity. Like him, she wanted retribution for the broken woman who had lived the horror she had for so long. Her smile was strained, and Jake wanted to wrap her in his arms and tell her how proud he was of her for handling everything the way she was. First her father, now Macy, and then the small matter of someone threatening her.

"Sure you are, never met anyone who likes people as much as you, all that soft mushy stuff you're always spouting tears me up."

Macy was watching the sheriff as he moved to take the seat across from her. Declan took one end of the table and Jake the other, closest to Branna. Taking her hand, he rested it on his thigh and threaded their fingers.

"Hey there, Macy, hear you're having a few problems?"

"This was a mistake, Cubby. I-I need to go home now."

"Here's the thing, Macy," the sheriff said in his calm voice. "I heard that Brian has been abusing you and that you're carrying a baby. Now, it seems to me that as there's another life besides yours involved, that you shouldn't think about going back to a man who has no respect for either of you."

"Y-you don't understand what he's capable of, Cubby!" Macy cried.

"Macy, you need to calm down now," Branna said, placing her hands over the ones Macy had clenched on top of the table. "You know you can't go back to him, you know it inside you. Yes, you're scared, and from what you've told me, you have every right to be, but it has to stop now, right here."

"Macy," Jake drew her eyes. "There are four people here in this room who will now watch over you. Four people who will do everything we can to keep you safe, and you know as well as me that there are plenty more like us in this town. This has to be stopped now, Macy, before Brian kills you and the baby."

Jake had no idea if Brian would get to that point, but from what Branna had told him, the beatings must have been bad.

"Wh-what should I do?" she whispered a few minutes later, to the relief of everyone.

CHAPTER
TWENTY TWO

Cubby had gone to arrest Brian Delray after he'd left Macy at Branna's, but he'd gone, apparently fleeing Howling sometime during the night. That he'd left in a hurry was obvious by the mess the sheriff found. Clothes were scattered around the bedroom, and papers in the office. After a thorough search, they found an envelope tucked down the back of a cabinet that Cubby reckoned Brian must have forgotten about, or lost. Inside it was a document that incriminated Delray, and gave Cubby more than enough, along with his treatment of his wife, to put the man away for many years.

"Seems he wanted Branna's land to build some kind of housing development on. Had people lined up and plans drawn up. He wanted to put Howling on the map, from what I gather." Cubby scratched his head as he looked at Jake.

Jake had called in to see Cubby and hear the news firsthand after the sheriff had called him. He'd left Declan at home with Macy and Branna, and he'd be home before it got dark. Because, even though the sheriff had assured him Delray had left Howling, Jake was taking no chances until the man was caught. Branna and Macy would be safe; he'd ensure it.

"I've put an APB out for the authorities to pick Brian up, and I'm hoping that won't take too long, because he's not exactly a man to hide out in the woods, if you know what I mean."

"I'd like a crack at him," Jake said.

Cubby nodded. "Wouldn't mind putting a pair of cuffs on him myself, and then watch him trip over and bang his head on something."

"We'll keep Macy with us until he's found," Jake added, as he climbed to his feet and headed for the door. "Mum's just left after checking her over. Both she and the baby are doing okay."

"Still can't believe it, Jake."

"Yeah, it messes with your head if you think about it too much."

"Hard not to."

Lifting his hand, he headed for The Hoot. It was getting late, but Buster was still there preparing stuff for tomorrow, and Jake had the idea of taking home a few muffins for his girl and Macy.

***

"You're cheating."

Macy laughed. "No, you're just really bad at cards."

Branna rolled her eyes and began to shuffle again. Her father was outside in the shed doing something, and she and Macy were playing cards in the lounge. Branna was on the floor, Macy sitting on the couch.

Jake had gone to town after taking a phone call from Cubby, and Branna was sure he was getting all the latest information on

Brian Delray. He'd promised to return before it got dark, and even though they had her father here, she'd feel better with Jake in the house too.

Jake had told her that Macy's husband had left Howling, but she was still nervous that he may try to come for his wife.

"Thank you, Branna."

What did she say to that, when she knew that what Macy was thanking her for was not the hand of cards Branna had just dealt her?

"Just look after you and the baby, and that will be all the thanks I need, Macy."

"I will, I promise."

Macy looked worn out and bruised, but Branna thought her eyes looked clearer, and she wondered if it was hope that she could see in them, and maybe relief.

"As soon as Dad and Jake get back, I'll make us some hot chocolate, it's better for you and the baby," Branna said, dealing the cards again.

"Brian hated hot chocolate," Macy said, picking up her cards.

"All the more reason to drink lots of it now," Branna added, picking up her hand.

"Doctor McBride said I will be tired for a while, and that rest and eating good healthy food is really important."

"Did she say how far along you were?" Branna asked.

"About thirteen weeks."

"What a shame you won't be going full term, wife."

Both women froze at Brian Reynolds' words. He stood in the hallway, and Branna realized he must have come in through the back door. In his hands was a gun, and it was pointed at Macy.

"You bitch," he said, pointing to Branna, "Get over here so I can tie you up before I teach my wife a lesson."

"Brian, no," the anguish in Macy's voice made Branna move to stand before her.

"You can't honestly believe you can get away with this, Brian? People know what you are now; you can't live in this town anymore," Branna reached behind her and grabbed a handful of Macy's robe to stop her from moving.

"People know what a whore she is; me, they like. I'm the gentle one they love, and she's the one people hate."

He wore a dark sweater and trousers, and the face that Branna had thought belonged to a nice man was now twisted in rage. He really believed what he was saying, Branna could see that. He thought people would turn on Macy and accept him. He was crazy, just like Macy had said he was...crazy and unlikely to see reason.

Branna looked to the front door that was closed, and wondered how she could get her and Macy out without one of them being shot. What if her father arrived? Would Brian shoot him?

"I won't let you take her." Branna took a breath to steady herself; panic would not help them get out of this unhurt.

"Then, I'll shoot you," Brian Delray said.

"Branna!"

Macy tried to get around Branna again, but she tripped and fell to the floor, and that was when he fired, the bullet hitting Branna in the arm. Her mind went completely blank, and it was

Macy's cry that made her look down. Blood was soaking into the sleeve of her shirt, and then she felt the pain. It was sharp and vicious, and literally took her breath away, and Branna was on her knees seconds later. She couldn't focus; her vision seemed to have narrowed and her head felt strange.

"No, dear God, no!"

Branna turned to face Macy as she cried out, but she couldn't move, and then suddenly she was falling.

Jake heard the gunshot as he climbed out of the car. To his right, he saw Declan sprint out of the shed, and they arrived on the porch seconds later.

"Branna!" Bursting through the door, Jake saw her on the floor, her body still, and then the blood; he was on his knees beside her two heartbeats later.

"I'm going to kill you!"

Ignoring Declan's roar as he charged Brian Reynolds, Jake turned Branna over slowly.

"Move the table, Macy; get me sheets or bandages and blankets now." He didn't look to see if she'd done what he asked; Jake had eyes only for Branna.

"It's okay, baby," his heart was thudding so hard in his chest he was struggling to breathe, as behind him, he heard the sound of fists hitting flesh.

The bullet had hit her in the arm. Pulling his shirt over his head, he applied pressure to the wound.

"Stay with me, Rosebud."

The sensory receptors completely overload the brain, and the victim goes into shock, forcing the patient to lose consciousness.

Pressure, elevation above the heart, and if bleeding won't stop, apply pressure directly to the brachial artery.

Lifting the arm, he used his other hand to check her pulse. It was weak, which told Jake that shock was taking hold.

"Get my phone out of my pocket," Jake yelled. "Call my mother, then Ethan…tell him to get the helicopter ready!"

He felt hands in his back pocket, taking out his phone, and then he heard Macy making the calls.

"Branna, love." Declan O'Donnell appeared on the other side of Branna, his face white, eyes on his daughter.

"She'll live," Jake vowed. She wouldn't be leaving him now, not when they'd just found each other.

Lifting his shirt, he checked the bleeding, but it was still flowing, and way too fast.

Wrapping his hand around Branna's arm, Jake pressed his fingers directly into the brachial artery. Pushing aside the fear, he relied on what he'd been trained to do, save lives, heal people, and care for the woman he loved. His mind raced through the things he'd learned in his years of study, whatever he would need to keep Branna alive.

"I've called Cubby, Jake, to come get him…Brian," Macy said.

Jake didn't speak, just tried to keep himself controlled as he held Branna's arm, feeling the blood pump over his fingers and out of her body. She needed this from him now, needed the doctor that he was to take charge.

"Is it s-slowing...the blood?" Macy was crying, tears streaking her face as she knelt beside Declan and looked down at the still unconscious Branna.

"Yes. Now get her van as close to the house as you can, and we'll take her to the helicopter," Jake said, and he could hear the rasp in his voice that fear had put there.

Cars started arriving as he bound the wound and prepared her to travel. His parents were the first.

"The bullet severed the artery; I've stopped the bleeding."

His mother didn't speak, just opened her supplies, and between them they started treating Branna.

"She's as stable as we can get her now, Jake. Let's move her to the van," Doctor McBride said minutes later.

Slipping his arms under Branna, he picked her up while his mother held her arm and they walked slowly to the van that Declan had running.

"Macy, you and I will follow in my car and pick up Declan. Then we'll collect Annabelle and follow in the van to the hospital," these words were from Jake's father.

Jake heard Buster say something to Macy, his voice deep with worry.

Branna was still unconscious, her face white, pulse weak, and Jake wanted to shout at her to open her eyes and stop scaring him. He needed her to look at him, needed that as much as he needed the next lungful of air.

"Let me have a crack at him, Cubby. I want to make him hurt for both Macy and Branna," Buster was now saying to the sheriff.

Add a round dozen for me, Buster, Jake thought, as he walked into the back of the van with Branna in his arms, his mother at his side.

"You know I can't do that, Buster. Aww hell, I'm sure there's like seven rules as to why I shouldn't let you kick Brian while he's lying trussed like my ma's Thanksgiving turkey."

"She'll be all right, son. I'll get to the hospital as soon as I can." Jake nodded as his father said the words, then closed the door. Seconds later, Declan was driving down the driveway.

"Someone should just put a bullet through Delray's head and save everyone a bucket load of trouble," Jake's mother said, as she sat beside him and wrapped and an arm around his neck.

"I may just do that for you, Mom, when I know Branna is okay."

"She will be, son, you have my promise on that."

Ethan had the helicopter ready as they drove up Jake's drive, so they had to duck under the blades to get in. His handsome face was lined with worry as he met them at the door and helped maneuver them all inside.

"How's our girl doing?" Ethan's hand gripped Jake's shoulder briefly.

"She's stable at the moment," Nancy McBride answered him.

"Okay, good." He stood back to let Declan move closer.

"I can't fit in here, Jake, so look after my daughter for me."

"Count on it," Jake said, squeezing the hand the man held out to him. The doors then closed and they were taking off. The others would follow by vehicle.

"I've radioed ahead. We'll land on the hospital roof and they'll be ready," Ethan said, and then they were in the air.

"Jake?" Branna had regained consciousness. Her eyes were dazed as she looked up at him.

"It's all right, baby, we're on our way to the hospital." He leaned over her, resting his cheek beside hers. "You scared me."

"It was Brian; he shot me. I-is Macy all right?"

"She's fine, and your dad dealt with Brian. Christ, Rosebud," Jake said, breathing in the scent of her. "I thought I'd lost you."

"But, because you're my hero, you saved me," her words were weak, but the best sound he'd ever heard.

"Something like that. I love you, baby."

"You too."

She didn't speak again, just pushed her face into his and kept it there until they landed.

They took her away from him and he tried to follow, telling them he was a doctor and that she was scared of hospitals, but they said Jake needed to get cleaned up before he saw her again. Branna was then wheeled through a set of doors that swung closed behind them, shutting her away from him.

"Mum," he whispered, as he started to shake. Jake felt her arms close around him, and he held on as he let the tears fall.

"She's going to be all right now, son; you know it just as I do."

"Can you just keep reminding me of that every second or so?" Jake said into her shoulder.

"I'm proud of you, Jake. You did exactly what needed to be done, no panicking, no drama. You saved her, son."

"Maybe, but you would have arrived in time to do the same."

"Where is she?" Ethan arrived then.

"Through there," Jake stood and pointed at the closed doors.

"Aren't you two doctors? Shouldn't you be in there too?" Ethan demanded.

"It's a hospital, Ethan; there are plenty of capable doctors here." Nancy McBride took Jake's hand and then Ethan's in the other one. "Now, let's find the waiting room and some really bad coffee."

Slowly, family and friends started to arrive. Buster burst into the room with his hair standing on end, turning the air blue with Declan O'Donnell, Jake's dad, and Annabelle at his side. Macy had been taken away at Annabelle's insistence to be checked over.

"Buster, calm down!" this from Jake's dad, who had an arm around Declan's shoulders and was leading him to a seat.

"I'm giving Branna the recipe to every mystery muffin I've made since she arrived."

Jake regained his feet and walked to where his friends stood.

"You okay, bud?" Buster questioned him.

"No."

"Do I have to hug you?"

"Had plenty of that already," Jake said, looking to the doors as they opened behind Buster.

"Doctor McBride?"

"Yes," both he and his mother said.

"Miss O'Donnell is doing well; she's stabilized and the bullet went straight through the arm."

"Can I see her?"

"I'll have a nurse come and get you as soon as she's out of recovery."

Jake paced around the room, while everyone sat silently staring at either their hands or the walls. Belle, who was sitting beside Declan, cried into his shoulder, and Jake heard Branna's father speak softly to her.

People pushed cups of coffee into his hand, and Jake drank without tasting a drop. Newman arrived with Mikey in his arms. The boy was crying and looking terrified, but Jake couldn't do more than place a hand on his head and kiss one damp cheek before he continued his pacing. His mind was on her, Branna, his love. Finally, after what felt like hours, a nurse finally arrived.

"Mr. McBride, if you'll follow me, I'll take you to Miss O'Donnell."

He looked at Declan, who nodded that he wanted Jake to go to her first, and then followed her from the room.

She had her eyes closed when he walked into the room, lying there in the blue hospital gown, looking small and vulnerable connected to machines with her heartbeat beeping on the monitor. Bending over her, he placed a kiss on her lips, and kept it there for long drawn out seconds.

"Jake?"

Her eyes were unfocused, still coming out of the anesthetic. "Hey, Rosebud." Stroking her cheek, he tried for a smile and failed.

"You okay?" She lifted her good hand and touched his cheek.

"I am now that I know you are."

"Is Macy all right?"

"The doctors are checking her over, but she seems okay," Jake said.

He couldn't stop touching her, running his hands over her hair, and stroking her face. He could have lost her today.

"I'm all right, Jake, really." Her smile was soft and sweet.

"Jesus, Branna," he bent at the waist and got as close to her as he could without causing her pain. "Seeing all that blood and you lying there—"

"Shhh, Jake I'm here with you now, everything's okay."

It would take him awhile to get that fact into his head, because right now all he could think about was that she could have been taken from him tonight.

"Did they get him…Macy's husband?"

"Cubby got him, and he and Buster put a few in for both of us, plus a few for Macy, before he locked him up nice and tight."

"Good, now Macy is really safe," she whispered, as her eyelashes began to lower.

"I need you to know how much I love you, Branna, and how much you mean to me." He kissed her again.

"I know," she whispered, as sleep pulled her under. "And ditto," she added, and then Jake felt her body grow weightless as she succumbed to the sleep her body so desperately needed. He stayed there, breathing her in, feeling her heart beat until he had himself under control. Only then did he go and tell the people who loved her almost as much as him, that she was going to be all right.

CHAPTER
TWENTY THREE

"I want to take this brace off."

They'd let her out of hospital a week later, and Branna was not what you would call an easy patient. Luckily, Jake had experience with the difficult ones, so he was up for the task.

"Funny girl."

They were on the front porch of her house. He was sitting with his feet braced on the railing, and she was in his lap, her feet between his.

"Macy's doing well, don't you think, Jake?"

"She is, but it will be a slow process, Rosebud. Brian has abused her both physically and mentally for years; it will take time to reverse those effects.

"Did you know that her parents blame her for the humiliation they're now suffering since this has come out?"

"You're kidding me?"

"No," Branna looked up at him. "I told her they were just as worthless as Brian, which was probably not respectful, considering they're her parents, but seriously, who does that to their only child when she's already hurting?"

"They'll have their share of guilt under all that B.S., baby, and you can bet that and the fact that they've always believed themselves to be above everyone else, will be driving their reactions."

"They better not come near me."

"I'm scared."

"You should be."

He kissed her because he could, and her lips would tempt a saint…plus the fact that he wouldn't have her alone for too much longer, not that she knew that yet.

"Jake, would you be okay if I let Dad live here and I moved in with you?"

He'd known this discussion was coming. They couldn't keep going back and forth; sooner or later, they had to call one of their houses home, and things were getting better between father and daughter every day. The bonds were strengthening, but they didn't need to be living on top of each other for that to happen.

"It'll be a bitch, but I'll manage, I guess," he drawled. "Plus, with you comes Geraldine, so it's a win-win all around."

"Ha."

"I can't reach my pocket, Branna, can you get that envelope out that's in there?"

"Who gave it to you?" She sat upright, and using her good arm, stuck her fingers into his pocket and pulled it out.

"Ethan."

That wasn't strictly a lie. Ethan had picked it up for him, but Jake had chosen it.

"Here," she tried to hand it to him.

"You open it."

She did, slowly, as she was one handed. Opening it wide, she looked inside. Her eyes then went to his before putting her hand in and taking out the ring.

"Marry me, Rosebud. Be my wife, and let me love you the rest of our days."

"Oh," Jake watched as she bit her lip. "I-I," she sniffed. Branna didn't like to cry, especially not in front of people.

"I'm dying here, baby."

"Yes, oh yes. I love you so much." She threw herself at him, then yelped as she hurt her arm.

"Will you take care?" He eased her away from him, lowering his head to look in her eyes. She had dark smudges beneath her eyes and was still too pale, but he was working on that.

"I keep forgetting."

"How? You're wearing a brace and have a hole in your arm."

"You make me forget."

"Nice answer." Taking the ring, he put it on her finger, then kissed her soundly, only pulling back as the first car arrived, followed by the second and third a minute after that.

"Why are there cars pulling up outside my house?"

She didn't seem particularly worried about the fact that doors were slamming and their friends and family were making their way towards them, arms loaded down with food and bottles clinking.

"We're celebrating our engagement, Rosebud."

"Cool!" She climbed off his lap and went to greet Belle, who folded her gently into her arms, and then her father, whose smile was almost as wide as Jake's.

His girl had worked it all out now. Howling was home and she was one of them. Smiling, Jake took the beer Buster handed him and went to join her.

THE END

The next book in the **Lake Howling Series** is **The Texan Meets His Match,** turn the page for an excerpt.

THE TEXAN MEETS
HIS MATCH

This is insane Gelderman. The woman can't stand the sight of you and you still want her.

Swallowing the last of his soda, he crushed the can then went into his bedroom to pack an overnight bag. Maybe that was why Ethan wanted Annabelle Smith so much, because she showed no interest in him, and that questioned his sanity because; he had enough warm willing women in his life, but he wanted the cold abusive one.

Zipping the bag shut, he picked up his keys and headed out the door and took the lift to the basement. Climbing into his Bronco, Ethan left the building and headed out onto the streets of Brook. Ten minutes later, he pulled into a park beside the water and went to find the woman who occupied far too many of his thoughts.

She was sitting on the bench where he'd left her thirty minutes ago, although now she was relaxed with her head resting on the hard wood behind. Stopping before her, he realized she was sleeping. Ethan had no idea how she'd managed to achieve that state, given that around them were cars, people and a fair amount of noise.

He'd never observed Annabelle Smith still, her luscious mouth silent. She was a beautiful woman. Her face was oval, her nose perfectly straight, cheekbones brushed with soft color, and her lips a deep raspberry that invited him to touch. He'd fantasized about that mouth wrapped around various parts of his body or kissing him senseless.

Stepping closer Ethan ran one finger down her cheek. "Annabelle honey, time to go now."

She didn't wake slowly, instead sitting upright, eyes wide with panic.

"Hey." He touched her arm. "It's me, Ethan."

Her eyes closed again briefly and then when she opened them, there was Annabelle Smith.

"Christ you nearly stopped my heart, Gelderman."

"Well now that would be a shame." Ethan took her bag to his Bronco and she followed.

"Did he like the car?" She climbed in beside him, already fully awake. Ethan envied that; he took a while to function after opening his eyes.

"He did. He went straight to his bank and gave me this."

Ethan turned the ignition as she began to unroll the notes. He saw her hands clench briefly before she began counting.

"But surely this is too much?"

It was, but Ethan was banking on her lack of knowledge about car prices to pull this off.

"I drove the car up, then said take a look and name a price." He shrugged as he slipped on his aviators. "He did, I agreed, and that was that. We need to sort the paperwork, but other than that you are now carless."

Her hands clenched again and Ethan could tell that selling her car had been hard; he just had no idea why she had done it. Obviously, she needed the money, and he guessed that phone conversation he'd overheard also had something to do with it.

"Thank you, Ethan."

He placed his hand over his heart. "God's truth, honey, I'm not sure I can take much more of you thanking me, when in the normal course of a day you would have abused me at least twice by now."

She snorted. "It's not like I don't want to. It's just that now you've done something nice for me I need to hold off a bit."

"It's unsettling, is what it is."

She opened her bag and he noticed it didn't have the normal clutter that he'd seen inside other women's. Like her car, it was neat and tidy.

"You a neat freak or something?"

"I like things orderly, Gelderman. There's no crime in that."

"You want me to take you to the bank so you can deposit that?"

"No...thanks."

"It's a lot of money to have lying around, Annabelle."

"I know that."

So she didn't want to put it in the bank, which just confused him more. Did she owe it to someone?

"Something in your bag is buzzing, Annabelle."

He watched as she pulled out her cell and turned it off. Her face didn't invite him to ask why, so he left it alone...for now.

Twenty minutes later Ethan drove through the gates of the small airfield, where he kept his bird. He'd phoned ahead and they'd had it readied for him, and sitting outside the hanger. He pulled the Bronco inside then got out, and Annabelle followed.

"You ever crashed that thing?" She looked nervously over at his gleaming helicopter where it sat on the landing pad.

"Honey, if I'd crashed it, then it wouldn't be still in one piece, but several of them. More importantly, I wouldn't have been able to put them back together." *Or me*, but he kept that thought inside his head.

"I'm not sure that's reassuring, Gelderman."

"You scared, Annabelle?"

"Hell, yes!" Ethan watched her fingers dig into the strap of her bag.

Most people would bluff their way out of it, spin him a line, or act tough, but not her, she told the blunt truth.

"So let me get this straight. You've never been up in anything?"

"Define anything."

Ethan just looked at her.

"No alright. I've never been off ground and never had a hankering to do so." She was glaring at him, brown eyes darker now she was angry.

"Oh now this is just too much fun," Ethan said as he took her bag out the back seat and headed to where his bird stood. "Annabelle Smith has a weakness."

"Fuck you."

He laughed as she stomped after him but didn't say anything else until he finished his pre-flight checks.

"Ok we're ready."

She muttered something like *I'm glad one of us is*, under her breath, but came forward as he signaled to her.

"In you get."

Annabelle climbed into the seat and tried to breathe. Why had she agreed to this? Her lungs had seized and fear was clawing at her throat. As Ethan strapped her in she tried to think rationally. Surely, he wouldn't put her in danger; after all he flew in this metal death trap all the time.

"You can talk to me and I'll hear your words, okay?" She nodded as he fitted a set of headphones over her ears. He then jogged around the front and climbed into his seat. He fastened himself in, then pulled on his headset and suddenly she panicked. It robbed her of rational thought and had her reaching for the headset.

"I can't do this!" Annabelle hadn't known she had a fear of flying, having never flown before, but now she did.

He stopped her by grabbing her hands, caging hers inside his, gripping them hard enough so that she was forced to look at him.

"Yes you can. The brave, strong woman I've come to know can do anything, and this, flying in a harmless helicopter, will be something you'll enjoy if you let yourself. Annabelle, you need to trust me on this."

"I-I don't think I can." She was totally undone, fear making her pathetic, and it was because of her weakness that he was able to lean over and lay a soft kiss on her lips before she could react.

"Hey!" She swung at him as he released her hands, but he was out of her reach.

"That'll give you something else to think about."

It did, for 2.5 seconds. The feel of his lips pressed to hers had produced an instant flare of heat, but now it was gone and the panic was back. Clenching her eyes shut she pressed her hands over them and prayed that the inside of her eyelids was not the last thing she would ever see. She should have caught the bus, but no, she'd allowed Ethan to provoke her into flying with him.

In minutes, she heard the whomp whomp of the blades and they were rising.

"Mother of God, I'm going to die."

He laughed softly into her head set. "Open your eyes for me, honey. Come on you have to see this."

Annabelle felt his hand touch hers.

"Pl-please keep your hands on the wheel."

"Collective Pitch Lever," he corrected her.

"I'm about to die and you're correcting me on the correct labels for your instruments?"

"Oh, I didn't realize we were talking about my instruments," he said, laughter in his voice. "I have other names for them."

"You're such a dickhead," she muttered as she opened her fingers and looked through them, then slowly dropped them to her lap, as he started talking, pointing out landmarks.

"Wow!" she said as they flew over the stunning landscape. Her heart was still thumping in her chest and her palms were sweaty where they now gripped the edges of the seat, but she couldn't take her eyes of what was before her.

"Pretty cool, huh?"

Annabelle couldn't take it in. She saw water and trees, land rolled into hills and dipped into valleys. It was spectacular, amazing and she could feel her smile getting wider with every new sight.

"I've never seen anything like this, Ethan. It's amazing."

"Maybe now when I tell you to trust me you should give it a shot."

"Is that Tillerby Lodge?" Annabelle saw the long low building to her left. It sat close to a lake and surrounded by trees with a mountain at its back.

"It is, and I think you can relax your fingers now before you lose the circulation.

"Ooooh," Annabelle squealed like a small child as he circled lower for her to take a closer look. She saw the horses running over the pastures, and then she found a person. Whoever it was raised their hands high, and she waved back.

"It's like…like—"

"Flying," Ethan inserted.

"Like nothing I can explain," Annabelle corrected pressing a hand to her chest. She still felt the fear, but she wouldn't have missed this for anything. "The perspective is so different from up here, seeing it all at once, the water, trees, hills and valleys, it's like being in a painting instead of looking at one. That probably sounds weird, but I can't explain it any other way."

"No, it sounds about right to me."

She looked across at him and he smiled, and it was the smile of a boy who was showing off his favorite toy, not the man who was trying to charm her. If possible, it made him look sexier.

God she was hot.

Ethan sucked in a breath as she looked away from him. Her smile had reached all the way to her eyes and the giggle had been sweet and so different from anything he'd ever heard from her before. Light and carefree, she was like a small child seeing something for the first time. Ethan loved being up here; he stepped away from life for a brief break. His troubles fell away when he flew, all the shit with his family left on the ground, and his only thoughts focused on the beauty of flying. He wanted that for the woman beside him, wanted to give her a few minutes of peace from whatever was riding her.

Annabelle kept talking. Even her voice was different, lighter somehow.

"Look at those Redwoods; they look huge even from up here."

She rattled on and Ethan let her. "How long have you been flying?"

"I was eighteen when I started."

"Does anyone else in your family fly?"

"Just the uncle who taught me, he's my father's brother and had no kids of his own, so he took me under his wing."

She smiled at him again, another genuine one that made his stomach clench.

"You are a lucky boy."

He had been but not for the usual reasons. Not because he had a loving supportive family or siblings that he actually liked. No, he'd been lucky because he had lots of money and plenty of food and a house many would envy. But more importantly he'd had his Uncle Mitch to keep him on the rails, even though he'd continually tried to step off.

They flew over tall stands of trees, then long ribbons of water and Annabelle made plenty of noises as she encountered each. Small humming sounds, gasps, a little squeal, and Ethan wondered what sounds she would make in bed.

The imagine of her naked straddling his thighs made Ethan's eyes cross with lust.

"Is that my lake?" She was pointing a long finger.

"Sure is. By air it's a short trip."

She watched Lake Howling grow bigger before her eyes.

"Where will we land?"

"That cleared space out back of Jake's place."

"No way is that big enough." The smile dropped from her face. "Tell me you're not for real?"

"I've landed there on and off for two years, honey. Remember what I said about trusting me."

He swooped over the lake and there was Jake's house. Branna's van was out front, beside the pickup. Smiling at the cars, he thought about the people who owned them.

"Why do you have that goofy smile on your face?"

"I was thinking about Jake and Branna."

She looked down at the fast approaching house and her smile became soft too. "Yeah, it's pretty cool to see isn't it? Two messed up souls finding each other and coming out the other side normal."

"Normal?" Ethan snorted. "Neither of those two is normal. What do you think that says about us?"

"That we're probably messed up too." She spoke the words softly and he heard the sadness return. He didn't say anything else, just brought the bird in to land.

"I'm not watching." Once again her hands were over her eyes.

"Have a little faith woman," he said going through the motions. Landing the bird gently, he undid his harness and turned to look at her, leaning forward to bring them closer.

"So I'm ready for that apology now."

He could see the emotions flick across her face as she looked at him. Her brown eyes were lighter here in this small space; he saw a touch of gold in their depths.

"What do I need to apologize for?"

"Abusing me."

"Which time?"

"The last time when you refused my kind and generous offer for this trip."

"Do I have too?"

"It's the right thing to do, Annabelle, after ripping up at me." Ethan kept his expression solemn as he leaned closer.

"Sorry," she leaned too.

"I forgive you." He smiled.

"That was easy."

"What can I say," Ethan moved closer so his breath brushed her lips, "I'm an easy kind of guy."

"I-I believe the term is loose." Her breath whispered across his lips.

"Harsh, Smith." Closing the last few inches, he kissed her soft lips. It was a touch, nothing more, a brush of his mouth on hers and Ethan felt as if an electric current had traveled through his entire body.

"Why did you do that?" She didn't pull away, her eyes still inches from his.

He couldn't answer that so he kissed her again, harder this time, his lips taking hers. She responded in kind, her lips taking his right back. Lifting a hand to her neck he cupped it and held her close. His heart hammered in his chest, the breath left his body and never had he felt such an intense reaction just from a kiss.

He'd brushed her lips before and his body had stirred, but this, this was an explosion.

She pulled back suddenly and he heard the sound of feet. Looking up he saw Jake approaching.

"Annabelle—"

"That was a mistake, Ethan, and one that will never be repeated."

She was flustered; color flooded her cheeks as her hands fumbled with the straps of her harness.

"You sure about that?" His voice was hoarse, the smooth Texan drawl nowhere in sight.

"Yes, it can't happen again."

"Why?"

She spun to face him again, eyes now lit with fire. "Because I won't be another notch in your belt, Gelderman, do you hear me? That kiss may have proved I want you, but damned if I'll ever let you near me again."

"Because I've supposedly slept with loads of women?"

"Yes!" She hissed out the word and that just pissed him off more.

"And you're just such a pure sweet gal that you could never sully yourself by letting me lay my hands on you?"

"Fuck you!"

"Well, now, haven't you just told me I can't?" Ethan said to annoy her and because he was unsettled himself. By insulting her, he was giving himself time.

Hardly a gentlemanly thing to do but it was all he had at that moment, especially as a furnace was still raging in his body. "You've just told me to keep my hands to myself and then you go and say something like that."

He'd seen her temper. It was a wild and wonderful thing, quick to ignite, but as she lifted her hand to take a shot at him, he gave her a look that stopped it moving. "I would advise against it, honey."

"Just stay away from me." The words where whispered as Jake McBride ran under the blades to her side of the helicopter.

"No fun in that."

ABOUT THE AUTHOR

Wendy Vella

Born and raised in the North Island of New Zealand, Wendy has been reading as long as she's been walking according to her parents. An incurable romantic she is always looking for a, happily ever after, ending to her books.

She shares her life with her husband of 30 years, son and daughter. They have two old dogs who rule their household, and life is busy and always full. She is a keen cyclist, and when time allows, is often found out on the roads with her family and friends, enjoying the beautiful scenery of her homeland.

For information on all of Wendy;s books, including updates on novels yet to come, visit Wendy's website at *www.wendyvella. com.*